The Long Way Home

The
Long Way Home

Sarah Storme

Five Star • Waterville, Maine

First Edition
First Printing: January 2005

Published in 2005 in conjunction with Tekno Books and Ed Gorman.

Set in 11 pt. Plantin.

Printed in the United States on permanent paper.

Library of Congress Control Number: 2004114998
ISBN 1-59414-306-4 (hc : alk. paper)

The Long Way Home

Acknowledgements

I want to thank Ruth Doyle for the many hours of dramatic reading and all the insightful comments, and Gordon Aalborg for being an efficient, kind, and entertaining editor. And I want to thank my family members for their unwavering support, especially my wonderful mother, Lydia Broussard, and my inspirational husband, Bob Zielkiewicz.

Prologue

"No! My wife does not work." Rick glared across the table. "You knew that when you married me."

Allie swallowed hard. "But I just want to go half-time. I talked to Hilda at the school and she said—"

"I don't care what she said. You are *not* going to work! My image is everything, and that image does not include a working wife!"

"But Rick, I need something—"

"No!" He slammed his coffee mug down on the table and rose.

His intensity scared her. Allie had never considered herself a cowardly person, but Rick seemed to be on the verge of madness.

She thought of news stories about mild-mannered people who go over the edge and shoot coworkers and family. No one ever seemed to know what had pushed that person past the breaking point. That was the image that came to mind as he towered over her at the table, daring her to speak.

She held her tongue.

He was right. He'd spelled out his intentions before they married. Unfortunately, she'd been too blinded by the promise of a home to consider the rest of it carefully. It was her own fault for agreeing; she couldn't, in all fairness, blame him now.

"Good. Now that that's settled, I'm going to work. Besides, the eggs are cold." He frowned at her accusingly. "I'll be late tonight. Make an appointment to get your hair cut. We're meeting with a prospective client this weekend, and you look like shit." He turned and marched from the room.

Allie stared at her coffee mug, fighting the hurt swelling in her throat.

A few minutes later, Rick returned to the dining room. He stood behind her with his hands resting gently on her shoulders, his voice calm and sweet again. "Allie, honey, you know how important you are to me. I don't mean to lose my temper. Forgive me?"

When she looked up and found him smiling down at her, she nodded as the hurt melted away.

Rick kissed the top of her head, and then hurried from the house.

Once he was gone, Allie threw herself into a dozen projects. She made an appointment with Albert for noon the following day, the earliest he could fit her into his busy salon, but that meant her hair would look good for the weekend. Stopping to glance in a mirror, she was horrified to realize how long she'd let it go. No wonder Rick had been annoyed.

As she cleaned house, Allie tried to imagine what it must be like for Rick, always having to be upbeat with clients and employees in order to maintain his image, working hard every day and well into most evenings. The home he'd given her truly was beautiful; he never denied her anything to make it more comfortable or presentable. Guilt took hold as she thought about aggravating him first thing in the morning.

Sometime around three, just as she finished the last load of laundry and washed out the mop, Allie decided to surprise her husband with dinner. Maybe, once he saw all the trouble she'd gone to, he'd reconsider letting her work before she went out of her mind with boredom. She drove at breakneck speed to the grocery, spent the last of the household allowance, and hurried home to fix his favorite meal. With the food, dishes, silverware, and even mood lighting packed in a paper bag, she hopped in her car a little before six.

Halfway to Rick's office, Allie realized she was still wearing the jeans she'd cleaned house in, and hoped Rick would be happy enough with her surprise to forgive her appearance. It was, after all, too late for him to be meeting with clients, and he never seemed to really care how she looked when they were alone. Relief washed over her as she pulled into the parking lot and found his car the only one there. The last thing she wanted to do was make him angry again.

Inside, as Allie followed sounds of cries and moans through the long empty hall and into the office, she couldn't immediately understand their origin. Was someone hurt? She clutched the brown bag tightly in both arms to stop dishes from rattling and eased around the corner.

Confronted with writhing, naked bodies, she froze in the doorway, fearing she'd entered the wrong office.

A framed wedding photo on the desk assured her that she hadn't.

Who were these people? Until they looked up, she was sure a couple of burglars had stopped to have sex in her husband's office. And then she saw Rick's face, flushed and dripping sweat.

"What are you doing here?" he asked.

Even after she realized what she'd interrupted, her mind wouldn't immediately accept it. She must have misunderstood.

"I . . . I brought . . . dinner," she mumbled, backing out of the room.

Rick followed her, hopping on one foot at a time as he pulled on his pants. Before she made it to his secretary's desk, he grabbed her arm, freeing the bag. Bowls shattered on the tile floor sending beef stroganoff and salad in all directions as matching silver candlesticks clanged and rolled across the room. Her purse slipped off her shoulder and fell into the middle of the mess.

Cursing through clenched teeth, Rick jumped clear of flying noodles without releasing her. "Allie, don't make more out of this than it is," he said, his voice amazingly calm and quiet. "I'm sorry you—"

"What . . . who . . ." Her thoughts wove themselves into jumbled knots.

"It's no big deal. Just go home—"

"No big deal? How can you . . . all this time . . ." Her chest burned, her heart raced, and her voice stopped working as she mouthed words that made no sense.

Rick shook her arm, treating her like a panicked child. "Calm down," he said. "This is nothing to get so worked up about. You're my wife. Everything is fine."

You're my wife. That's what he always said, as if he owned her, as if she were a pet or a car. When had she become a possession? Or had it always been this way, and she'd simply deluded herself into thinking she was more in his eyes?

She studied her husband's face, and realized that he saw her as a minor annoyance to be dealt with so he could get on with his life.

12

That's when the outrage flared, taking control of her reactions. "No, it's not fine!"

His eyebrows shot up. He must have been surprised that she hadn't backed down. "Yes, it is. Perhaps I've made a mistake, but it doesn't mean anything."

"*Perhaps?*" Her voice rose in pitch and volume. "Do you expect me to just go home and sit quietly while you finish with your *mistake?* What am I supposed to tell people when they ask where you are, that *perhaps* you're having sex with your secretary?"

Rick's face reddened with anger. "God dammit, Allie, I don't want to hear another word about this!" The muscles in his jaw tightened, and a frightening fury filled his eyes. She'd seen the look before. He lowered his voice, and it shook with the effort of control. "You know that any hint of this would ruin my business, and then you'd be sorry. You'd lose your precious home. I've worked too damn hard to let you spoil it. Do you understand?"

He sustained his viselike grip, waiting for her to nod; her hand tingled from lack of blood flow. She nodded and he released her with a shove that sent her stumbling toward the outer door.

"Go home," he said, his voice little more than a growl. "Get cleaned up and wait for me there."

She left him frowning at the wreck of food and broken glass with the young blonde secretary standing behind him in the doorway, clutching stray pieces of clothing to her naked body.

One

Truck headlights, appearing suddenly from around the bend, momentarily blinded Allie and sent the Volvo's right tires off the road. She fought the car back onto the pavement and then wiped her cheeks with the heel of her hand.

Why couldn't she stop crying? Rick hadn't physically injured her. It was amazing, though, how much betrayal truly hurt.

The car sputtered and jolted as it tried to climb. Allie downshifted to second and strained to see the narrowing roadway through vision blurred by tears. Where on earth was she? She'd lost track after getting off the interstate.

The road crested, and the Volvo seemed to sigh with relief as it started down the hill.

Her clothes still reeked of stroganoff, and the smell turned her stomach. How could she have been so blind? All those nights Rick had worked late and then come home too tired to make love. He must have been secretly amused that she was so ridiculously trusting and naive. He probably laughed every time he got away with it.

It must have been going on for years. The realization brought more tears.

After running from Rick's office, she hadn't gone home as ordered. Instead, she'd just started driving. She hadn't known what she was doing at first. All she knew was that she had to get away.

Allie wished she'd thought to pick up her purse. If not for the ten-dollar bill she'd found while doing laundry earlier in the day and shoved into her pocket, she'd have left town penniless. As it was, she'd had to pump seven dollars of gas into the car. But she couldn't go back. She could *never* go back. Her perfect home had crumbled into a pile of debris in a matter of seconds, and nothing could ever again be built on the worthless foundation of lies.

It was a hard way to learn a lesson, but she'd learned it. She wasn't meant to have a home. Why had she been foolish enough to believe Rick when he promised her one? And why had she let him dominate her life so completely?

Allie jumped at a loud pop that was followed by hideous grinding and then quiet. She guided the slowing Volvo to the edge of the road where the tires crunched on gravel until it rolled to a stop. Pushing in the clutch, she turned the key. "Please," she whispered. The headlights dimmed as the starter cranked for several minutes, and then even it refused to cooperate. She dropped her head to the steering wheel as more tears fell. "No, not now."

Wrestling with despair, Allie straightened. This was it— she was lost, it was late, and her car had just died. She couldn't even manage to run away properly. Leaning forward, she squinted at the view illuminated only by her dimming headlights. The road climbed a little in front of her, then disappeared. To the right a cliff rose straight up from the shoulder, and thick bushes blocked the view to the left. What was she going to do?

Even as she asked the question, the answer came to her, drying her tears. There was only one person in the world she could turn to. If she could just get to Melissa, everything would be okay, no matter how horrible it felt. Melissa would know what to do.

Allie tucked her hair behind her ears. Rick must be looking for her by now. It had been at least three hours since she'd left his office. But there was still hope. If she could get to a phone, she knew Melissa would come to her rescue. Unfortunately, in the middle of nowhere a phone might be hard to find.

Allie turned off the headlights, climbed out of the car, closed the door, and dropped the keys into her sweater pocket. She gasped at the strength of the frosty night air. Wherever she was must be high in the mountains.

The thought of walking wasn't appealing, but she had no choice. She couldn't sit and wait for Rick to find her. Better to face bears and mountain lions than be dragged back to Denver.

Squaring her shoulders against growing fear, Allie started forward. Stars filled the clear sky and helped light her path. It was hard to believe any place could be so quiet. There wasn't even a hint of traffic. In fact, there was nothing but the sound of her tennis shoes on pavement.

Had it been less than a day since she'd taken a chance and tried to talk to Rick during breakfast? It seemed more like a week. They'd discussed her going back to work once before—the first time he'd ever really yelled at her. This time she hadn't slept for two days while working up the nerve to broach the subject. That lack of sleep had her feeling a little groggy now as she recalled the way he'd glared at her and she'd felt guilty for making him mad.

Allie stumbled as she stepped off the edge of the pavement and fell onto her hands and knees in cold, damp gravel. Keys jingled as they hit the ground somewhere to her right. She waited a moment to be certain she wasn't injured, then felt around for her keys, but found no sign of them. "Great."

Well, the keys wouldn't do any good without the car. Allie straightened and continued, wiping small rocks and dirt from her smarting palms and jeans.

She glanced down at her clothes and considered the irony of Rick Tate's wife running around the countryside in old clothes soiled with stroganoff. Nothing was more important to Rick than appearance. Of course, the last time she'd seen him, he hadn't been exactly overdressed.

At the bottom of the hill, the road turned hard to the right. When Allie rounded the bend, she was stunned to find a building on the backside of the cliff. She stopped and stared. "What on earth—"

A red neon sign declaring "Last Chance" lit a huge dirt parking lot. As she watched, the sign buzzed and popped, and the *L* disappeared. Allie wondered if she had stepped into a *Twilight Zone* episode. At least the place promised warmth and perhaps phone service.

Parked in front of the building were three pickups and a car. A big black dog in the back of one of the trucks, illuminated by what was left of the neon sign, watched her. She saw no people, and only a hint of sound escaped from the building. Not exactly a hot spot.

Trying to push her hair into place, she sighed and headed for the stairs that led to a door. As she passed the pickup truck with the dog, the beast leaned toward her and sniffed the air, but he didn't bark. Allie gave him a wide berth. She had never been comfortable around dogs.

The door screeched to announce her entry, and the noise drew silent stares from patrons at the bar and tables. Old wooden planks creaked under her slow footsteps as she approached a tall, thin man with long, dark hair who waited on the other side of the dimly lit bar. Somewhere in the background, a cheap radio whined country music.

"Hi," she said, donning the best smile she could manage.

"Hi," the man answered. "Can I get you something?"

The edges of her ears stung as they warmed, and food smells made her stomach growl. Allie glanced around to find several people eating.

"A sandwich?"

"Sure." He shoved a soiled, paper menu toward her.

She ran down the meager list and found a chicken salad sandwich that sounded hopeful. The major selling point was that it cost less than two dollars.

"Chicken salad?"

The man nodded. "Anything to drink?"

"Water, please. And do you have a phone?"

He pointed to the alcove behind her.

"May I have change?" She pulled a one out of her pocket.

The bartender traded the bill for quarters, then disappeared.

Allie ducked into the alcove and sighed with relief at being hidden from prying eyes. A payphone hung between doors that sported "Cowboy" and "Cowgirl" signs.

Her hands shook with a mixture of excitement, fear, and anticipation as she dialed information, trying to remember how long it had been since she'd seen Melissa, her last true friend. A year? Maybe two?

At one time in her life, she'd had several friends. They weren't people who knew her deepest, darkest secrets, but she could have called on them in a pinch. Over the course of her marriage, Rick had convinced her to break all ties. He'd said he wanted her to himself, but now she wondered if he was only worried that she'd have someone else to lean on when things were bad. He couldn't afford a wife who was strong enough to make public accusations. Even Melissa could only take so much before she quit coming back.

"What city please?" a nasal voice asked.

"Steamboat Springs."

"What listing?"

"Melissa Melbane. M-E-L-B-A-N-E."

After a moment of silence, the voice said, "I don't have a Melbane listed."

When the news hit, it had the force of a hammer against her heart.

"What? But, you must."

"No, ma'am, I don't."

"What about, like, some other town near Steamboat?"

There was another thick, quiet moment. "I don't have a Melbane in the county. Do you want another listing?"

"Denver?"

More silence. "No, ma'am. There's no Melissa or M. Melbane in Denver. Another listing?"

Tears welled up again, driven by panic, as Allie stared at the black face of the phone. No Melissa? Without Melissa, she had no place to go, no one to turn to, no hope of success.

She was utterly, completely alone.

"Ma'am, do you want another listing?"

Allie shook her head and then managed to croak, "No." She used both hands to return the receiver to its cradle, then closed her eyes and fell forward until her forehead rested on cold plastic. Her entire body shook as she tried to silence her sobs.

It wasn't fair. She couldn't return to Rick, and he'd made sure she had no way to survive without him. She'd be-

19

come a prisoner without realizing it. How could she have been such a fool?

"I'm not . . . going back," she whispered through clenched teeth.

Sam speared the last bite of chicken-fried steak, swirled it in the gravy, and ate it with a tired grin. The steak was better than usual, but it might be because he hadn't eaten lunch. Whatever the reason, he'd polished it off quickly.

Frank, the bartender, picked up the empty plate and poured coffee. Sam nodded his thanks. Half a cup more and he'd leave. Coffee would keep him awake long enough to finish the work waiting at home.

"Hey there, Calvert. How's my horse doing?"

Sam stiffened at the familiar voice, trying not to choke on his coffee. "She's doing fine, no thanks to you, and she's not yours anymore."

Ron Stanley sneered as he slapped Sam's shoulder. His face reflected the extra weight the rest of his body held, and his breath reeked of alcohol. "That's true, she's yours now. You take good care of her, Sam, you hear?"

It was all he could do to keep from taking a swing at Ron as the man walked past. The thirty-year rivalry had soured over time, culminating in hatred when Sam found the mare Ron had abused. Ron Stanley didn't have an ounce of compassion in him.

The front door slammed and a few seconds later, a pickup roared out of the parking lot.

As soon as Ron was gone, Sam took several slow, deep breaths and released the anger. He didn't have the energy to hold on to it anyway.

He glanced across the room at the woman returning from the restroom. It was odd, first of all, to find a stranger in the Last Chance on a Wednesday night, and a young woman alone was even more unusual. He watched her over the top of his coffee cup as he sipped. She walked hesitantly to the bar where Frank waited with a sandwich on a plate. Sam couldn't quite hear their conversation.

Frank straightened and shook his head. The woman pulled money out of her pocket and placed it on the bar, then climbed onto a stool. The bartender shook his head again. The woman dropped her face into her hands and Frank left her alone.

"More coffee?" Frank lifted the pot.

"No, thanks." Sam nodded toward the mystery woman. "What was that?"

Frank leaned forward, dropping his voice to a whisper. "First she ordered a sandwich, then she decided she wanted tequila instead. But she doesn't even have three dollars on her. That's not enough for a drink, much less for a sandwich and a drink. I'll get fired if Mr. Dean catches me giving her a drink when I know she can't pay for it."

"Strange."

"Yeah. And she doesn't look too good."

"What do you mean?"

The woman hadn't moved.

"Looks like she's been crying," Frank said. "She made a phone call that must not have gone well. I sure hate to see a young lady like that, all upset and everything. And I didn't hear a car pull up before she came in. Maybe you could talk to her, Dr. Calvert. I don't want to let her go out into the cold without knowing she's okay."

"I'll try." Sam grabbed his hat from the bar and slid off the stool. "Give her the shot of tequila and put it on my tab."

Frank nodded.

Sam strolled around to the front and sat with one stool

between him and the woman. He placed his hat on the bar to his right. She didn't turn, and only looked up when Frank approached.

"What's this?" she asked.

"Tequila." Frank tilted his head toward Sam. "Compliments of the doc."

The woman glanced over and frowned. Frank was right; she had been crying. Red circles around her eyes and a bright red nose marred her otherwise attractive features. Her hair was a nice brown color close to her head, but much lighter at the ends and a little scraggly—a blonde from a bottle. She wore stained blue jeans and a dirty blue sweater over what appeared to be a good figure. There was no sign that she'd been wearing a coat.

Sam hooked his heels on the stool and leaned on the bar, his hands wrapped around his coffee cup. He returned her frown.

"I've never heard of a doctor prescribing tequila," she said.

"I've never seen someone who looked so much like she needed it."

She shrugged and turned to the drink, mumbling, "Thanks."

Sam discreetly studied the woman as she sipped from the shot glass, cringing and struggling not to cough halfway through. She looked young, maybe mid-twenties. She also looked a little desperate, and that had Sam worried.

"So what are you doing by yourself way out here?" He sipped his coffee.

"It's a free country." She cringed again and drank.

"True."

She stared at the shot glass as she took several deep breaths.

"I know you're not from Rocky Butte."

She didn't respond.

"Where are you from, Blondie?"

Sam grinned when she fired a nasty glare at him.

"My name isn't Blondie."

"Then, what is it?"

"That's none of your business." She finished off the drink.

He turned completely to his left to face her, propped his boots on the bottom rung of the stool between them, and leaned on the bar. "Well, something must be my business, 'cause I'm paying for the booze."

Her frown returned. "It's not my fault if you don't know better than to buy a drink for a stranger. I didn't ask you to, *Doc.*"

"You got a point there." He chuckled. "It wouldn't be so bad if you knew how to drink it."

"I'm getting it down."

"Yeah, but you got no *style.*"

She huffed. "What does a redneck, two-bit, cow-town doctor know about style?"

Sam laughed, which elicited another glare. He tried not to show that he saw the fear behind her quips. "Frank," he said, "two more shots, two slices of lime, and salt shakers." He pushed his nearly empty coffee mug aside and turned to face the bar.

The bartender returned quickly with the request, lining ingredients in front of each of them. Sam nodded at the woman. He poured a little salt in his hand, popped it into his mouth, upended the shot, and sucked the juice from the lime slice. He then dropped the slice into the empty glass, flipped the glass upside down, and turned to his drinking partner.

She watched him intently, and dropped her gaze when it

23

met his. Taking a deep breath, she emulated his actions, except she missed about half of the salt and gagged on the lime. When she flipped the glass over, she turned to him and shrugged.

"Not bad for a beginner, Blondie."

"I'm not a beginner, and don't call me Blondie." She leaned farther forward, gripping the bar with her left hand.

Sam hoped it wouldn't take much to loosen her up. It had been years since he'd consumed more than one beer in a night.

"What am I supposed to call you?" he asked.

"Why do you have to call me anything?"

"I have to talk to you. We're drinking together."

They both watched Frank replace the shots and lime.

"Allie," she said. "My name is Allie."

"Is that short for Alicia?"

"No. It's short for Allison."

Sam slid his shot glass toward her and moved to the closer stool. He offered his hand. "Nice to meet you, Allison. I'm Samuel. Everyone calls me Sam."

Allie looked at his hand and then returned her attention to the bar.

Sam shrugged. "Ready?" He poured salt into his palm.

This time Allie matched his actions, except she spilled more of the salt. They pounded their shot glasses onto the bar almost simultaneously.

He sighed and pushed the glass forward. "So, Al, have you eaten dinner?"

"No."

"That sandwich looks good. Aren't you going to try it?"

Allie shook her head vigorously. Sam watched her, grabbing her sleeve momentarily when she almost fell off the barstool. Either she'd been drinking before she appeared in the Last Chance, or she didn't have much tolerance for alcohol.

"Not hungry, huh?"

"No, I've lost my appetite."

From across the bar, Frank raised the tequila bottle questioningly, and Sam shook his head.

"How bad can it be? What could cause a pretty young thing like you to look so miserable? A man?"

"Oh, shut up, Doc. I don't need your redneck questions."

He coughed back a laugh. "Well, Al, you need something. Looks like you're lost. Don't you know that you can die from hypothermia out there on a night like this?"

"Yeah?" She didn't look the least bit surprised, or even interested, as she stared at the bar.

"It's been that bad a day?"

Allie nodded.

"There's one good thing about today being so terrible. Tomorrow has to be better."

"I doubt it."

"You know, Al, you need practice as a drinking buddy. You're way too depressing."

Allie slid off of the stool, steadied herself on the bar for several seconds, then turned.

Sam rose. "Hey, don't leave yet."

Tears started down her face as she took two shaky steps toward the front door and then stopped. Sam dove for her as she collapsed like a rag doll. He winced at the pain that shot through his right leg when his knee banged against the wooden floorboards.

Allie's eyes were crossed and half closed when he turned her over in his lap. "Doc . . . I don't feel so good." Her eyelids fluttered and she went limp in his arms.

Sam checked her pulse, which was steady and strong,

then gathered her up and groaned as he rose. She was tiny and light, but he'd really smacked his kneecap. Damn, it hurt. He shook his leg until the pain subsided, then carried Allie to the bar. When he leaned forward, Frank placed his hat on his head for him.

"Thanks," Frank said.

Sam shrugged. "If anyone comes looking for her tonight, she'll be at my place."

The bartender nodded, and Sam limped toward the door. He pushed it open with his foot and let it slam behind them.

Two

Sam looked over the parking lot, but didn't see any vehicles he didn't recognize. Stars filled the cold night sky, and claws clicked in the metal bed as he started toward his truck.

"Don't worry, Blue, we're headed home."

The dog whined in response.

Sam opened the passenger's door, placed Allie carefully in the seat, and waited to be sure she wouldn't fall. Then he pushed the door closed and climbed into the driver's side. The old truck started on the first try.

Allie glowed blue-green from the dash lights. Sam kept an eye on her as he drove. When he turned off the highway, she sat up and groaned, looking considerably less blue and more green, and fumbled with the door handle. Sam pulled over and dashed around the truck in time to keep her from falling out. He held her as she leaned over and vomited. After several minutes, her stomach stopped convulsing, and she groaned again as she straightened.

She looked at him with one eye open. "Where am I?"

Sam turned her toward the truck and urged her in. "You're okay. It's me, Sam, your drinking buddy."

Allie muttered an unintelligible reply as she crawled up onto the seat and lay down. Sam had to lift her head out of the way to get back in, and he put it down on his thigh. By the time he pulled into the driveway, she was snoring.

She should never have walked outside. Fortunately, though, what she'd heard was true—freezing to death was just like going to sleep.

Was this heaven? Her guardian angel held her, and the place was a fuzzy peach color. Allie had expected white, but peach was close. It had to be a good sign. There was no fire or brimstone that she could see. Not that she would have recognized brimstone. What exactly was it, anyway?

Her guardian angel touched her cheek. His cool, wet hands washed away the dirt of life. His face was rugged but kind, with green eyes and wavy brown hair, and he spoke softly. A halo surrounded his whole face. Interesting.

"Lift your arms," he whispered.

Allie tried to comply, but her arms were filled with lead. The angel lifted them for her and pulled her blouse off over her head. It felt good to shed the rags of mortality. Then he helped her into a robe and wings. Was she really going to be given wings so soon? Wasn't there a training period, or a learner's permit?

Why was she so tired? Who would have guessed you had to sleep in the afterlife? Maybe this was an adjustment period. She wanted to ask her angel, but she couldn't form the words. He let her fall slowly to her side.

"Sleep now," he commanded softly.

She clutched the cloud he gave her for a pillow, and squinted to watch her angel cocoon her in the giant white wings. They were warm and soft and safe. She closed her eyes.

Allie smiled as she drifted into sleep. Heaven was wonderful.

★ ★ ★ ★ ★

Sam knelt beside the bed, studying Allie's face. Her eyes moved quickly under the lids—she was already dreaming. What could have happened to make her so completely miserable? Even with her scraggly hair, she was certainly attractive. Her delicate features were well proportioned, and her eyes were the lightest brown he'd ever seen. In fact, they were almost golden.

He realized when he undressed her that she was too thin and pale. She needed a few good meals and some time outdoors. She also needed a bath, but a quick sponge bath was the best he could do. His T-shirt swallowed her.

He groaned as he pushed himself up to his feet. Allie didn't stir. He switched off the lamp, deciding to leave a light on in the bathroom in case she woke in the night. Then he picked up the pile of clothes and limped out of the room, pulling the door closed behind him.

He really wished he hadn't had the tequila. It made him tired as hell. But there were patients to check on before he could go to bed. He stopped in the laundry room, dropped Allie's shirt and jeans into the washer, and tossed her sweater into the laundry basket, deciding it probably needed the gentle cycle. The washer hissed, and he left the machine to do its job.

The old wooden floor creaked as he continued down the hall. When he opened the double doors to his office, whines and meows and the yaps of Tina Miller's Chihuahua greeted him. With overhead lights blazing, he opened each of the stacked cages, lifting out inhabitants one at a time and inspecting them. He held the sleepy Chihuahua up to look at the stitches that were healing nicely.

"You're looking good, Tiger. I'm sending you home tomorrow, but I want you to stop eating out of the garbage.

29

You understand? If I have to take another toothpick out of your intestine, you might not make it."

The tiny dog stuck out his tongue several times in response.

"Okay, you go back to sleep." Sam placed him in the cage, and the dog curled up on the towel.

"Good night everyone. I don't want any disturbances out here unless something's really wrong, okay?"

Sam flipped off the lights and pulled the doors closed. He tiptoed down the hall, stopping at the laundry room long enough to drape Allie's clothes over a drying rack, then walked back to his own room where he mechanically went through the motions to get ready for bed. As he brushed his teeth, he stared at the white porcelain sink.

Six more days and Tracy would finally arrive. He wasn't looking forward to the first day or two. After spending all but a few weekends of the school year with her mother, she was always angry at the beginning of their summers together, and it was definitely getting worse as she got older. Christ, could she be fifteen already? Where had the time gone?

She'd been five years old the day her mother put her in the car and drove the two of them out of his life. Tracy had pressed her little face to the car window, tears streaming down her cheeks, and his heart had broken. Sam remembered it like it was yesterday. He could forgive Lisa for a lot, but he'd never forgive her for taking his daughter from him.

He spit out the toothpaste and rinsed his mouth, then turned off the bathroom light and stumbled to bed. The bruise on his knee made the joint stiff as he crawled under the covers. He took a deep breath, blew it out slowly, and closed his eyes.

What was he going to do about the young woman sleeping in his guest room? Allie had no identification on her. In fact, her pockets were completely empty. And she must have walked to the Last Chance from somewhere. He couldn't imagine where. Or maybe she'd been hitchhiking. As much as anything else, he was concerned by the bruise on her upper arm about the size of a handprint. The poor girl probably *did* have a really rough day. He was glad, for her sake, that it was over. But what would happen tomorrow?

Sam wondered if she'd intended to walk out into the cold night and die. It was possible—she certainly looked desperate enough. From everything he'd read, he understood that the desire to commit suicide was usually temporary. Assuming Allie really intended to do herself in, he guessed that he only needed to make her stay until she was over the hump. Hopefully, that wouldn't be too long. He had a lot to do before Tracy arrived. If it looked like Allie had bigger problems than a few days would take care of, he could always call Bill. The sheriff must have the authority to check her into the county hospital.

Sam hoped it wouldn't come to that. But at the moment, his most immediate concern was sleep. He dropped his hands to his sides and shut down for the night.

Allie jumped at the sound of dogs barking. She opened her eyes and stared at the ceiling, and the barking stopped.

Where was she? As she lifted her head to look around the room, she winced. Why did her head hurt so badly? And her tongue was thick and furry. She returned her head to the pillow for a moment to work up the energy to rise. Then, lifting the puffy white comforter with her, Allie pushed herself up against the headboard and opened her eyes again.

She sat in the middle of a large bed in a strange room. The wall to the right held several windows—the old-fashioned kind with lacy curtains. A huge oval rug covered a dark wood floor and disappeared under the foot of the bed. Blinking to clear blurry vision, she focused on the furniture across the room—a bookshelf full of books, and a secretary-style desk and chair.

Allie turned slowly and dropped her feet over the side of the bed. The clock on the nightstand said ten-thirty. Could that be right? Another chair, beside a bureau, held a set of folded clothes that looked a little like hers. In fact, they looked exactly like hers.

Forgetting her headache, she threw the comforter aside and stared down at the giant white T-shirt she wore and gasped. Someone had undressed her.

She jumped up and closed her eyes to the pain sudden movement caused. Holding the sides of her head with both hands, she tried desperately to remember how she had ended up here, and where *here* was.

The whole scene in Rick's office came back quickly, bringing with it a wave of nausea. Then there was the drive into the mountains and car problems. She remembered walking and finding a bar and trying to get Melissa's number. She'd felt like a beggar asking for a drink she couldn't afford. She'd never had tequila at a bar and had no idea how much it cost. There were drinks, though, and someone called Doc, but she couldn't remember what he looked like. Then she'd started to walk out of the bar.

The dream floated back into her mind, as soft as cotton candy. She'd been in heaven being tended to by an angel. It was such a nice dream.

Allie took a deep breath, dropped her hands to her sides, and opened her eyes. She needed to discover what she'd gotten herself into and to find a way out. And then she needed to decide what she was going to do. Things certainly had not improved overnight.

She picked up her clothes and tiptoed to the closest door. Finding a bathroom on the other side, she slipped in and locked the door behind her.

On a tiny stool beside the tub were a folded towel and a paper bag that held an assortment of toiletries. Amazed, she pulled out a bottle of fairly expensive shampoo.

Allie glanced around the room. No matter what had happened to her, she didn't think she was in immediate danger. Maybe a warm shower would make her feel better.

"Here he is." Sam placed the tiny brown dog in Tina Miller's arms.

The woman cooed into the dog's ear.

"The incision is healing and the stitches should come out in a week. I'm giving you a head guard that I want you to put on him if he starts trying to bite the stitches."

"You mean one of those lampshade things?" Tina asked.

Sam nodded. "That's it."

"Okay, Sam. I'll do whatever it takes. I'm just so happy to have my boy back." The woman kissed the top of the dog's head.

"And, Tina, you really need to work at keeping him out of the garbage. It could have been worse."

"I know. He'll never go near the garbage again." She stepped closer. "In fact, I've already rearranged the kitchen. Why don't you come over for dinner and check it out? Say, tomorrow night?"

Sam forced a smile. He'd made the mistake of accepting a dinner invitation from Tina Miller once. He wouldn't make it twice. "Thanks anyway. Maybe some other time."

The shapely woman shrugged and turned away. "You don't know what you're missing." Tina exaggerated the swing of her hips as she walked down the concrete steps.

Sam handed her a bag of medication and supplies after she was in her car, and Tina waved and drove off with the tiny dog in her lap.

Sam shook his head as he walked back into the office. He washed his hands, then opened his roll-top desk, pulled a check out of his pocket, and tossed it onto a pile of checks.

He closed the office doors quietly and ran his fingers through his hair as he walked down the hall. He would gladly pay for a few more hours of sleep, but there was just too much to do.

As he rounded the corner into the kitchen, his heart stopped and he jumped back when he nearly ran into his guest.

She flattened herself against the wall like a terrified rabbit, clutched the front of her shirt, and stared at him.

"Whoa! I didn't know you were up." Sam caught his breath and continued around her. "How are you feeling?"

She didn't answer, or even move except to follow him with her eyes.

"You drink coffee?" He glanced over as he filled his cup and saw her nod. Without looking up again, he pulled down another cup, filled it, and handed it to her on his way to the dining room. "Glad to hear you're not on a strict tequila diet."

Sam sat at the table and waited. In a moment, Allie walked in, her eyes wide.

"Have a seat." He nodded at the chair across from him, and she took it. He watched as she sipped the coffee.

Allie placed the cup in front of her and looked up, frowning. "Where . . . who . . ."

"It's me, Sam, your drinking buddy from last night. You're in my house, just outside of Rocky Butte."

"My clothes . . ."

"I had to get you out of your things. You'd kind of made a mess of them. But it was strictly business, Al. Scout's honor."

Allie stared at him for a moment until recognition lit her golden eyes. "Doc," she said.

He nodded. "That's me."

She suddenly jumped up from the table, nearly upsetting her coffee in the process. Steaming liquid sloshed over the sides of the mug before settling down.

Allie backed into the wall. "Look, I don't know what you think you're doing, but I can take care of myself. If you think you're . . . that I owe you something for what you did, you're wrong. I didn't ask you to help me. You come near me and I swear you'll be sorry!" Her hands were fists at her sides and her voice echoed in the room when she stopped yelling.

Sam got up from the table and marched into the kitchen. He hated being yelled at. Trying very hard to maintain his calm, he picked up a dishtowel and carried it into the dining room. After wiping up the spilled coffee, he took a deep breath and tossed the towel onto the table.

"Allison, I know you're frightened. I promise, I have no intention of hurting you, but I won't stand by and watch someone throw her life away because of a bad hair day. I'm not going to live with that guilt for anyone. I'm giving you food and a place to stay, and I expect you to stay here until I say you can leave."

"You can't keep me here," she said through clenched teeth. "Kidnapping is illegal."

"So is attempting suicide."

35

Her eyes widened. "I had no intention—"

"Whatever you say. But if you try to leave before I tell you it's okay, I'll have the sheriff pick you up. You can talk to him about it. Do you understand?"

She nearly snarled.

Sam sighed. "In the meantime, stay out of my way and everything will be fine. When you're ready to act like a civilized human being, let me know." He picked up his coffee and walked through the den and out to the yard.

Once he was out of sight of the house, he stopped and kicked a fence post. The rattling that the kick produced dissipated some of his anger. How dare she get mad at him for trying to save her miserable life?

Allie stared at the spot vacated by Doc and suddenly remembered him introducing himself at the bar. Samuel. Sam. The angel she'd dreamt was Sam putting clean clothes on her. Allie slid down the wall, dropped her head into her hands and let the tears flow. Anger and fear flowed out with them.

He had probably saved her life. When she'd tried to leave the bar, she hadn't really thought about freezing to death. All she'd thought about was escaping. She'd had fuzzy plans to hitchhike somewhere, although now she wasn't sure where she'd planned to go. Alcohol on a sleep-deprived, empty stomach had affected her quickly. Allie lifted her head and let the tears drip from her jaw.

What was she going to do? She had no money, and she had no car, but she couldn't just wait for Rick to find her. He would probably convince the world that she was some troubled woman he had tried to help by marrying, and that he was the one mistreated. He was so good at his disguise that he'd had her fooled for a long time. He could probably get her committed or locked away somehow. Then he would be able to continue his outside *activities* and not worry about tarnishing his image with divorce.

Was her imagination just running wild? It sounded far-fetched, but she wouldn't put anything past him anymore. And no one would miss her if he made her disappear.

Besides, no matter what happened, she couldn't live the lie anymore.

She had to keep moving. Where could she go? For that matter, where did Sam say she was? Rocky Butte? She'd never even heard of it, and she'd lived in Colorado for five years. It must be the middle of nowhere.

A thought suddenly occurred to Allie. At the moment, no one in Rocky Butte knew who she was, and no one in Denver knew *where* she was. She could drop Tate and pick up her maiden name. Allie Parker. It was a name she hadn't used in a long time. The tears slowed. The car was in Rick's name, so no one would connect it to her if she didn't claim it. Rick would think she'd abandoned it and hitchhiked away. Who in their right mind would stay in a place like this? It could work. At least until she decided on her next move. Threads of hope began weaving themselves into a lifeline.

Allie jumped at the sound beside her. She looked down to find an orange cat sitting on the floor, just out of reach, studying her. The cat meowed again and tilted its head.

"Hi. I'm Allie Parker," she said, practicing her new introduction. "How do you do?"

The cat meowed, as if replying to her question.

"Sorry, I don't speak feline."

Allie wiped her eyes and rose from the floor. She sat at the table and took another sip of bitter coffee. She would have enjoyed it more with a little sugar, but she didn't want to snoop around for a sugar bowl.

Okay, so if she decided to change her identity, how would she make a living? Getting a job wasn't easy without references. Although she'd been out of the workforce for five years, she knew that if she was willing to do anything, there was a job out there somewhere. She could make enough to buy food and get started on her own. All she needed was an opportunity. The lack of ID might be a problem, but she was certain she could get around it, given time to think.

One thing for sure: she couldn't give Sam a reason to call the sheriff. The whole thing could blow up in her face if Rick had reported her missing to the Denver police and they had circulated her picture.

Allie drank the last sip of coffee. In another room, a phone rang. She listened. It rang again.

After a dozen unanswered rings, she got up, followed the sound into the kitchen, and lifted the receiver. "Hello?"

"Hello! Is Dr. Calvert around?"

"Dr. Calvert?"

"Sam. Is Sam Calvert around?"

"Um, yes, I think he's here somewhere. You want to hold on while I look for him?"

"No. Tell him Clancy called. We have a cow down and it looks bad."

"Um, okay, I'll tell him."

The line clicked and Allie returned the receiver to the cradle.

A cow? The local doctor worked on cows, too? It must be a *really* small town. With a sigh, she followed the path Sam had taken from the dining room.

The only room left before the exterior door was a den, and he wasn't in there. Allie walked outside, surprised by the size of Sam's place. To her left were a garage and a huge barn surrounded by a high wooden fence, and to her right the mountains glistened in the sunlight. She couldn't see any other houses from the back door.

"Sam?" Allie started toward the barn. "Sam?"

"Yeah?"

She rounded the corner of the garage to find him standing in front of the barnyard fence, one cowboy boot propped on a rail about a foot off the ground, the coffee mug empty at his side. His brown, wavy hair brushed his broad shoulders and seemed to glitter in the sunshine. A large black dog sat near him, watching her.

"I, um, answered your phone. Someone named Clancy said to tell you he has a cow down and it looks bad, whatever that means."

Sam nodded and dropped his foot to the ground. "Thanks." He walked past her and into the house without another word. The black dog followed him, glancing warily back at her.

Within a minute or two, Allie heard a vehicle start on the opposite side of the house. Dust rose behind a blue pickup truck, presumably with Sam behind the wheel, that roared off down the dirt road.

He hadn't given her any instructions, except to stay out of his way, and Allie's stomach burned with hunger. She had no choice but to search Sam's kitchen for food; she hoped he wouldn't be too angry.

As she turned back to the house, bright silver metal reflecting sunlight caught her eye. Curious, she walked to the side of the house and peered around the corner.

The old frame building had shiny fences attached to it. Allie continued around, trying to figure out exactly what they were. As she approached, two dogs barked from inside the fences. One dog had a front leg in a splint and the other had its shoulder shaved and the skin in the middle stitched together.

The fences were dog kennels, a dozen of them. Allie turned back and stared at the barn through narrowed eyes. A huge barn, dog kennels, a call about a cow . . .

Somehow, the idea of Sam undressing her wasn't so bad when she thought he was the town doctor and used to seeing people disrobed. But he wasn't a people doctor—he was a veterinarian. The only patients he saw naked were dogs and cows.

Allie held the top of her head as she walked toward the door. "Oh, God," she muttered, wondering how she'd ever face him again.

Three

By the time Sam pulled the truck into the driveway, the smell of fried chicken was driving him crazy. It must be almost five, and he hadn't eaten anything since breakfast. He drew the brown bag out after him and carried it into the house. On his way to the bathroom, he left the bag on the table.

After scrubbing his hands, Sam changed into a clean T-shirt. He had already washed his boots at Clancy's. The rest could wait until after he ate.

"Al?" Sam called down the hall as he left his room. "Hey, Al!"

There was no reply.

Dammit, she hadn't skipped out on him, had she? Sam stopped at the guest room and opened the door slowly. "Allie?"

The room was empty.

"Damn."

He slammed the door and started back down the hall. When Allie backed out of the laundry room and ran into him, they both jumped.

An instant wave of relief washed over him. "There you are."

"What's the matter, Doc? Did you think I'd run off?"

"Well, Al, the possibility had occurred to me." Sam

walked around her. "Dinner's here. Want to call a truce and eat?"

"Okay."

As he passed through the kitchen, Sam picked up two plates and two sets of silverware. "Grab a cold drink out of the fridge for me, would you? And get whatever you want."

Allie followed him into the dining room, a Coke can in each hand.

"You want a glass?" he asked.

She shook her head.

Sam opened the bag and extracted the dozen fried chicken pieces, wrapped in foil, as well as containers of coleslaw and biscuits.

"Dig in."

They filled their plates in silence, and Sam devoured a chicken thigh. Slowing after the initial attack, he worked on three more pieces and the slaw, and watched Allie. With her hair pulled back and her face clean, she had almost a child-like innocence about her. He sympathized with her; she must have been confused and frightened when she first woke in a strange place. She picked at a chicken wing in silence.

"You're going to have to do better than that," he said, "or you'll starve."

Allie grinned at him sheepishly. "Actually, I fixed myself a sandwich. I hope you don't mind."

"No, I don't mind."

"And I had a piece of the apple pie that's in the refrigerator."

Sam laughed quietly. He could probably stop worrying about her getting enough to eat. "Fine."

She finished the wing and started on a drumstick. "You didn't tell me you're a vet."

"You didn't ask." He glanced up and found her frowning at her plate.

"I'm sorry I yelled at you," she said. "I . . . I appreciate your help."

He looked up again to catch her studying him with those golden eyes.

Allie looked away.

"Don't worry about it," he said.

Her voice got quieter; he had to stop chewing to hear her. "I, um, don't have anywhere to go."

Sam dropped the chicken bone to his plate, wiped his hands, and took a large swig of Coke. He returned the can to the table. "I guessed that." He sighed. "You're welcome to stay here as long as you need to, and I can help you get a job in town, if you want it."

Her eyes snapped up to his. "I'm *not* a charity case. I can earn my keep. Just give me work and I'll do it. And I can get my own job in town."

Damn, she could go from meek to feisty without any warning, which he found more than just a bit annoying. "Okay, if that's what you want. There's plenty around here to do. You can start with the barn tomorrow morning. The stalls need mucking out, and the walls need washing."

She narrowed her eyes. "Mucking out?"

"Cleaning. It's not easy work, especially for a little thing like you, Al."

"Don't worry, *Doc*. I can handle it. You just tell me when and where."

"Fine. Seven o'clock tomorrow morning at the barn."

"I'll be there."

Sam poured honey on one of the biscuits and ate it while he watched her working on the drumstick and slaw. She ate the chicken with her pinkies sticking out, like she was in a fancy restaurant, and visibly relaxed as she worked her way through the food. Her face was actually pretty when it wasn't tight with anger.

"What happened to Clancy's cow?" she asked.

Sam swallowed the last bite of the biscuit. "She didn't make it."

"What was wrong with her?"

"She was old. Milk cows get old and die just like everyone else."

"That's sad."

"Yeah. But it's part of life."

Someone pounded on the door. Sam jumped up, walked to the den, and found Bill standing on the steps, dressed in his uniform.

"Hi, Bill. What can I do for the sheriff's department this evening?"

"I'm sorry to catch you so late, Sam, but Thor wrestled with a porcupine today."

"Let me guess who won."

The gray-haired man huffed. "Yeah."

"You bring him around to the office and I'll meet you back there."

"Thanks. I really appreciate this."

"No problem."

Sam closed the door and started through the dining room. "Sorry, Al—"

She was gone, but her plate hadn't moved from the table. She must have run to the bathroom or something. He drank the last of his Coke, washed his hands, and walked quickly to the back of the house. When he opened the exterior door, Bill waited with the German shepherd in his arms. The poor dog had a dozen quills sticking out of his shoulder and face.

"Put him up here on the table and let's have a look."
Sam switched on the lamp. "It's okay, Thor," he said.
"We'll get these nasty quills out of you." He looked at each
quill, checking the depth and tissue penetrated. None of
them looked too bad.

"We can take care of these with locals. I'll give him a
mild sedative first. Can you hang onto him while I get them
out?"

"You bet." The older man wrapped his arms around the
dog, holding Thor's head still with his own.

Sam smiled. These two had been buddies for a long
time.

After Sam's footsteps faded, Allie stepped cautiously
from the bathroom. She'd heard the conversation at the
door and decided to hide. There was no point in taking
chances. The light at the end of the hall must be coming
from Sam's office. She hadn't looked down there today,
mainly because she'd stopped at the laundry room. She'd
found her sweater in the dirty clothes and washed it, along
with a few loads of clothes for Sam.

She slipped silently down the hall and returned to the
dining room. From there she could duck outside and hide if
she needed to, and she could keep an eye on the visitor's
car. As quietly as possible, she cleaned the table and
washed dishes. By the time the work was done, the sun had
started to drop below the mountaintops.

Sam was still in his office. Allie walked out and sat on
the steps, enjoying the chilly evening. A pair of ravens circled above in the clear mountain air. She filled her lungs,
appreciating the lack of carbon monoxide. How long had it
been since she'd been out of the city?

Allie straightened at the sound of a car starting. It pulled out of the driveway and raced down the dirt road.

Sam's boots thumped on the wooden floor as he entered the den. "Allie?"

"I'm out here."

Sam pushed the screen door open just enough to slip out. He eased down onto a step two below her and leaned back. "Nice evening."

"Yes."

"Sorry about the interruption, and thanks for cleaning up."

He surprised her. Judging by most of his comments, she would have thought Sam enough of a redneck to expect her to clean the kitchen. Allie smiled at the back of his head. "No problem."

They watched the sky for several long minutes in silence as the ravens dropped into the tops of distant evergreens.

Sam sighed. "Well, there's still too much to do. I can't sit here dawdling." He pushed himself up, groaning as if he'd aged ten years since dinner.

"Anything I can help with?" she asked.

He turned to face her, towering over her and blocking out what was left of the sun. He must be at least six-two, and he was big. Allie guessed that most of his bulk was muscle. She could picture him wrestling a horse to the ground.

And yet, when he stood there with his head tilted and one eyebrow raised, he looked like an overgrown boy.

"You can help fill food bowls if you want," he said.

Allie grinned. "I can probably do that." She took the hand he offered, and he effortlessly pulled her to her feet and released her. She followed him through the yard.

Allie slowed as they approached the kennels. When Sam

opened the first gate, she even took a step backwards.

Sam frowned. "Are you afraid of dogs, Al?"

She took a deep breath. "I guess so, a little."

"What happened? Bitten when you were a kid?"

"No."

"Haven't you ever been around dogs?"

"Not really."

Sam couldn't remember meeting anyone who hadn't spent any time with dogs. "You don't need to be afraid of the dogs around here. Come on over and I'll introduce you."

Allie folded her arms across her chest and took half a step forward. "Why don't we just call this good, and you tell me what to put in their bowls?"

"Come on. Come say hello." He stepped into the first kennel with Joey. The black Lab hopped around, pushing his head into Sam's hand. Sam knelt and rubbed the dog's ears, and was rewarded with a decent licking. "See? He's friendly, to say the least."

Allie cringed as she moved slowly closer. "That's gross."

"No, it isn't. He's just expressing his gratitude and friendship with a kiss. You're telling me you don't like kisses?"

She rolled her eyes and frowned. Standing with her arms folded, the orange sky behind her, her golden eyes flashing caution and her lips pushed out in a pout, she was a whole lot sexier than she should have been.

Sam swallowed and turned back to Joey. He scratched the dog's chest to calm him as he looked at the stitches. The cut was healing well.

"Why is he standing so still?" Allie's voice startled him because of its closeness.

Sam scooted over to give her room and she squatted tentatively near him.

"He likes being scratched here. Most dogs do. You want to try it?"

"I don't know—"

Sam grabbed her left hand and put it next to his. "Just like this, up and down gently." As soon as she had the rhythm, Sam withdrew his hand. Joey's eyes crossed and his head turned sideways.

"Hey, you've got the spot. See? It almost puts some dogs in a trance."

Allie's apprehension relaxed into a smile.

"Now, if you stop scratching, he'll give you a kiss."

Allie sighed. "Oh, all right." She pulled her hand back to her knee and squeezed her eyes shut. When Joey's tongue first hit her chin, she flinched, but after about the fourth lick, she started to laugh as she tried to get away. When Allie fell over, Joey took advantage of the situation and licked her neck. Allie's laughter was contagious, and Sam chuckled as he pulled the Lab away.

"He doesn't know when to stop, I'm afraid." Sam led Joey out and to the last kennel. "You should be ashamed," he said to the dog. "Total lack of self-control."

Joey barked twice.

"Yeah, I know she's cute, but that's no excuse."

Joey dropped his head as if in shame. Sam scratched his ears before closing him in the pen. He returned to find Allie wiping her face on her sleeves.

"Cute, huh?"

Sam held up both hands. "His words, not mine."

"Right, Doc. Is your last name Calvert or Doolittle?"

"Whichever you prefer, Al." He tossed the towel and

chew-toy through the open gate and picked up the water bowl.

Allie shook her head and then looked up as he walked past her. "What should I do?"

"You can grab the plastic bottle of disinfectant out of the shed over there. I like to clean the kennels out before I feed the inmates."

Allie nodded and walked toward the shed. As Sam opened the second kennel gate, he glanced over at her. She had a nice walk—very sensuous in its simplicity, as if she didn't know she was attractive.

He took a deep breath. Good thing he wasn't interested, because he could see where Allie could be very distracting.

At five minutes to seven, Allie inhaled crisp morning air that filtered in through the kitchen window as she finished her last sip of coffee. She left the mug in the sink and walked out to the barn.

Sam must be around somewhere. She hadn't seen him since they finished feeding the menagerie the night before, but he had left fresh coffee for her in the coffee pot.

When she arrived at the barn, she found the same orange cat she'd seen in the house and knelt in front of it. "Hi, cat."

The cat studied her for a moment, and then approached and let Allie rub its back, purring loud enough to be a wind-up toy.

"I see you've met Popsicle."

She looked up to find Sam standing before her in a white T-shirt almost black with dirt, well-worn leather gloves, blue jeans, and cowboy boots, and wearing a tattered straw cowboy hat low on his forehead. Locks of brown hair flipped up from under the hat, dripping sweat that ran down the sides of his face. As she watched, he lifted his hat just long enough to wipe his face on the sleeve of his T-shirt.

"Popsicle?" she asked. "Isn't that a strange name for a cat?"

Sam smiled, pushed his hat back a bit, and crouched in front of her. He gently grabbed Popsicle's tail and the cat meowed in response.

"I guess it is. When I found her in town three winters ago, it was the middle of a cold spell. Must have been fifty below. She was frozen to the sidewalk, crying for help. Poor little orange cat, frozen to the sidewalk. She looked like an orange popsicle."

"What did you do?"

"I poured a bucket of warm water around her and melted the ice. She jumped right into my truck and rode home with me."

When Allie looked down at the cat, Popsicle winked at her as if to verify the story.

"Look," Sam said, "about the barn—"

They stood at the same time.

"Don't start this macho crap with me again," she said. "I told you I'd clean it, and I intend to do just that. Show me what to do."

Sam sighed. "Okay, fine, this way."

He gave her a pair of gloves, a rake, a shovel, a pitchfork, and a wheelbarrow, and he explained the process. Then he showed her how to lead the horses out to the corral. Her lack of experience with horses must have been obvious, because Sam gave very detailed instructions on exactly how to hold the halter and lead the beasts around. A large white one started neighing and snorting as soon as they got close.

"I'll go ahead and take Hattie out," Sam said. "She's not

very good with strangers."

The horse backed into the wall when Sam eased into her stall. He spoke calmly, and after several tense moments, Hattie finally let him touch her halter, but she continued to stomp and snort. Allie moved out of their way when Sam led the horse out.

"She's so fat," she said, noting that the horse was at least twice as wide as the others.

"She's about to foal." Sam closed the horse in the second corral and walked back to the barn.

"To fold?"

"No, to *foal*," he said. "She's very pregnant."

"Oh. Is that why she's so jumpy?"

Sam looked out at Hattie and frowned. "No. I got her from someone who whipped her on a regular basis. I've had her for six months, but it'll take years for her to get over it. If she ever does." He turned back and started toward the door. "And she was too damn old to be bred." Muttering, he left the barn.

Allie watched the large white horse. Now that she was alone, Hattie calmed down and began nibbling on grass that grew up along the fence. Poor thing. With the sun on her, Allie could see long scars on the horse's back and sides. How could anyone be so cruel?

Pulling on the gloves, Allie walked to the pile of tools. She gathered them together and pushed the wheelbarrow into the first stall. Cleaning the barn might be a stinky job, but it didn't look all that difficult. And her nose had already started to adjust to the stench.

An hour later at the door to the fourth stall, Allie lifted the handles of the wheelbarrow, which was heavy and listed to one side. When she tried to straighten it, she tripped over her own feet and fell to her knees. The wheelbarrow turned over, spilling its contents back onto the ground.

"Dammit!"

She pushed herself up and marched to the corral, stripping the oversized gloves from her hands and throwing them down in disgust. She dropped to the ground in the shade, leaned back on the wooden slats, and closed her eyes.

Cleaning a barn was a lot harder than it looked. The muscles in her arms and back burned. Out of all the jobs she'd ever had, this was definitely the toughest.

She could give up. She could walk into the house and tell Sam that the job was more than she could handle. He'd probably give her a redneck grin and make some snide remark.

She took a deep breath. No matter what, she wasn't going to give him the satisfaction of saying, "I told you so."

The blast of hot air on Allie's shoulder sent her scrambling across the ground. She spun around and stared at the pink nose protruding from between two rails of the corral. Nostrils flared and the horse snorted, then pulled its nose back in and made a funny little neighing sound.

Allie stood and walked slowly to the corral. This was the white horse that Sam had said was afraid of strangers. What was her name? Hattie?

"Hi, Hattie."

The horse raised her nose toward Allie. Tentatively, Allie reached over the fence and touched the horse's head. Hattie closed her eyes and Allie rubbed her face.

"What's the matter, girl? You tired, too?"

The horse moved her head just a little as if in response, but her eyes remained closed. Allie rested her chin on her arm as she continued to rub, and silence settled around the two of them like dust after a breeze. Allie closed her own eyes to enjoy the strange sense of peace, feeling for the first time as if she truly had a shot at a new life. Maybe she'd get the same chance Hattie had been given when Sam rescued her. Allie felt as if all she had to do was finish cleaning the barn.

By eleven-thirty, Sam had moved the rest of the hay to the loft, replaced rotten siding on the garage, cleaned the dog runs, and seen three patients. He was hungry and tired, and a little worried about Allie.

When he'd secretly checked on her before he showered, he'd found her nearly halfway through. She'd looked worn out, but she hadn't given up. He'd seen her getting water from the hose a couple times, and letting the water run over her head. One thing for sure, she was no wimp. Cleaning such a huge barn wasn't easy for anyone, and especially for someone not used to that kind of work.

He was relieved to see her finally headed for the house. She walked slowly, with a tired but steady gait.

Sam had searched Tracy's room for some clothes that he thought might fit Allie. Allie was taller and thinner than Tracy, but he'd managed to find a dress, a pair of shorts, two long-sleeved blouses, a T-shirt, and some blue jeans. Tracy would never miss them. She brought new clothes with her every summer anyway.

The screen door slammed as Sam emptied the contents of a soup can into a pot. He glanced back at Allie in time to see her straightening defiantly in his presence, and he couldn't help but smile.

"How did it go?"

"Just fine."

"Well, good, I'm glad to hear it. You've got time for a quick shower before lunch. I put some clothes on your bed.

53

You're welcome to them if they fit."

She continued through the kitchen and disappeared into the hall without another word.

By the time Allie walked back into the kitchen, Sam had sandwiches made and was dishing up soup. She wore Tracy's jeans, which were a little short for her, and one of the blouses. Her brown and blond hair was wet and combed back, and she definitely smelled better than she had twenty minutes earlier.

"Sandwiches and iced tea are on the table. Go ahead in. I'll be right there." He followed her into the dining room, carefully carrying bowls of soup. Once the bowls were placed, he took his chair.

"Whose clothes are these?" she asked.

"They're my daughter's."

"You have a daughter?"

"Yes, I have a daughter."

Allie didn't say anything.

"Her name is Tracy. She's fifteen and she lives in California with her mother during the school year. Spends the summers here. She'll be here in four days. Anything else you want to know?"

Allie shook her head and smiled at him, but the smile was forced. He watched her with furtive glances as she worked on her soup. It wasn't until she picked up the sandwich that he realized what was wrong.

Four

Allie held her sandwich between the very tips of her fingers.

Sam put his own sandwich down and leaned across the table. "Let me see your hands."

"What?"

"Let me see your hands."

"Piss off, Doc."

He reached out and grabbed her wrist. "I'm not joking around, Allie. Put the sandwich down and show me your hands."

Frowning, she slowly complied. As he'd feared, huge blisters full of fluid marred both palms. She flinched when he gently touched one.

"Dammit, didn't I give you gloves?"

"Yes, you gave me gloves, but they were too big. I didn't know this would happen."

Sam shook his head and jumped up from the table. "I'll be right back."

When he returned with salve, antiseptic, and bandages, he pulled an empty chair around to Allie's side and placed the first aid supplies on the table.

"Turn this way and give me your right hand first."

Sam filled a cotton cloth with antiseptic and dabbed it on her skin, careful not to break the blisters. He then applied the salve and loosely wrapped it, taping the bandage in place. He repeated the process on her left hand.

As she turned back to the table, Sam closed the salve and antiseptic.

"These are serious blisters," he said. "If they break and get infected, you could be in big trouble. The bandages are to keep them clean and protect the skin, but you need to make sure you're getting air to them. Questions?"

Allie shook her head.

Sam put the supplies away and returned to the table. Allie worked carefully on her sandwich again. He refilled her glass with iced tea before returning his attention to his food.

When they had finished eating, Sam carried the plates to the counter. "I want you to take the rest of the day off, Al. You've definitely earned it."

Allie followed him into the kitchen. "Actually, Doc, I was just thinking that a nap sounds good." She ambled from the kitchen, her feet dragging.

Sam stopped up the sink, dropped in the plates, and added dish soap. As the sink filled, he stared at the massing bubbles.

He couldn't believe how bad the blisters on Allie's hands were. They must have hurt like hell while she was cleaning. She would certainly go to great lengths if challenged. That was the last time he'd put her in a situation where she had to prove herself to him. It was his fault that her hands were in such bad shape.

As he'd tended to her hands, sitting close to her and leaning closer, Sam had noticed just how good Allie smelled. And there was something about being near her that made it hard for him to breathe. Damn. When she'd walked into the Last Chance, he'd recognized her as a good-looking woman, but it was only a passing observation. Suddenly, she was much more than just good-looking.

This was stupid. He turned off the water, lifted a plate, and scrubbed it. Allie was the first female, other than his daughter, who had spent any time in his house in the past ten years. That was the problem. It had nothing to do with her. He had simply forgotten what it was like to have a woman in close proximity all the time.

Now that he'd thought it out, everything would be okay. He had no time in his life for a woman. Years ago, Lisa had accused him of being married to his work. It may not have been true then, but it was now, and his job was a very demanding mistress.

Sam rinsed the plate and stood it in the drain pan.

Allie stretched out on the bed, sighing as muscles in her back relaxed one at a time. She'd never realized how many muscles the human body had.

Why had she continued when her hands started hurting? There was absolutely no reason she needed to impress Sam. What difference did his opinion of her make? None. None at all.

So, why had his look of approval made her feel so good when she first walked into the kitchen?

The worst thing that had happened that day was that she'd realized she found Sam attractive. This big man, tremendously masculine and muscular, leaning over her hands and touching them with such tenderness, made her knees weak. She'd wondered how his arms would feel around her and was horrified by the desire to touch him. Fortunately, he had finished bandaging her hands quickly and released her before she'd made a fool of herself.

The year of abstinence must be getting to her. Why else

would she find a redneck cowboy attractive? She hated rednecks. And she had more important things to worry about, like how she would make a living and where she would go.

Allie gently placed her hands on the bed, palms up, and wondered how hard it was to get a job in Canada. As she was wondering, she fell asleep.

Friday night was bad. After a four-hour nap, Allie had risen to stiffness she'd never experienced before. A hot shower helped, but shortly after dinner she'd gone back to sleep. Sam had suggested she move around. She'd told him to get stuffed or something similar because she was unable to keep her eyes open. The apocalypse would have passed unnoticed.

But Saturday morning she was fairly sure she'd discovered hell. It took a half hour just to get out of bed. Every inch of her body screamed with pain. She couldn't even close her hands, and her back hurt no matter which way she moved. It took another half hour to get dressed. What she needed now was a little food, and then she might just go back to bed. Maybe she could sleep until the misery was gone.

Allie filled a mug with fresh coffee from the pot. As she was stirring in the sugar, Sam strolled in and filled his own cup.

"Morning." He was much too cheerful.

"Yeah."

He must have just showered, because his hair was wet, and his T-shirt and jeans were clean, as were his brown, muscular arms. Allie had realized that he worked several hours in the morning before she even got up. He seemed to have an endless supply of energy.

Sam leaned back on the counter, crossed one boot over the other, and watched her as he sipped from his mug. After a moment, he narrowed his eyes. "Just how sore are you?"

Allie lowered her coffee mug, working hard not to groan at the effort. "Pretty sore."

"What hurts?"

"I think it would be faster to ask what doesn't hurt."

Sam cringed. "I'm really sorry, Allie. I should have known better than—"

"Oh shut up, Doc." She turned toward the dining room, walking as fast as she could. A sickly snail could have outpaced her. By the time she managed to sit, Sam was across the table, watching. From the look in his eyes, she would have guessed he was the one suffering.

Allie sighed. "So, how do I make it stop hurting?"

"You need to stretch out those muscles," he said with the enthusiasm of a coach. "It's tough at first, but it'll help in the long run."

She frowned. "I'm not really good with the long-run stuff. Are you sure I shouldn't just go back to bed?"

Sam smiled into his cup. "I'm sure. Stick with me for a while this morning and we'll get you moving again."

She sighed and nodded.

Sam's smile disappeared. "But I want you to be really careful with those blisters."

"No problem there."

Allie felt like a worthless blob as Sam fixed breakfast and served her a plate of eggs scrambled with ham, mushrooms, and onions, complete with homemade biscuits and a glass of orange juice. It was all she could do just to eat. He then cleaned up the kitchen and met her at the back door where she stood, staring helplessly at her tennis shoes. She couldn't bend down to put them on.

Sam frowned at her for a second, then grinned. He knelt in front of her and held her right shoe open. Allie slid her foot in, but she had to use his shoulder to keep from falling over. He pulled the laces snug and tied them, then checked to make sure they weren't too tight.

His shoulder was a rock under the soft, cotton T-shirt he wore. Allie felt muscles flexing beneath her fingers as he tied her shoe. Her stomach fluttered and she swallowed the lump in her throat. God, he was more muscular than she'd realized, and she found that fact more exciting than she should have.

When he finished her left shoe and rose, she had to force herself to release him. She couldn't look at him, afraid her face would betray her, and he didn't say anything until he was outside, holding the back door open.

"Come on, Al. There's lots of work to do."

Together they cleaned cages and bowls and yards. They fed horses, dogs, cats, a calf, and two sheep. Sam did the actual scrubbing and anything else that required the use of tools or muscles. Allie followed him and carried smaller objects. She was sure he could have done the work in less than half the time by himself, but he didn't say a word about her lack of speed. Before she realized what had happened, she was walking at nearly her normal pace and was able to bend down to the ground. Everything still hurt, but the pain was manageable.

They were walking back from the barn together when a car pulled into the driveway and skidded to a stop. As soon as the engine quieted, a woman's voice could be heard yelling for help.

Sam trotted toward the car, and Allie followed as quickly as she could. When she reached the driveway, she saw Sam pulling a cardboard box out of the front seat. A young woman held the car door open with one hand and a small child by the wrist with the other. Both the woman and child were crying.

"Oh, please help him," the woman said through tears. "The car that hit him didn't even stop."

"I'll do what I can, Mrs. Halley. You two wait out here for a few minutes, okay?"

The woman nodded as she wiped her eyes.

Sam turned to Allie, frowning. "I need your help."

She nodded and followed him to his office.

Sam put the box on a metal table in the middle of the room and washed his hands and arms in the sink as he spoke over his shoulder. "Fill this pan with lukewarm water, and then bring it and one of these sponges to the table."

Allie followed his instructions, glancing at the table as she did. Sam switched on a spotlight, lifted a small dog from the box, and placed it gently on the table. The dog was soaked with blood and its tongue hung from its mouth. It didn't move or make a sound. Allie was sure it wasn't alive. Fighting shaking hands, she carried the pan of water to the table, placed it within Sam's reach, and moved the cardboard box out of the way.

"Is it . . . dead?"

"No. We need to wash off enough of this blood to see where it's coming from." He grabbed the sponge and squeezed it above the dog's shoulder. Red water ran to the edge of the table and then down to the drain at the end. Allie held the pan closer.

Just as Sam finished washing off most of the blood, the dog opened its eyes and whimpered.

"It's okay, boy. We're taking care of you." Sam spoke softly as he worked. The dog was only slightly bigger than his hands.

Sam looked up. "See that tray on wheels? Push it around to this side."

Allie found the tray filled with tools neatly arranged on top of a towel and holding several small bottles and hypodermic needles in one corner. When she reached him, Sam released the dog and lifted one of the bottles. He filled a hypodermic, turned back to the table, and, holding the needle up in the air, looked at Allie.

"You okay?"

She nodded.

It was only half true. Her stomach did flips and her hands shook. She'd never spent much time around either blood or needles, but both seemed to make her a little queasy.

"Don't forget to breathe," he told her. "Take slow, deep breaths."

She nodded again and inhaled through her nose. He was right, she'd been holding her breath without realizing it.

Sam injected clear liquid into the back of the dog's neck. Then he dropped the needle onto the tray and held the dog's head, rubbing one ear with his thumb.

"That's it. You just close your eyes for a while," he whispered. After a minute, he lifted one of the dog's eyelids and then let it close.

Allie watched his face as he straightened and sighed. He pressed a piece of gauze to the canine's shoulder.

"Is he going to die?"

Sam smiled at her. "Not if I can help it. Unless I'm missing something, it's not quite as bad as it looks. I see two deep cuts. I don't see signs of internal injuries or broken bones yet, but there could be something hiding from me. Will you do me a favor?"

Allie nodded.

"Will you take Mrs. Halley and her daughter inside and get them something to drink? I'll be in there shortly."

"You don't need help in here?"

"Not right now. I'm used to doing this part alone, and he's out." Sam leaned over the table and checked the dog's eye again. "I need to get started before he loses much more blood."

Allie was quite happy to get out, but she felt bad about leaving Sam alone. Stopping in the doorway, she watched him pull a metal stool up with the toe of his boot and sit. He lifted utensils from the tray and leaned over the table, completely absorbed in his work. Allie closed the door behind her.

Mrs. Halley leaned on her car, hugging her daughter, and straightened as Allie approached. "How is he?" she asked.

"I don't really know. The doctor asked me to invite you in. He said he'd be out in a little while."

The woman nodded and followed Allie into the dining room, where she sat at the table and pulled her child onto her lap. Allie guessed the little girl must be five or so—older than she'd first seemed.

"Juice, Coke, water, or coffee?"

The woman looked down at her daughter and back up at Allie. "We could share a Coke. That would be nice."

Allie poured a Coke into two glasses. Her hands still shook, but they were getting better. She filled a glass of water for herself and then carried all three glasses to the table and sat at the end. Mrs. Halley and her daughter wiped away tears, and they drank in silence for a while.

Allie had been able to ignore her sore muscles until a sharp pain in her lower back caused her to straighten quickly, wincing as she did.

"Are you okay?"

She smiled across the table at the woman. "Yes, it's just a sore back."

"Oh?"

Allie nodded.

"You're not from around here."

"No, I'm not."

Mrs. Halley, at least five years Allie's junior, studied her intently. "I'm Jennifer Halley, and this is my daughter Trish. Everyone calls me Jen." The young woman extended her hand.

Allie took Jen's hand gingerly with her own bandaged one. Fortunately, the woman was afraid to squeeze. "Allie. Allie Parker."

"What happened to your hands?"

She shrugged. "It's just blisters."

"Oh. Are you a relative of Dr. Calvert's?"

"No. I'm a houseguest."

"Oh."

Allie hid her grin in her water glass. She could see wheels turning in Jen's mind. This was a "small town" part of the state where everyone knew everyone else.

Her grin faded as she thought about what that meant. She would stand out here like a sore thumb, and people wouldn't be satisfied until they knew exactly who she was. Or, at least, thought they knew. She'd have to come up with a believable story. Maybe she could be Sam's cousin and her mother had just died. Sam was comforting her. Or maybe she was a vet student on sabbatical.

Neither one sounded very convincing. She'd have to work on it. God, she hated the thought of having to lie.

They continued to sit at the table, drinking, for another half hour. Trish gave Allie her puppy's life history, and then went on to talk about her neighbor's Great Dane. Allie felt

Jen's scrutinizing stare the entire time, although the woman would look down when Allie returned it. It was a great relief to finally hear Sam's footsteps in the hall.

Sam stopped in the kitchen for a moment, then continued to the dining room and joined them at the table, sipping from a half-empty glass of water. Jen's face suddenly filled with concern that she'd almost forgotten.

Sam sighed. "That's one lucky puppy. What's his name?"

"Lucky," Trish answered.

Sam gave the girl a smile that could melt ice cubes. "Good name."

The child beamed.

"He has a couple of cuts that required stitches, but so far, I don't see any signs of internal damage. The car must not have run over him. I need to keep an eye on him for a few days, to watch for hidden problems. I'm not guaranteeing anything, but it looks good at the moment. I'll know more by Monday."

Jen wiped away fresh tears. "Thank you, Dr. Calvert." The woman glanced at Allie and then turned back to Sam and spoke quietly. "I don't know how we're going to pay you for all of it."

Allie felt like an intruder, yet she couldn't stop watching the exchange. Sam smiled at Jen and drank the last of his water. He got up from the table, walked around it, crouched by Trish's chair, and held the girl's shoulder as he spoke to her mother. "Right now we need to concentrate on getting Lucky well. We'll worry about the rest of it later."

Jen nodded in silence as she wiped her eyes again.

Sam picked up the child and carried her outside, and Jen and Allie followed.

"I'm going to keep Lucky with me for a few days," he

said to Trish, "okay?"

The girl frowned at Sam, her arm draped across his shoulder. "He'll be lonely here. He sleeps in my bed."

"He won't be lonely. There are lots of other dogs here to keep him company, and I'll check on him a lot."

As if on cue, the black dog appeared from around the corner of the house and watched them all from a safe distance.

"You won't forget to feed him?" the child asked. "It's bad to forget that."

"I promise I won't forget," he said.

Sam opened the car door and placed the girl in the back seat. She buckled her seat belt and then looked up at him. "I guess he can stay here for a little while."

"Thanks. I'll take good care of him."

Trish nodded, and Sam pushed her door closed.

"Thank you," was all Jen could manage before she slipped on her sunglasses and climbed into the car.

Sam waved as they pulled out of the driveway, and then he walked back into the house. Allie followed him to the kitchen where he refilled his water glass. He smiled at her, holding her gaze longer than he usually did.

"Thanks for the help," he said. "You do well under pressure."

Allie rotated her shoulders, trying to work out the kinks. "Thanks, Doc. You're pretty good at this stuff, aren't you?"

His smile turned into a grin. "I'm the best around, Al."

Allie grinned back. She liked the way his green eyes twinkled when he called her Al. And she was starting to get used to the name. "What now?"

"I've got some cleaning to do, and then I need to work with the horses. I think you could use a good soaking."

"Oh?"

"I have just the stuff for you. A little in a warm bath will pull the soreness right out."

Sam disappeared and returned with an unmarked bottle.

"What is it?" Allie opened the top and sniffed. It didn't smell too bad.

"My own special brew."

"You mean to tell me you get sore muscles?"

"You have no idea." His gaze ran down to her toes and back up, and he chuckled. "Well, maybe you do." His eyes glistened with mischief. "You need some help getting out of those clothes?"

Allie raised one eyebrow. "No, thanks, I think I can manage."

"Whatever you say. Try four capfuls, but wait until the bath is half full before you add it."

"Okay."

"And keep your hands out of the water as much as you can."

Allie felt his eyes on her as she walked slowly from the kitchen. At the doorway she looked back and caught him. He just smiled and shook his head.

Five

"Whoa, Prince." Sam pulled gently on the rope and the gelding stopped and turned. The horse walked slowly up to Sam and lowered his head.

"Yeah, I know, you're just a big baby." Sam scratched the horse's face and tugged on his forelock. "Okay, that's enough for you today."

As he led Prince back to the barn, Sam spotted Allie walking across the yard. He tried not to smile, but he couldn't help it. He decided he liked having her around. In just two days her face had lost its pallor and taken on a healthy glow. Her cheeks didn't seem quite so sunken, either. She already looked good—a little too good, in fact— and was looking better every day.

Sam wiped Prince down with a wet cloth and the horse whinnied appreciatively. As soon as he was sure the gelding was cool, Sam led him into the stall and unhooked the lead rope. He turned to find Allie watching him from across the barn.

"Feeling better?"

"Much. You could make a fortune selling that stuff. It's a miracle cure."

He laughed. "Actually, the exercise this morning probably did you the most good."

She shrugged. "Whatever you say. I just know I feel a lot better."

"I'm glad to hear it." Sam latched Prince's stall and walked into the next one. "Come on, girl, you're the last one today." He snapped the lead to the gray filly's halter and led her into the corral.

Allie followed them. "Anything I can do?"

"Not right now, but you can help me rub her down once we're done."

"Okay."

Sam lifted Lady's right front leg and inspected the hoof. The split was under control, and she had stopped favoring it. He lowered her leg, and stood and glanced over at the corral where Allie was talking to Hattie.

The old mare whinnied at Allie's approach. Sam nearly fell over when Hattie walked directly to the fence, raised her head over the top rail, and closed her eyes as Allie rubbed her jaw. It was the first time since he'd had her that Hattie had willingly let anyone touch her, much less enjoyed it.

"I'll be damned," Sam muttered as he let out the lead and sent the filly away. With a few clucks, Lady began trotting around the corral, kicking her heels and tossing her head, feeling her oats. On each pass, Sam glanced over Lady's back at Allie and the mare. They stood together quietly during the entire exercise.

"Whoa, girl." Sam pulled Lady in and patted the filly's neck. Her nostrils flared as she worked at catching her breath, and sweat outlined her chest. She followed him with her head lowered.

In the barn, Sam wrapped the lead rope around a post and walked to the hydrant to rinse out the rags. Allie joined him. He handed her a rag and they stood on each side of the horse and wiped her down with Allie copying his movements.

"Looks like you and Hattie are friends," he said.

"Yeah. We bonded when I was cleaning the barn."

"I have to admit, I'm surprised."

Allie shrugged.

Sam watched her wiping the horse's flank. Some scars were more visible than others. He wondered if Allie and the mare shared a similar background. Had abuse been the cause of the fear he'd seen in Allie's eyes and the bruise on her arm? The thought made him sick at his stomach. Sam dropped his gaze to Lady's hide.

"I think that does it," he said, as he tossed the rag over the top rail of a stall and unwrapped the lead rope. Allie backed away and Sam put Lady in her stall. "You want to try bringing Hattie in?"

"Sure."

"Here's the lead rope." Sam held it out to her.

"No thanks, I won't need it."

Allie walked to the corral, opened the gate, and let Hattie out. The mare stopped at the gate while Allie closed it, then followed her to the stall. Allie never even touched the halter.

Sam lifted his hat and wiped his brow on his sleeve.

Allie walked up, grinning smugly.

"You're a showoff, Al."

"When you've got it, you flaunt it, Doc."

With the barn closed, they walked to the house.

He called back to the black dog that followed several steps behind them. "Come on, Blue."

"Okay, so why Blue?"

As if keeping secrets from the canine trotting behind them, Sam lowered his voice. "Well, old Blue's a shy dog, had a tough childhood. Not much of a watchdog, I'm afraid. He's not real comfortable around people, and he thinks he's camouflaged when he's riding in the back of my blue truck. I'm not going to be the one to tell him that everyone can see him back there. I don't want to burst his bubble, so I call him Blue."

Allie raised her arms and dropped them to her sides. "Of course. It's so obvious."

They both laughed and Sam held the door open for her. Blue ran under the edge of the house to wait for dinner.

Allie sipped on the glass of red wine that Sam had poured for her. He explained that it was part of a payment, as was much of his food and drink. The wine was quite good, but she wondered how he managed to pay his bills.

Sam placed supplies on the table and pulled up a chair again. "Okay, let's have a look."

Allie gave him her right hand, and he carefully cut away the bandage. He held her palm close to his face and tilted it left and right in the light. A wavy strand of hair threatened to fall into his eyes, but he ignored it.

"Not bad," he said. "It's healing quickly. Give me the left one."

He repeated the process.

"Good. Let's leave the bandages off until you're ready for bed. Let the skin breathe."

"Whatever you say."

Sam left the table with the spent bandages and returned with his own glass of wine. He pulled the chair back around and sat in his usual place across the table from her. With a groan, he lifted his right leg and rested it on an empty chair.

"What's the matter, Doc, old football injury?"

"No, Al. I bruised my knee the other night in the bar trying to keep you from hitting the floor. It hasn't quite healed yet."

"Oh." Allie's face burned as she thought back to the scene she must have caused. "Did I really throw up on you?"

He took a sip of wine. "Actually, you mostly got yourself. It was kind of hard to tell where you hit my nasty old boots."

Allie dropped her gaze to the table. When she looked up, he was watching her, neither smiling nor frowning. He looked tired.

"I'm sorry, Sam."

"Don't be. I'm the one who gave you all the tequila to begin with. I think I gave you one too many."

"You never asked me what happened that day."

"No, I figure you'll tell me when you want to. It's your life."

True, it was her life, and she wondered if she'd ever be able to tell him about it.

Allie sighed. "Don't you get a day off around here once in a while?"

Sam smiled at that. "I try to go for a ride on Sunday mornings, but I don't always make it."

"On horseback?"

He nodded and sipped.

"Are you going tomorrow?"

"I don't know. I've got a lot to do before Tracy gets here. She's flying into Denver Tuesday."

"I think you should go. You definitely need a rest."

"Think so?"

Allie nodded.

"I'll go if you'll go with me."

Her eyebrows shot up. "Me? I've never ridden a horse in my life."

"It's not difficult, Al. If a bunch of redneck cowboys can do it, I'm sure you can."

She shook her head slowly. "Okay, I'll give it a try. I don't have to get up at five in the morning or anything, do I?"

"Not unless you want to."

"No, I don't think so."

Sam dropped his leg from the chair. "You want a refill?"

"Sure, but let me get it."

He nodded and propped his leg back up.

Allie brought the wine bottle from the kitchen and handed it to Sam. "I can't pull the cork out," she said. "My hands are still sore."

"We make quite a pair tonight." Sam removed the cork and filled both of their glasses.

Allie winced at the remnant stiffness as she returned to her chair. She suddenly recalled the puzzled look on Jen Halley's face, and she laughed.

"What?"

"I was just remembering how Jen Halley looked today when she was trying to decide who I was."

Sam laughed quietly. "We're probably the talk of the town by now."

"Think so?"

He nodded. "It's not often that an attractive young woman comes to town alone and moves in with one of the most eligible bachelors around."

"One of the most eligible?"

"Right up there at the top."

"Wow."

"I know, it's impressive as hell. I have a plaque and everything. Just can't remember where I put it."

His green eyes sparkled with merriment and held hers until she felt uncomfortable and looked away. Allie wondered if the wine made the light in his eyes shine a little brighter. It definitely affected her. Even after finishing off fried chicken, coleslaw, and apple pie, she felt light-headed from only a glass and a half. How much of that was the altitude, and how much was the fact that she was so tired? Whatever it was, she caught herself thinking again about how attractive Sam was.

Allie took a long drink and frowned at the table. It was one thing for them to sit there and joke about what the town might think of them, but it was another thing entirely when considering Sam's daughter. Fifteen was a tough age. She remembered it well. It had mattered very much to Allie what people said about her when she was fifteen.

"I should be out of here by Tuesday."

Sam frowned, all the merriment gone. "Why?"

"Your daughter might be uncomfortable if she finds me here."

"Why should she be uncomfortable? It's not like we're sleeping together."

Allie's face warmed at his words.

"Look," he said, "you told me three days ago that you didn't have anywhere to go. As far as I can see, that hasn't changed. My guest room is yours for as long as you want it. Tracy's a bright kid; she won't be bothered by small town gossip."

"Are you sure? I mean, I can't just stay here indefinitely as a houseguest."

"Okay, then, you can work as my assistant. I usually hire a high school kid for the summer to help out, but I haven't lined anyone up yet. And I can't count on them to be around for emergencies."

"I don't know. So far I think I've only managed to slow you down."

"That's bull. Everyone has to go through training, and you'll be up to speed in no time. And the barn hasn't been this clean in years."

Allie smiled at her wine glass, then drank the last sip. "Okay, I'll think about it. You understand, I'm not guaranteeing I'll be around that long, right?" She looked up at him.

Sam returned her smile. "I understand." He lowered his leg again and stood. "I've got to check on the puppy, and tuck in the rest of my boarders. Let me put fresh bandages on you before I get too tired to tell your paw from your foot."

"Hand, Doc. Hand, not paw."

"Oh, yeah." He grinned as he pulled the chair around the table and straddled it.

Sam cleaned the skin and replaced the ointment on her right hand first, and then her left. As he wrapped the left one, he glanced up at her several times. They sat very close, and she found his gaze exciting.

By the time he taped the bandage in place, his hands were shaking. Or were hers the ones shaking? After smoothing the last piece of tape, Sam looked into her eyes and frowned. Neither of them seemed to be able to look away, and Allie found it difficult to catch her breath. His eyes dropped to her mouth, and she wanted nothing more than to feel his lips on hers. He leaned forward slowly until his breath caressed her face.

Sam's eyes snapped up to hers, and a look of absolute terror replaced his frown. He backed out of the chair, catching it just before it fell completely over, and turned away from her. He gathered the first-aid supplies and then turned back, the fear gone.

"Good night, Allie. See you in the morning."

"Good night, Sam."

As soon as he left the room, Allie closed her eyes and took a deep breath. Her heart pounded.

This was absurd. She couldn't afford to get attached to Sam. She may have left Rick, but she was still legally a married woman—a situation that wasn't going to be easily remedied. And if Rick figured out where she was, she might end up on the run again. As difficult as the possibility would be to face under the best of circumstances, she couldn't imagine the added problems an emotional bond would produce. It wasn't worth the risk.

Allie stood with determination and carried the wine glasses to the kitchen. She would have to guard her heart closely while in Sam's house. She'd never felt such attraction before.

Tomorrow, she'd go for her first horseback ride. She wasn't really looking forward to it, but Sam was a good, kind man who needed a rest. If she had to learn to ride a horse in order for him to get it, she could make the sacrifice. Besides, she'd undoubtedly be too terrified to find him appealing.

Sam closed the office doors, turned, and dropped his forehead to the wall. He closed his eyes and took slow, deep breaths.

It's not like we're sleeping together.

As soon as he'd said it and seen Allie blush, he'd realized that he wanted very much for them to be sleeping together.

Sam groaned. He was hard just thinking about her.

Pushing himself away from the wall with both hands, he walked to the sink and splashed water on his face. He leaned over the basin, letting the water drip from his chin and nose, trying to catch his breath.

He really needed to get over this. It was completely unfair to Allie. No telling how desperate she was. She might even feel obligated to sleep with him in order to stay in his house. God, he couldn't imagine anything more humiliating.

He took a deep breath and straightened. What scared him the most was that he really liked Allie, and enjoyed being around her. She could stand her ground, but she had compassion. He saw it in her eyes. In her beautiful golden eyes. It would be much too easy to fall for her, and she'd been brutally honest tonight about the fact that she might not be around for long. He doubted he could stand the heartache he knew she could inflict. He wiped his face with the hand towel and then tossed the towel in the corner.

"Okay, Calvert, shape up." Sam flipped on the lights and started for the cages. He had work to do before he went to bed. Tomorrow, when he wasn't so tired, he'd be in control again and tonight's struggle would seem ludicrous.

Lucky sat up when Sam approached—certainly a good sign.

Sam opened the door and lifted the puppy out. "Welcome back to the world, boy."

The dog's tail wagged slowly in response.

"How are you this morning, Al?"

Allie looked at the two horses, saddled and tied to posts, and sighed. "I'm okay right now, Doc, but I don't have much confidence in the immediate future."

Sam smiled. "How are the boots?"

She pointed the right boot out in front of her. "I really have to wear these?"

"Yes, you do. I'd hate to see you dragged along behind a

horse because you were worried about being mistaken for a redneck."

"I'd hate to see that happen, too. And the hat?" Allie held up the old straw cowboy hat Sam had fished out of a closet.

"After an hour in the sun at this altitude, you'll appreciate it." He handed her a pair of leather gloves. "With these and the sunglasses, I think you're set."

She took the gloves from him and carefully slipped them on over the bandages. Gloves were one thing she wouldn't complain about. Then, fumbling in oversized leather fingers, she managed to put on the sunglasses.

Turning slowly, Allie grinned. "What do you think?"

Sam studied her, his arms folded across his chest. "Yikes, Al. I'd have to say you're the cutest little thing west of the Mississippi."

She put her fists on her hips. "Can it, Doc, and show me what to do, now that I'm all dressed for the occasion."

"Yes, ma'am." He led her to a huge brown horse. "This is Prince. He's a sweetheart, so be nice to him."

"Oh, don't worry about that. He's way too big for me to be anything but nice." Allie's stomach knotted at the thought of sitting on top of the gigantic beast.

Sam took the reins from the fence, tied a knot in the end, and looped them over the horse's head. "It's important for you not to drop the reins. Now, come over here and step in my hands." He laced his fingers together and leaned over.

"I don't know—"

"Come on. There's no turning back now. Give me your left foot."

Allie put her foot in Sam's hands, and, after a moment's hesitation, gripped his shoulder with her left hand and the saddle with her right. Suddenly, she found herself sitting on the saddle, holding on with both hands.

When Prince shifted his weight, Allie realized just how huge he was. "Oh, Sam, I don't think this was such a good idea."

He looked up at her and pushed his hat back on his head. His green eyes reflected the morning sun like emeralds. "You're okay, Allie. I promise I won't let anything happen to you."

"You swear?"

"I swear."

She took a deep breath and blew it out. "All right. I guess I'm committed. How do you steer this thing?"

Sam explained how to rein the horse as he worked on shortening her stirrups. When the task was complete, he stood at Prince's shoulder and rested his hand on Allie's knee.

"Okay," he said, "we're ready. A couple of things. First of all, horses can sense fear. You need to take a deep breath and relax."

"Oh, great. He must be on sensory overload right now."

Sam laughed. "I mean it, you'll be fine. The other thing to remember is that the reins are attached to a metal bit in Prince's mouth. When you want to stop, pull back gently. Don't jerk the reins around or you'll hurt him. Okay?"

Allie nodded.

"Good. And talk to him. Prince likes the sound of your voice."

"Are you sure?"

"Yep. He told me so."

"I didn't know you converse with the horses, too."

"There's a lot you don't know about me, Al."

"Likewise, Doc."

He quickly squeezed her knee and released it.

Before Allie even had the reins situated in her hands, Sam hopped up on the big white horse and pulled away from the fence. He made a clucking noise, and Prince turned and followed him.

Allie grabbed the saddle horn to maintain her balance.

At first, each movement was amazing. Muscles rippled in the horse's shoulders as he stepped. Trying not to hurt his mouth, Allie moved the reins in time with his head. After a few minutes, she began to pick up the rhythm and didn't have to concentrate quite so hard.

She felt Sam glancing back at her periodically. Once she was comfortable enough, she looked up and returned his smile, although his was probably the more sincere.

Actually, the whole experience both thrilled and terrified her. At any moment, the horse could take off like a runaway freight train and she'd have no way to stop him. Was the ground really as far away as it looked?

Sam slowed his horse and pulled alongside her. "You're doing great."

"I'm not doing anything. Prince is doing. I'm just along for the ride, so to speak."

They exchanged honest smiles.

Sam looked natural sitting on top of the horse, slouching just a little, his hat pulled down to protect his eyes. If a line of covered wagons had suddenly appeared behind him, it wouldn't have surprised Allie at all.

"Well, then," he said, "sit back and enjoy."

Six

The path narrowed as Allie rode along behind Sam into the trees and they climbed the side of a mountain. The air felt thick and smelled sweet with pine for the first half hour, then it thinned and cooled among the aspen. They followed a tiny trickle of a brook to its headwaters at a blue lake surrounded by groves of aspen. On the far side of the lake, Sam stopped his horse and hopped off.

"We're here," he said as he walked to Prince's left. "Want a hand?"

Allie swung her leg over, popped her left foot out of the stirrup, and slid down to the ground, careful not to wince at the tingling in her feet when they hit harder than she realized they would. "No thanks. Getting off isn't so bad. It's staying on that's the challenge."

"How true."

Once he'd loosened the saddles, Sam led the way to the edge of the lake. Allie stayed behind him so he wouldn't see her trying to work the kinks out of her backside. By the time they got to the water, her feet had nearly started cooperating, but she couldn't shake the annoying feeling that she was only two feet tall.

"Won't the horses run away?"

Sam glanced back. "No, I don't think so."

"You don't *think* so? I'm not about to walk down this mountain."

"Don't worry. If the horses run away, I'll carry you down."

Allie narrowed her eyes. "Don't think I'll let you off the hook, either."

"Of course not."

They sat in the grass at the edge of the water. Sun on the lake's glassy surface turned it into a shining blue jewel. Long-legged bugs scooting across the top provided the only sign of movement.

One bug disappeared into a tiny whirlpool.

Allie pointed. "Did you see that?"

Sam nodded. "It's good fishing here."

She turned to look at him.

He sat with his knees drawn up to support his arms, gazing at the lake.

"Is this where you usually ride?"

"Most of the time. It's my favorite place."

Across the lake, snow-covered peaks rose above the tree line. Allie felt as though they were the only people who knew this magnificent place existed.

Sam sat very still beside her.

"We're here for you to rest," she said. "Don't let me stop you from doing whatever you normally do. I can entertain myself."

"Okay."

Allie turned at the flurry of motion to find Sam stripping off his cotton outer shirt. When it was off, he pulled off his boots and socks, and stood up and loosened his belt.

"Wait a minute! I didn't . . . I mean, give a girl a chance to turn around, will you?"

Sam pulled his belt off and dropped it and his hat to the

ground. "Why, Al, I didn't know you were shy." He unsnapped his jeans.

"Dammit, Sam, stop!" Allie jumped up and started back toward the horses.

"Wait, Allie, I was just kidding." He grabbed her shoulder and turned her around, then quickly released her. "I'm sorry. Don't run away."

Allie crossed her arms and frowned at him.

He stood before her in a white T-shirt and blue jeans still unsnapped, his hands at his sides. The shirt clung to him, accenting the lines of his chest and shoulders. She hoped he couldn't see the lust he evoked in her. The thought of Sam continuing the striptease made her insides squirm.

"Really, I was just messing around. This is a great place to swim, but it's still a little early in the year. Why don't we go for a walk?"

Allie held her stance. It probably looked like she was considering his offer. In truth, she wanted to be sure her voice would work before she answered. Finally, she shrugged. "Okay."

"Good. Wait right here." Almost as quickly as he'd stripped, Sam put his socks and boots back on and fastened his jeans. He left the shirt, belt, and hat in a pile. "Come on, I want to show you something."

Allie followed him away from the lake. They walked through the woods for a few minutes, then stopped.

Sam stepped aside so that she could see the view.

They stood on the edge of a rock face overlooking a pristine valley filled with aspen and evergreens and divided in half by a wide, lazy creek that bulged with beaver ponds every hundred yards or so for as far as she could see.

Sam sat on the cliff and dangled his legs over the side.

He raised his hand to her, and Allie took it. She sat carefully beside him, not looking down until she was safely seated. Even then, the height made her lean back. "That's quite a drop."

"Yeah. It's impressive."

Sam looked out over the valley. The wind blowing up the cliff lifted his hair from his neck and made brown waves dance around on his head. He closed his eyes for a moment, then squinted out against the breeze. Something about his face looked both fearless and kind, and full of life.

He was so close, she could feel his body heat on her side between gusts, and the realization made it difficult to swallow.

"You can almost always see wildlife from here. Look."

Allie followed the line of Sam's arm to a clearing halfway across the valley where at least two dozen dark brown animals grazed in a meadow still thick with spring flowers.

"Are they elk or deer?" she asked.

"Elk."

"Cool."

He smiled. "Yeah."

They sat in silence for a long time, enveloped by a sense of peace unlike anything Allie could ever remember feeling before. Little more than large spots, the elk made their way slowly across the distant opening, then disappeared into the woods.

Sam sighed and rose. He stepped back and offered her his hand again, which she gladly took. Getting up from the edge was worse than sitting on it.

"Hungry?"

She shrugged. "A little."

On the walk back to the lake, they stopped at the horses. Sam pulled a bulging towel out of his saddlebag and carried it to one of the larger aspen near the lakeshore, where he sat and stripped off his boots and socks again. "I just can't enjoy a picnic with shoes on."

Allie decided to join him. Warm air felt good on her feet, which had been suffering from the unfamiliar confinement of boots. She also took off her hat and sat in the shade near Sam.

He unrolled several items from the towel, one at a time. "Sandwich?"

Allie accepted a plastic bag. "What kind?"

"Peanut butter and raspberry jam."

"Sounds good."

Sam pulled out a second sandwich and placed it on his thigh. Then he took out a corkscrew and, finally, unwrapped a wine bottle.

Allie raised her eyebrows. "Peanut butter and wine?"

"Hey, have you ever tried it?"

She shook her head. "No, I admit I haven't."

Sam pulled the cork out and handed her the bottle.

"What am I supposed to drink out of?"

"The bottle, Al. We're roughing it."

Allie took a long drink of wine. It was good: not too sweet but slightly fruity. She handed the bottle to Sam and took a bite of the sandwich, shocked to find the tastes a perfect match.

She laughed until she almost choked.

"What's so funny?"

"It's just too good," she said.

"What is? The wine?"

Allie leaned back on one hand, holding up her sandwich to the cloudless sky. "No, the whole thing. The place, the sky, the lake, the peanut butter and wine. It's all just too good. It makes me want to laugh."

Sam smiled at her. "Good."

They ate and drank until the food and wine were gone. Then they lay back in the soft, short grass, their feet close together, and Allie fell asleep.

A soothing, silent breeze blew across the lake. Sam considered allowing himself to go back to sleep, until he realized that the sun shown from directly above them. It must be close to noon, and he still had a lot to do before the day ended. Silently cursing his busy schedule, he sat up.

Allie slept soundly. The light ends of her hair had fallen across her face. Fighting the urge to brush them aside, he hesitated for a moment, his hand poised above her shoulder, then he gently squeezed her arm. "Allie."

"Hmm?" She stretched her arms over her head.

"Time to wake up. Places to go, people to see."

"Um-hmm."

As she continued to stretch, Sam slipped into his boots and long-sleeved shirt.

He'd been surprised by Allie's reaction earlier. He wasn't *about* to really take off his pants and had expected her to call his bluff when he started stripping. Instead, she'd almost flipped. He must have accidentally wandered into sensitive territory. Whatever the cause, he'd regretted upsetting her. Her laughter at the picnic had made him feel better.

Allie sat up, glancing around with one eye closed. She looked warm and tired, and Sam clenched his jaw against the desire to hold her in his arms. He scooped up his hat and walked back for the picnic trash.

"Awake?" He smiled at her as he picked up the wine bottle.

"A little. Too much wine."

Sam offered a hand, which she took, and he pulled Allie to her feet.

Without the boots, she was more than a head shorter than he was, and she looked up at him with both eyes open. Wide open.

He held her hand, and she held his, squeezing the back of his hand with her thumb. He couldn't stand the longing she caused for another second. He had to either step away, or kiss her. Now. And her precious lips looked moist and inviting.

Stepping away wasn't the choice he wanted to make, but it was the one he needed to make.

Sam turned and walked quickly to the horses, gripping his shirt against the pain of his pounding heart. Why on earth did he want her so badly?

By the time Allie made it to the horses, he had the girths tightened and trash loaded into saddlebags. Prince stood ready and waiting. Sam laced his fingers together and leaned over.

Her hand on his shoulder made his skin tingle all the way down to his toes. It also caused a reaction that embarrassed the hell out of him, and which he hid by checking a troublesome connection on his saddle. As soon as he was able, they started back down the trail.

Allie had completed the morning ride more than just a little sore again, but after soaking in some of Sam's miracle mixture, she felt much better. The tub in the guest bathroom had a skylight overhead, a modern concession in the old house. She enjoyed watching clouds sail by and found it difficult to leave the bath.

As soon as the horses were unsaddled and wiped down, Sam was on to other things. The morning of rest seemed to have revitalized him, and he worked like a man possessed. Allie tried to help and stay out of his way, but it wasn't easy to do both. He even rushed through dinner like a Tasmanian devil.

When the sun finally set, he wound down—a locomotive running out of steam. As soon as he'd cared for the boarders, Sam joined Allie in the den. He stretched out in an overstuffed armchair.

She brought him a mug of hot cocoa, and then curled up with her own mug at the end of the sofa.

"Thanks." He sipped the steaming drink with his eyes half-closed.

"Do you always make up for taking the morning off by working like a maniac?"

"Not always."

"Why now?"

Sam sighed. "I guess I'm starting to get nervous. Tracy comes in day after tomorrow." He sat up suddenly, nearly spilling his drink. "What time is it?"

Allie glanced at the VCR. "Eight-ten."

"Good, it's only seven-ten there." He hurried into the kitchen.

Allie didn't plan to listen to the phone conversation, but it was hard not to in such a quiet house.

"Lisa, Sam. May I speak to Tracy?" There was a long silence. "No, I understand. I just wanted to get the time of her flight in . . . yes, I'll be there . . . no, I won't be . . . okay."

He walked slowly into the den, returned to his chair, and, after a long drink from his mug, wiped his mouth with the back of his hand and sighed.

"I don't get it, Sam. Why are you nervous about your daughter coming here?"

He looked at her. "You got any kids, Al?"

Allie frowned at her lap. The way her life was going, she'd never have kids, or anyone else in her life to devote herself to. With Rick, she'd thought she was finally part of a real family, but it had only been a dream. "No."

"They can tear your heart out. Trust me on this." Leaning back and resting his mug on his stomach, Sam closed his eyes. "And they don't even have to try."

Pain flickered momentarily in his face and disappeared.

As soon as she saw his head starting to fall to the side, Allie jumped up and grabbed Sam's cocoa before it also fell. He squinted up at her as she loosed the mug from his fingers.

"Doc, I think you're done in."

"Yeah."

"You need some help getting up?"

"No thanks." He yawned and stretched. "I can make it."

Sam pushed himself slowly to his feet and started toward his room. He stopped at the doorway and looked back at her. "Thanks for riding with me this morning. I needed that."

"My pleasure."

He turned and left.

Allie sat on the sofa and looked down at her drink again, watching the swirling cocoa darken with her thoughts. Maybe she *had* stepped into the *Twilight Zone*. She certainly seemed to be in some kind of time warp. Riding horseback in the mountains with Sam, she found it easy to believe that the past five years had never happened. And had she just left Denver on Wednesday?

Maybe this had been some divine respite, designed to let her gather her wits. She really needed to decide what to do next, before she forgot that she didn't actually belong in Sam's house.

Allie grunted at the mild ache as she straightened her back. She'd never spent so much time in pain and felt so good about it. Fortunately, her hands were past the critical stage. Sam had declared them healed before dinner and un-wrapped them for the last time. The fact that they wouldn't have an excuse to sit close every evening disappointed her, but at least she could use her hands again. She'd never con-sidered having useful hands a luxury before.

After drinking the last sip of cocoa, she carried both mugs to the kitchen. Dishes filled the sink, but they could wait until morning. And so could her decision on what to do. Right now she needed sleep.

In her dreams that night, she and Sam rolled together in the grass by the lake, tangled in each other's arms, their clothes gone. And they kissed—deep, passionate kisses. But as soon as they started to make love, Sam turned into Rick, and Rick was angry.

Allie screamed and fought, but she couldn't get away.

She woke in a panic, and spent a full three minutes sit-ting in bed, clutching the comforter to her chest, staring at the sunlit window, before she could relax enough to get up.

She rose and walked to the bathroom. A long, hot shower would wash it all away.

When she returned to her room, refreshed and wrapped in a towel, Allie found two dresses, two pairs of jeans, and three blouses laid out on her bed. Under a brown cotton dress were a half dozen pairs of panties. "What on earth?"

Upon closer examination, she realized all the clothes were new. They were practical, but in colors that she would have picked out for herself.

Allie couldn't believe her eyes. She'd outgrown fairies

years ago. Obviously, Sam had bought the clothes for her. It was one thing for him to pass on used clothes his daughter didn't want, but something totally different for him to go out and buy new clothes as if she were his to take care of— to dress.

Her face burned at the thought of Sam seeing her as a *cause*. Clutching the brown dress, shaking with anger, she stomped from her room to the kitchen. "Sam!"

"Yeah?" His voice came from the den.

Allie rounded the corner to find Sam standing in the middle of the room, talking to a man in dirty jeans who held a cigar in one hand. The stranger's eyebrows shot up and they both stared at her.

She stood just inside the room, still wrapped in a towel. "I . . . uh . . ." She couldn't think of a thing to say.

"Allie, this is Clancy. I believe you two spoke on the phone a few days ago. Clancy, Allie."

"The man with the cow." Allie remembered the urgent phone call.

Clancy swallowed hard and grinned at her. "Yes, ma'am."

The whole thing was absurd. She couldn't stand around, pretending to be dressed.

Allie started backing out of the room, bumped into the doorway and continued. "Excuse me."

As soon as she was out of sight, she ran back into her bedroom, closed the door, and fell against it, fanning her flaming face. Sam could have said something to hint that he had company. Anything. He didn't have to stand there, grinning, and introduce her like there was nothing wrong.

Allie took a deep breath and blew it out. She wanted to punch him.

With control starting to return, she placed the dress on

the bed and put on her own clothes. They might be dirty, but at least she didn't owe anyone for them. Zipping her jeans, she glanced over at the knock on her bedroom door.

"Allie?"

"Go away."

"May I come in?"

"No. Go away."

"Come on, Al. I just want to talk to you."

She glared at the door. "I don't want to talk to you right now. Go away!"

"Why are you mad at me? What did I do?"

What did I do? Could he really not know?

Allie yanked the door open to find Sam standing with one hand on each side of the doorframe.

She frowned, stepped back, and crossed her arms. "What's the idea of buying me clothes? I'm not a charity case—some cause for you to spend money on."

"That's what you're mad about?" Sam's frown matched hers.

"Yes. That and the way you just stood there and introduced me to . . . to . . . ."

"Clancy."

"To Clancy."

"What was I supposed to do? You came running in with nothing on but a towel. And looking pretty foxy, I might add. I couldn't act like you were invisible."

"Oh shut up, dammit!" Allie turned and walked several steps away.

"As for the clothes, I picked them up this morning while I was in town, and I was hoping at least some of them were things you'd like. I know you don't have any money, and you need new clothes, Allie. You really do."

She looked down at her jeans that were not only dirty, but also a little ragged. Granted, she did need clothes, and Tracy's hand-me-downs didn't quite fit.

"If I promise not to do it again, will you do me a favor and try these on? Think of them as payment for all the work you've done around here. Or, think of them as an early birthday present, if you'd rather."

Allie looked over at the clothes and back at Sam. Why was she really so upset? He wasn't trying to buy her off and probably had no intention of telling her how to dress. He was just trying to help.

She sighed.

He gave her half a grin and left.

Sam threaded a rod through the last clean curtain and then returned it to the hooks. He smoothed out the fabric and tied it to the side. There, that did it. Once the sheets were on the bed, Tracy's room would be ready.

"Need some help?"

He spun around.

Allie walked into the room in the brown dress he'd bought. It was just a shade darker than her eyes and looked a hell of a lot better on her than it had on the hanger. The fitted waist hugged her figure, and the skirt fell well below her knees. The old-fashioned cut looked anything but old-fashioned on Allie.

"What do you think?" She twirled in place, smiling at him coyly.

She was a siren, a vixen, and he wanted her. He wanted to touch every inch of her.

"Not bad." Sam hoped she didn't notice the trouble he had swallowing.

"You were sweet to get the clothes for me. I'm . . . I'm

sorry I got mad. I'm not used to people giving me things without expecting something back. I guess I don't handle it well."

Sam turned to the bed and stripped off the comforter. "Hasn't anyone ever just *given* you anything?"

Allie stood across the bed from him and grabbed a corner of the sheet when he threw it out. "Not really."

"What about birthday presents? Or Christmas presents? Didn't your parents give you Christmas presents when you were a kid?" They made the bed as they spoke. Sam tried not to think about how much he wanted to reach across the mattress and tackle her.

"I didn't have parents until I was fourteen, and they didn't like me much."

"No parents?"

"No, I was raised in an orphanage and foster homes."

Sam glanced up as he threw the comforter over the top of the sheets. Had there always been a touch of sadness around her mouth? Sorrow tightened his chest, and he wanted to take back his words.

"I'm sorry."

Her eyes flashed when they met his. "Don't be. I don't want your pity."

Sam nodded and tucked the comforter over and under the pillows.

He understood not wanting pity. Looks from the people around Rocky Butte after Lisa left had just made him feel worse. He would have been happier if they'd acted like they hadn't known whom he was.

"What do you think? On the bed or on the dresser?" Sam grabbed two of the dozen stuffed animals from the top of the dresser and held them up.

Allie narrowed her eyes and studied the toys. "She's fifteen?"

He nodded.

"I'd leave them on the dresser and let her move them if she wants to. She might see it as you implying that she's still a child."

"She *is* still a child."

Allie laughed. "She may be, but I suggest you don't tell her that."

Sam frowned at the stuffed dog and cat and returned them to the dresser. How could he possibly think of Tracy as anything other than his little girl? Why the hell did she have to grow up?

"Come on, Doc. Show me what else I can help with."

Sam sighed and turned from the dresser.

"You have any patients coming in today?" she asked.

"Not any scheduled, but you never know. I have to call Jen Halley about Lucky."

They walked from the room together.

"How's Lucky doing?"

"Good. He really was appropriately named."

She smiled up at him, and he hoped he'd make it through the rest of the day without acting like a fool.

Seven

Sam had found a hundred things that absolutely needed to be done right away, but most of them he did himself. Allie had to practically beg for assignments, and she got all the cushy jobs. As the day wound down, she insisted on being allowed to cook stew. Slicing vegetables was about the most challenging work she'd done all day.

The most challenging *thing* she'd done all day, however, was maintain control around Sam. Whenever they were within ten feet of each other, the air seemed to crackle with electricity. At first she'd thought it was just her imagination, but she caught Sam looking at her several times when he had no reason to do so, which only made things worse.

As she sliced carrots, Allie thought about the attraction. She couldn't give in to it, no matter how much she wanted to. Sam was too kind and nice—someone it would be easy to get attached to. Not only did she refuse to risk it for her own sake, but now she found herself thinking of Sam. How could she live with herself if she hurt him?

"Excuse me. May I move you over for just a second?" Sam waited until she stepped aside, then raised the kitchen window and unhooked the screen. "I decided to wash these."

Allie stood close enough that their arms almost touched. Her heart raced, and her entire right side burned by the time he stepped away. She knew she was playing with fire but just couldn't resist.

"Thanks," he said, grinning a little too much.

"No problem."

Allie returned to the cutting board. The only way to get out of the situation in one piece was to find a job and leave Sam's house. Tomorrow morning she would get a ride into town and start looking for work. There had to be something out there, even in a town as small as Rocky Butte.

By the time they sat down to dinner, Sam finally felt like he had the house ready. At least, as ready as it would ever be. He could always find one more thing that needed to be done, especially in such an old house.

Allie filled a bowl with beef stew and handed it to him. She'd added some spices he wouldn't have thought of adding, giving the stew the most wonderful aroma.

Sam glanced up and caught her golden gaze. She looked incredible, and a shiver ran through him in response.

"Are you all right, Doc?"

"You bet, Al. The stew smells great." He took a bite and grinned. "And it tastes even better."

"Glad you like it."

They ate in silence until they'd both finished a bowl and Sam had started on his second.

"I think I'll go to town tomorrow and start looking for a job," she said.

"But . . . but, Allie, you have a job here, if you want it."

She looked down at the table and then up at him, her eyes wide and serious. "Thank you, Sam, but I can't stay here much longer."

His heart thumped. "Why not?"

"I . . . just can't."

97

Sam put his spoon down, his appetite suddenly gone. Maybe he'd misinterpreted her reaction to him. Could this be nothing more than a one-sided crush? Somehow, he'd thought there was more.

God, it was probably wishful thinking by a man who had been out of circulation for way too long. He felt as dumb as a teenager at his first school dance.

"Okay. I can give you a ride in on the way to Denver." He couldn't look at her.

"Thanks," she said.

Allie stood on the curb in the morning sun and watched the pickup disappear down Main Street. The back of the truck seemed empty without Blue, but Sam said he didn't feel safe taking the dog to Denver. Within a moment, dust in the truck's wake settled into desolate silence.

She took a deep breath and looked around downtown Rocky Butte. There were seven buildings that didn't appear to be houses, and one of them was the sheriff's office. That left six places to try. She wouldn't exactly wear herself out job-hunting.

Which one should she try first? The biggest was Joe's Motel, but the grocery store looked more lively.

Allie chose the store. She brushed off the front of her calico dress and started in with confidence.

Her confidence had waned by the time she walked into the last place, Maggie Mae's Beauty Parlor.

A woman with large, frosted hair sat in a hydraulic chair, thumbing through a magazine. She rose when Allie entered. "Hi, hon. You need a cut?"

"Actually, no, I'm looking for a job."

"Oh." The woman dropped back into the chair. "I'm afraid you're looking in the wrong place."

"Is there a right place in this town?"

The woman huffed. "This *town* is the wrong place I was talking about."

"Oh. Well, thanks." Allie turned toward the door.

"Wait. You want a cold drink?"

She turned back. "No, that's okay. But, thank you."

"Come on, have one with me. I need someone to talk to. I'm certainly not going to have any customers to gossip with today at this rate."

The woman disappeared into the back room without waiting for an answer and reappeared with two bottles of root beer. She handed one to Allie.

"Here. Have a seat. I'm Maggie."

"Maggie Mae?" Allie glanced back toward the sign in the front window.

"No, just Maggie. Maggie Mae sounds better though, don't you think? And I've always been a big Rod Stewart fan."

"I'm Allie. Allie Parker."

"Allie. Nice name. Short for Alicia?"

"No, Allison."

Maggie nodded. "You're not from Rocky Butte."

"No, I'm not."

"Have you just moved in?"

"No, not really. I mean, I'm just staying here for a little while with a friend. If I don't find work, I guess I'll have to try another town."

Maggie's eyes lit up. "I know who you are. You're the woman staying at Sam Calvert's place."

Allie nodded and drank a sip of root beer.

"Honey, if Sam Calvert asked me to move in with him, wild horses couldn't drag me out of there."

Allie blushed at Maggie's words. "It's not like that. I'm

staying in his guest room for a week or so."

"Oh?"

She considered all the lies she'd practiced, but couldn't bring herself to tell any of them. "I was . . . having some problems and Sam was nice enough to offer his help."

Maggie grinned. "That sounds like Sam."

They both drank from their bottles.

"You know him fairly well?" Allie asked.

Maggie's grin softened to a smile. "Yeah, we went to school together. Sam Calvert, Ron Stanley, and I are the only ones left here from our class."

"Where's everyone else?"

Maggie smiled again. "The rest are either dead or gone. Of course, there were only eleven of us to begin with, and half of those were from Simpson's Bluff, a little town eight miles down the road. It isn't really a town anymore, though, just old abandoned buildings."

"Was Sam always a nice guy?" This was her chance to get the scoop on Sam's background, although Allie wasn't sure why she wanted it.

"Always. Every one of us had a crush on him. He was tall and handsome and nice. What more could a girl want?"

"So he had lots of girlfriends?"

"No, Lisa caught his eye in about seventh grade, and no one else could ever get his attention. I guess he really loved her, although, for the life of me, I don't know why."

"Lisa?"

Maggie nodded. "His ex." Her answer held a hint of a sneer.

"They married right out of school?"

"Not quite. Lisa was a grade behind us. Sam left for college while she was a senior. I thought Ron would end up with her, since he stayed behind to *look after* her."

"Ron?"

"Ron Stanley. He had the hots for Lisa for as long as Sam did, and she was forever playing them against each other. Ron saw his chance when Sam left. And it might have worked if Ron hadn't gotten Cindy pregnant. Since she was only a freshman, he had to marry her before her father had him charged with statutory rape."

"Sounds like a soap opera."

Maggie laughed and slapped her thigh. "You bet. *As Rocky Butte Turns*."

"Lisa must have been special."

"Oh, she was gorgeous, all right. You know, tall, blonde, and all legs. But that girl was sneaky. She knew Sam would make good, and she expected him to carry her away from here. It's a shame she was too blind to see what a sweetheart he is."

Allie sighed. "Did Lisa remarry?"

"Not right away. She took their daughter and moved to L.A. For a while, she was living with a movie director, but it didn't last long. Lisa has always been domineering, and Sam used to put up with it. Sounds like Mr. Hollywood didn't like being bossed around. Anyway, she married an artist two years ago. From what I hear, though, it isn't working out too well." Maggie sipped her drink.

"And what about Ron Stanley? You said he's still here."

"Yes, he runs the local real estate agency. He buys out starving ranchers and sells to developers and mining companies. Ron's a bitter old man, and his son is just like him. Doesn't give a damn about anyone or anything. The kid's only twenty-three and he has already been to the state pen. He's just plain mean."

"What about Ron's wife?"

Maggie glanced around, frowned, and dropped her voice to a whisper. "He did her in. That poor girl. The county coroner said she died of injuries from the wreck, but I swear, Ron beat her to death, put her in that car, and pushed it off the cliff. Who in their right mind would believe that a young woman who never drank a drop in her life, and who was the slowest driver on God's green earth, would get drunk on a Monday morning after dropping her son off at school and drive eighty miles an hour off a cliff? I guess we all look pretty stupid around here."

Allie upended the root beer bottle, marveling at Maggie's stories. Of course, her own story wasn't much better. Apprehension wormed its way in as Allie considered what kind of gossip Sam's daughter might hear about her.

"Thank you for the root beer. I should go. I need to catch a ride back to Sam's."

Maggie rose as Allie did. "Wait, I'll get you a ride. My nephew is going that direction this morning. I'll see if he's ready. You don't want to get a ride with just anyone."

"Thanks, Maggie. And I really enjoyed the talk."

The woman smiled warmly. "Me, too. You come back anytime, Allie." She reached for the phone. "Keep your eye out for a beat-up station wagon with a redheaded kid driving. That's Ralphie, my nephew."

"Okay." Allie waved and walked outside, closing the door gently behind her. She started walking slowly in the direction of Sam's house, thinking about the stories Maggie had told. Even a town this small had its share of scandal. It was hard to imagine how much a city like Denver held.

Before she got to the end of the block, an old yellow station wagon screeched to a halt beside her.

"Hi, I'm Ralph. Aunt Maggie said you need a ride."

Allie exchanged smiles with the friendly redheaded boy

and climbed in. She hoped he was really old enough to drive.

When she heard Sam's truck pull into the driveway, Allie dashed into the bathroom to check herself in the mirror. She brushed off the front of her dress, more out of nervousness than need, and trotted to the door.

A teenage girl in holey blue jeans and a red T-shirt, carrying a suitcase, walked quickly from the driveway. Sam pulled two more suitcases out of the back of the truck and followed her, frowning at the ground.

Allie held the door open for Tracy and the girl stared at her for a moment before walking in. She had Sam's eyes, but her shoulder-length hair was much lighter, a sandy blond.

"Hi, Tracy, I'm—"

The girl continued across the den, ignoring Allie.

Sam stepped through the door. "Tracy!"

His bellowing voice stopped the girl in her tracks. She turned around slowly, her green eyes sending daggers through the air.

"Tracy, this is Allie."

Allie stepped forward. "Allie Parker," she said, extending her hand.

The teenager glared first at Allie and then at Sam. "Fine. Can I go now?"

Sam sighed. He followed Tracy, carrying her suitcases, and returned quickly. Stopping in front of Allie, he sighed again. "I'm really sorry."

"Problems?"

Tracy walked back into the room. "I'm going out with Sandy and Matt. Is that okay with you, *Pops?*"

Allie cringed at the sarcasm in the girl's voice.

Sam turned around. "Already? You just got here."

"Big deal. I'll be here for almost three whole months. I called Sandy and she's on the way over. Can I go or not?" Tracy stood with one fist on her hip, glaring.

"Fine, go. I've got paperwork to catch up on anyway. But be home by ten."

Tracy walked outside, muttering as she went. "Why? Worried I'll get lost in this stupid town?"

Sam's hands clenched into fists at his sides and he marched out and down the hall. Allie heard his office doors close with enough force to rattle the panes of glass in the den.

Her heart went out to Sam. He had been so excited about Tracy's arrival.

"Jeez." Allie tucked her hair behind her ears as she walked to the kitchen. Maybe a cup of tea would make him feel a little better. She couldn't stand to see him hurting.

Sam walked around the office twice, mad enough to hit something. Anything. Since he found nothing that would be able to withstand his wrath, he walked around the office three more times. Then he stopped at the roll-top desk, opened it, and sat in the ancient wooden office chair. With his elbows on piles of paper, he dropped his head into his hands.

Why did they always have to go through this? Every year it got a little worse. Nine months of Tracy listening to stories of what a bad husband and father he'd been, and she hated him by the time the summer started. He wanted to strangle Lisa for doing this to his daughter, and for doing it to him. Last year he'd gone through a week of Tracy telling him how perfect L.A. was, and how much she wanted to go home, and how much she hated Colorado. She'd eventually come around, but it had been a week of pure hell. This one wasn't starting off any better.

Sam sighed. Two and a half hours in the truck, trying to get her to talk about anything, and all he'd gotten were biting, sarcastic comments and snapped statements about all the fun things her friends were doing that she was missing. She didn't respond to his questions about school or the volleyball team or anything else.

Damn, he hated Lisa.

The door to his office squeaked, and Sam raised his head. He lifted one of the pieces of paper in front of him and pretended to study it.

"Sam?"

"Yeah?"

"I brought you a cup of tea. May I come in?"

Sam turned to find Allie leaning through the doorway, a mug in her hand. He smiled as much as he was able and dropped the piece of paper. "Yes, thanks. Come on in."

Allie walked in, closing the door behind her, and placed the mug on his desk.

He picked it up and sipped. As soothing as the steaming brown liquid was, it didn't compare to the comfort of Allie's presence. He sipped again and then rested the mug on top of the papers.

"Is that your heart bleeding on the floor, Doc?"

Sam nodded and his smile broadened. "Yeah, Al, that's mine. How did you guess?"

"Is it always like this?"

"Oh, this isn't so bad. At least her hair isn't purple this year."

Allie strolled around the office, looking at counters and utensils and shelves. "Anything I can do?"

Sam turned back to his drink. "No, but thanks. It's always bad for a while, but we manage to work it out." He sipped the tea.

When Allie's fingers touched the tops of his shoulders, he jumped. After a moment's hesitation, she ran her hands back and forth on his shoulders twice and then began to rub them.

Sam put his mug down before it could leap from his hands and he closed his eyes. Her touch sent magical waves of heat rolling through his body.

"Oh, that's wonderful."

Her hands went part of the way down his back and then up to his neck, rubbing sensuous circles.

His heart hammered against his ribs. "Allie, I don't—"

She stopped rubbing and walked around to the front of his chair, and stood before him as an angel in a calico dress, her golden eyes caressing him. Then she leaned forward, put her hands on his shoulders, and lowered her face to his.

Sam closed his eyes and a groan escaped against his will as their lips touched. Her lips were warm and moist and full of life, and when she pulled them away he thought he would die.

He opened his eyes and found her leaning over him, her eyes half closed and her lips slightly parted. Aching for another taste, needing her lips and her mouth, he reached up with both hands and pulled her face back to his. He urged her mouth open and their tongues danced together in a soulful duet, as he climbed into heaven.

And then he realized what he was doing.

He pushed Allie's face away and dropped his hands to the arms of the chair. "Allie, stop."

"Why, Sam?" she asked, her voice throaty.

"I can't . . . I don't have the strength to resist you right now."

She raised one eyebrow. Holding his shoulders, she

raised one leg at a time and squeezed her knees between his thighs and the chair, straddling his legs. The old chair was just wide enough for both of them.

She pressed her forehead to his. "Good, Doc, 'cause I'm tired of resisting."

Allie kissed his cheek and then his ear and then the side of his neck. Her hands slid down the front of his chest.

"Oh, God, Allie—"

He felt her heat against him as she settled into his lap, and he feared he might explode. It had been so long. Too long. And he wanted her now. Here.

Sam ran his hands up the outside of her thighs, under her skirt, touching her warm, smooth skin. He turned his head until he found her lips again, and he was lost. He slid his hands to the back of her nylon panties and drew her into him.

She groaned against his mouth as her tongue lured his in, and she pushed her fingers into his hair.

He pulled her closer as the suction of her kiss tugged at his very soul. He needed to be inside her more than he needed to breathe.

And then she pushed against him, ripping her mouth away. She might as well be slicing open his chest.

He resisted her efforts until he realized why she was pushing. "Son of a bitch," he muttered.

"You want me to answer it?" Her breath danced sweetly across his face.

He inhaled and sighed, releasing the pressure on her buttocks. "No, I'll get it. It could be Tracy."

Allie nodded and backed off the chair. She panted just as hard as he did, but at least she could stand.

Sam reached across the desk and lifted the phone. "Hello."

Eight

Allie stood back and watched Sam's chest rapidly rising and falling as he held the phone to his ear with his eyes closed.

She couldn't believe what she had just done, and she couldn't believe how badly she wanted him. His kiss was the most amazing she'd ever experienced, hot and demanding. And when she'd felt him hard beneath her, she'd nearly lost her mind. She'd never felt desire like this. What was it about Sam that got to her? He was gorgeous, no doubt, but it was more than just his looks. She had only meant to console him, but as soon as she'd touched his muscular shoulders, she forgot her original intent. The thought of what might happen when he got off the phone made her belly quiver.

"Yeah . . . no, don't try to move him . . . okay, I'll be right there." He replaced the receiver with his eyes still tightly closed, then he took a slow deep breath and blew it out before he turned to her. "I can't believe this, but I have to leave."

"Now?"

Sam nodded, looking at her with pain glistening in his eyes.

"Maybe we can continue this later." She leaned over and kissed his forehead, then turned around and left the room.

She needed a glass of cold water . . . immediately.

In the kitchen, Allie filled a glass and drank it. She rolled the cool glass back and forth on her forehead, trying to douse the raging flames. It didn't help much. After another sip, she rinsed the glass and placed it on the counter.

A few minutes later, Sam stepped into the kitchen, his jeans jacket and his hat in one hand. He walked directly to Allie, slid his hand behind her neck, and guided her mouth to his. As his tongue swirled hungrily around hers, he pinned her to the counter. Her knees were about to give out when he leaned back to look at her with smoldering eyes.

"Dammit, Allie, you've started something that we're going to have to finish. You'd better be here when I get back."

She nodded and he kissed her again.

A mixture of desire and fear had her stomach in knots by the time Sam walked out. No matter what the consequences, she'd be waiting for him. Her only hope was that neither of them would regret it.

Sam eased the old truck into second as he approached the turn at the bottom of the hill. Although he was tired as hell, it was all he could do to keep from speeding home. Allie waited for him.

He'd had a hard time concentrating on his work, even when faced with a broken leg. It had taken hours to get the horse into the sling and explain the procedures to Jim so that he could keep the animal's digestive tract working properly. As soon as Sam turned away from his patient, the thought of Allie's golden eyes burning with desire had made him smile.

The Last Chance was surprisingly crowded for a Tuesday night, with a dozen cars and trucks in the parking lot, and it wasn't even eight o'clock yet. There were also a half dozen people outside. One couple lay across the hood of a black Mustang, locked in a heated embrace. Sam shifted into third as he passed them, shaking his head in disgust. They were practically having sex in public. They couldn't be locals, could they?

He hadn't gotten a good look at the guy, but the woman had on a red shirt and jeans.

And she had blond hair.

Sam slammed on the brakes, causing the truck to slide sideways. As soon as it stopped, he threw it into first, spun a circle into the parking lot, roared across it, and stomped on the brake again, sending gravel flying. He jumped out as the engine sputtered.

They hadn't even noticed the disturbance. The man who held his daughter was on top of her, pushing her shirt up.

"What the hell do you think you're doing?" Sam grabbed the young man by the back of his collar and pulled him straight up, then turned him to study his face. "I should have known."

Tommy Stanley had just started to realize what was going on when Sam tossed him aside. He fell to the ground in a heap.

Tracy, reeking of alcohol, lay on the hood of the car, laughing, her eyes half-closed. Sam pulled her by the arm until she sat, then he walked her to the truck.

Tommy jumped up and tried to get in the way, but was weaving too badly to resist a shove. He fell to the ground again, muttering a string of slurred curses.

Once he had Tracy in, Sam slammed the door. Three young men and a woman stood around, watching in silence.

Sam turned to Tommy, who sat on the ground. "I catch you with your hands on my daughter again, and mine will be the last face you ever see. You understand?"

The young man was too drunk to respond.

Sam had difficulty shifting with his hands shaking so badly. He managed to get the truck into gear and pull out onto the road. Tracy leaned against the door, her eyes closed.

He glanced at her. "What the hell were you doing?"

"Having fun, until you came along and spoiled it." Although bombed, she wasn't too drunk to speak.

Sam gritted his teeth, opting for silence, afraid he might run off the road.

Blue jumped out of the truck as soon as it stopped and he ran under the house. Sam started around to Tracy's door, but she was already out by the time he got there. When he grabbed her arm, she jerked it loose.

"Leave me alone. I can walk by myself."

He walked directly behind her, just in case she fell.

Allie opened the door for them. When Tracy got to the sofa, she plopped down.

Sam stood by the sofa, his hands clenched at his sides. He was so angry he could have put his fist through the wall. Knowing it wouldn't do any good, he took several deep breaths, trying to relax.

"Tracy, do you realize what you were doing?" Surprisingly, his voice sounded almost calm.

"Sure I do."

"You could have been raped, do you know that?"

She sneered. "It wouldn't have been *rape.*"

"At your age, it would have, no matter what you think."

Tracy stood up, weaving a little. "Oh, so you can be screwing some slut you picked up in a bar, and tell me that I can't have sex when I want to? That's a laugh, *Pops.* You're a goddamn hypocrite. You know—"

"Tracy! That's enough!" Sam stepped toward her as he yelled. "What the hell's the matter with you?"

"I'm not your little girl anymore, and it's not easy for you to handle, is it? Well, you better accept the fact, *Pops*, or this whole summer will suck." Tracy tossed her head and walked from the room, bumping into the doorframe as she left.

Sam just stared. Who was this person who looked like his daughter? He stepped back, fell onto the sofa, and dropped his head into his hands.

"God Almighty, what am I going to do?"

Allie watched him crumble as soon as Tracy left the room. The girl's words hung in the air like a frost, trying to kill everything there.

Sam sat on the sofa, holding his head. Her heart bled for him. She wanted to hold him, to soothe away the pain. But she couldn't move.

Where had Tracy heard such a horrible thing? Surely it wasn't something she would have thought up on her own. And how would she have known where Allie met Sam?

Allie had been right; she needed to leave. The last thing in the world she wanted to do was drive a wedge between Sam and his daughter.

Sam rocked back and forth in silence, and she couldn't stand it anymore—he needed comforting. Sitting on the arm of the sofa, she wrapped her arms around his shoulders, put her head on his back, and rocked with him.

"Allie, I'm so sorry. What she said—"

She held him tighter, whispering. "It's okay, Sam. She doesn't mean it. It's okay."

After several minutes, he quit rocking and she felt him take a deep breath. "What did I do to deserve this, Al?"

She smiled at the use of her nickname and sat up. "I'm sure you don't deserve it, Doc."

Sam raised his head and dropped his hands. "I sure hope you're right."

Reluctantly, she slid her hand across his shoulders and down his arm until they no longer touched.

After a moment he stood and flashed a smile that might have convinced a total stranger. "I've got to check on the mare. You want to come with me?"

"I don't know. This doesn't seem like—"

"Please, Allie, come for a walk with me." His green eyes pleaded.

"Sure."

When they had their boots on and stepped into the yard, Allie was surprised to find the sun still setting. As they started toward the barn, Sam reached for her hand and she took his without looking at him.

He squeezed her hand, and the need she felt in his grip terrified her, but how could she refuse Sam her support after all he'd done? And why would she want to? She squeezed back.

At the barn, they walked inside and closed the door. Sam turned on the single light that hung in the walkway, providing just enough light to see by but not enough to disturb the horses. He walked to the last stall and leaned on the top rail.

Hattie whinnied. Allie stepped up beside Sam, peeking in between the top two rails. "Hi there, girl," she whispered.

The horse turned around and stuck her face toward Allie, snorting to get the scent. Allie rubbed the velvety end of the horse's nose.

"It still amazes me the way she's taken to you," Sam whispered.

Standing together in silence, they watched Hattie until

she started to doze. Quietly, Sam backed away from the stall. Allie followed him out and waited while he secured the barn.

He stopped at the corral fence and leaned back against it. Above them, the moon brightened as the sun disappeared. They watched it together for a moment. Allie loved the way the tops of the mountains changed from red, to purple, and then to blue.

"Nice, don't you think?" Sam spoke softly in the still evening air.

"Yes, very nice."

He sighed. "Mood kind of got ruined, didn't it?"

"Yeah, kind of."

"Think we'll get another shot at it?"

"I don't know."

"Allie, hold me for a minute, will you?"

"Sam—"

Still leaning back on the fence, Sam scooted his feet out and in front of him until he and Allie were the same height. He grabbed her hand and guided her, slowly, to stand in front of him.

"Nothing else, Allie. Just hold me. I need to put my arms around you." With one hand on her waist, he drew her forward gently.

Allie raised her hands on his chest. He pulled her closer and she slid her arms around his neck.

Sam wrapped both arms around her as she rested her cheek on his shoulder, and he sighed.

His chest and stomach felt wonderfully solid, and she loved the way he smelled. It was an earthy smell, not perfumed, not artificial. Real. His right hand ran slowly up and down the middle of her back, and he rested his head against hers.

They stood together in silence until well after dark.

With a nearly imperceptible squeeze, Sam sighed again and released her. He whispered into her ear before completely letting go, "Thank you."

"You're welcome," she whispered back.

Walking very close together, but not actually touching, they made their way back to the house.

"What do you think about Hattie?" she asked.

"I'd say she's due any day."

"What about Tracy?"

"That one I don't know about. I wish teenage girls were as easy to figure out as horses."

Allie smiled. "Then there wouldn't be any mystery left to life."

"No, I guess there wouldn't."

Allie warmed leftover stew while Sam showered. When the meal was ready, he slipped down the hall to offer Tracy a chance to eat.

The lamp by her bed lit the room, but she was sound asleep. He tiptoed in and stood beside her.

Tracy looked so innocent when she slept, like she was his little girl again, and it just made him more miserable. How was he supposed to let go?

Sam pulled off her boots and took her sunglasses out of her shirt pocket. Then, moving slowly, he turned her legs, pulled the comforter up over her, and sat on the edge of the bed.

"No matter what, I love you," he whispered. "I always will." He pushed the blond bangs off her face and kissed her forehead. "Good night, Trace." He turned out the light and gently closed the door behind him.

Allie waited in the kitchen. "Is she coming?"

He shook his head.

Allie filled two bowls from the pot. Sam leaned back on the counter, studying her. Her strong hands were capable, newly browned by the sun, and sensuously feminine. They should be adorned with silver and turquoise. Watching her grip the bowl and the ladle, he remembered the wonderful feel of her hands on his chest and shoulders. He had to shake himself out of his reverie when she handed him the bowl of stew.

They ate in their usual places at the table. Allie glanced up after every second or third bite.

"I never got a chance to ask you how your morning went, Al."

"Not that great, Doc. There are no jobs in Rocky Butte."

"There's one. My offer stands."

She grinned. "I'm still thinking about it."

"Well, don't think too long or I'll have to hire a high school kid."

"Give me a few days?"

"Okay, deal."

They ate a couple more bites.

"I ran into an old friend of yours," she said.

"Oh? Who?"

"Maggie."

Sam nodded.

"She knows a lot about you, and everyone else here."

"Don't believe half of what Maggie tells you. She's always had a flair for exaggeration."

"She thinks you're a prince."

"Well, okay, she's right about some things."

They both smiled.

"How did your call go?" she asked.

Sam told her about the horse whose broken leg he'd tended. Allie asked questions, and he found himself going into great detail just so he had an excuse to look into her eyes. He felt like they were lovers, even though they weren't. Somehow, pretending it was true for a few minutes made him happy. He thought about how wonderful she felt in his arms. He hadn't held anyone in a long time, but that wasn't the reason. It was her. And her mouth sparked a fire in him that he couldn't explain, or control. Maybe, if circumstances were right, they would end up in bed together in the future. God, he hoped so.

It was all Sam could do to remember not to kiss Allie good night when they parted at the kitchen door, whispering against the darkness.

"Good night, Allie."

"Good night, Sam. Good luck in the morning."

"Thanks. I'm sure I'll need it."

Allie woke to Sam's and Tracy's voices. Long silences between harsh sentences came from somewhere past the kitchen. She climbed out of bed and dressed, and with everything brushed and in place, she walked to the kitchen and filled a coffee cup.

Sam and Tracy sat at the dining room table.

"Good morning." Allie took her usual chair.

Sam handed her a bowl of scrambled eggs. "Good morning."

Allie filled her plate as she looked around the table. Sam had only a cup of coffee in front of him. He'd probably eaten hours ago. Tracy worked on a plate of eggs, sausage, and toast, and ignored Allie's smile.

Sam passed the bowl of sausage.

"Thanks," Allie said.

"It's not like it's the first time I've been drunk, you know." Tracy spoke in a low, poisonous tone.

"Maybe not, but it's the last time you'll get drunk here," Sam said.

"And how are you going to stop me?"

"First of all, by grounding you. You are not to leave this house unless you're with me."

"For how long?"

"Until I tell you otherwise."

Tracy took a bite of eggs and glared at Sam. He returned her stare with his own relatively calm one. Neither of them had raised their voice, but Tracy's bitterness and Sam's thinly veiled anger were impossible to miss.

Allie ate quickly.

Tracy narrowed her eyes. "How are you going to keep me from leaving?"

"I'm bigger than you are. If I have to physically carry you back in the house, I will."

"Yeah, well, you can't stay awake all the time."

"Maybe not, Tracy, but if you sneak out on me, you'll find out just how miserable your life here can be. You hear me?"

Tracy rolled her eyes and then dropped her gaze to her plate.

Sam watched her for a few more minutes, and then glanced at Allie, apologizing with his eyes.

Allie smiled at him. "So, Doc, what's the plan for today?"

Sam's face immediately lit up and he smiled back. "Well, Al, I've got a patient coming in soon, and I need to get Lucky out of his cage. The horses need exercising, and everything needs cleaning. Just another typical day on the farm."

"Why don't I start with the dog runs? After your patient leaves, I can move to the inside cages."

"That would be great. And, knowing how important it is to Tracy for her to pull her own weight, I'm sure she'll be thrilled to help you. After I'm done, the three of us can work the horses together. Sound all right?"

"Sounds good."

They both looked at Tracy.

The teenager glanced up long enough to sneer, then returned her attention to her food with a total lack of enthusiasm.

Sam raised his cup. "Sounds like a plan to me."

As soon as the table had been cleared and the dishes washed, Sam headed to his office and Allie stopped at the back porch. She hadn't realized how late it was; morning birds had already abandoned the yard. She stepped into rubber boots Sam had left for her and picked up rubber gloves on her way out. After turning on the water to the hose, she grabbed tools from the shed.

Cleaning dog runs wasn't glamorous, but Allie found that the smell didn't bother her much, especially if she breathed through her mouth. And she kind of liked the dogs. Even the big, sloppy kisses weren't as bad as she'd first thought. The three current visitors were all large dogs that craved attention.

Allie led each dog to the far end of the runs. As she put them in new cages, she knelt and rubbed their necks and chests, careful to avoid any stitches. By the time she finished moving the third one, her face was wet with dog slobber.

"What do you want me to do?"

Allie closed the third gate, wiped her chin on her sleeve, and looked over at Tracy. The teenager stood with her arms folded across her chest, boredom glued to her face. She wore holey blue jeans, a black skull-and-crossbones T-shirt, and a hint of black eye shadow. She'd painted her fingernails black sometime before breakfast.

"There's poop to scoop and water bowls to scrub. Which would you prefer?"

Tracy heaved a dramatic sigh. "I'll take the water bowls."

"Okay. They're all yours."

As she scooped the cages clean, Allie glanced at Tracy now and then. The teenager scrubbed the bowls and rinsed them, definitely taking her time and never changing her expression.

Allie sprayed down the cages, then asked, "Will you get the bottle of disinfectant for me?"

Tracy complied without a word.

Allie squirted the floors with disinfectant and scrubbed the concrete with a long-handled brush. She heard a car drive up to the house. Sam's patient must have arrived.

With the scrubbing done, Allie rinsed out the runs and then started toward the garage with soiled towels. At first, she thought Tracy had ducked out. When Allie got farther away from the runs, she spotted the teenager sitting on the ground under a cottonwood tree. Popsicle stood in the girl's lap, twirling under Tracy's fingers. The two looked like old friends, so Allie decided not to disturb them.

Allie put a load into the ancient front-loading washer in the garage that was just for animal towels and blankets, and was returning to the dog runs when a tan sedan pulled out of the driveway and started down the dusty road.

As Sam rounded the corner, Allie slowed. "Hey. That was a fast one."

"Yeah. Just needed a quick check and puppy shots.

Those are the easy ones." He stopped in front of her. "Is Tracy helping you?"

"Yep, some."

"Where is she now?"

"She's resting."

Sam frowned and started to walk toward the yard.

Allie grabbed his arm. "Sam, leave her alone for a little while, okay?"

It took a moment for his frown to disappear. "Okay." He sighed. "I'll be back when I'm done with Lucky."

Allie nodded and returned to the runs. She grabbed clean towels from the shed, filled water bowls, and moved each dog back, receiving three more face-washings in the process. She stepped from the third cage just as Sam rounded the corner again.

"Okay, Allie, Tracy!" Sam continued to the barn. "Let's go exercise the horses."

Popsicle ran from the tree as Tracy slowly rose. Allie heard the teenager grumble, but couldn't hear what she said. Assured that Tracy would join them, Allie walked on ahead.

She needed to find a way to reach the girl. Sam said the friction was normal, but it was important to Allie to know if she was causing more problems between Sam and his daughter than would otherwise exist. She would have to watch for the right moment.

"You want to take Hattie out?" Sam asked.

"Sure, I can do that." Allie opened the mare's stall and walked to the farthest corral with Hattie clunking slowly behind. As soon as Hattie was in the corral, the horse turned and rested her head over the fence where Allie could rub it.

"I think she's slowing down a bit," Allie said.

Sam walked out leading Prince. "She's getting close." Allie nodded.

"See if you can get her to follow you around the corral a few times, will you? She needs the exercise."

"Okay, I'll try." Allie slipped through the gate and started walking slowly around the corral. After every couple of steps, she had to wait for Hattie to catch up, but the mare continued to follow.

"What am I supposed to do?" Tracy stood with her hands on her hips.

"You can lunge Prince in the corral over here, and I'll use the pasture." Sam dropped the lead rope over the top rail and waited at the gate.

Tracy huffed as she walked to the corral.

Sam stopped her by stepping in front of her. "Can you do this?"

"Yeah, Pops, you taught me how years ago, remember?"

"I remember, Trace. I just want to make sure you do."

The girl nodded as Sam moved out of her way and she continued into the corral. She took the lead rope and walked to the middle, giving the horse slack on the rope and clucking the way Sam did. Allie decided she needed to learn to make that noise.

As Prince circled the corral, Sam led Lady into the pasture, walking with his hat low on his forehead. Allie couldn't see his eyes, but she was sure he watched Tracy and Prince while speaking softly to Lady. Horses' hooves pounded the dirt, and a gentle breeze carried puffs of dust into Hattie's corral and Allie's eyes.

"Switch directions, Trace," Sam said.

Tracy tugged on the rope. Prince stopped and then started around the other way. As soon as she'd completed the maneuver, Sam did the same.

Hattie slowed to the point of stopping, and Allie decided to let her. She leaned back against the fence and scratched the mare's jaw, as Hattie balanced one back hoof on its edge and went to sleep.

"Okay, that's enough." Sam guided Lady to him and started back toward the barn.

Tracy held Prince's lead tight. As she walked through the gate, the horse bumped into her so that she hit the post with her shoulder.

Tracy swung around and slapped the horse's neck with a resounding *thwak*. "Stupid horse!"

Prince jumped back with his head high and his eyes wide. He stomped and snorted, trying to back away.

Faster than lightning, Sam had Tracy by the arm. He pulled her around, held her just inches from him, and spoke in a low voice, filled with anger. "Don't you *ever* let me see you do that again. A horse may be big, but that doesn't mean you can't hurt him. You *know* better. I've taught you better."

Boredom completely disappeared from Tracy's face. She stared up at Sam, her eyes as wide as Prince's, and nodded slowly.

He released her and stepped aside, propped his elbow on the fence, and held the front of his hat. "Leave him there."

Tracy dropped the lead rope. She walked quickly to the barn, her head low. Allie couldn't see her face, but she suspected the girl was crying.

Nine

As soon as Tracy disappeared, Sam jerked his hat off, threw it to the ground, turned to the fence and dropped his head to his arm.

Allie slipped quietly out of the corral. She picked up Sam's hat, dusted it off, and stood silently behind him.

Sam raised his head and shook it slowly. His shoulders rose and fell as he fought for control. "Damn."

Allie wanted to touch him, but she felt like she was intruding, so she put his hat on a post near him. Speaking softly to Prince, as she'd seen Sam do, she led the horse into the barn and tied him to one of the hitches.

At the corral, Sam leaned back against the fence, his hands on his knees. He straightened when she approached. "Thanks, Allie. God, I can't believe she can make me so damn angry." He took a deep breath and shook his head again, then turned and grabbed his hat from the post. He walked to the pasture fence where he'd left Lady, putting his hat on as he went.

Allie followed them into the barn.

Sam wiped Lady down and brushed her as Allie did the same to Prince. They worked in silence. She had never seen anyone look as completely unhappy as Sam did.

"If you'll bring Hattie in," he said, "I'll exercise the other two."

"Okay." Allie closed Prince's stall, then opened the gate to the corral for Hattie. The rotund mare followed her.

As soon as Sam had the smaller white horse circling the corral, Allie slipped out of the barn and headed for the house. Just before she got to the back door, she spotted toes of boots sticking out from behind a tree. Quietly, she strolled to the tree and sat in the grass to Tracy's left. The teenager had her knees drawn up and her head on her arms.

Tracy raised her head. She wiped the tears away with her palm and stared off to her right. "I didn't mean to do it," she said. Her chest convulsed with a stifled sob, and fresh tears started down her cheeks. "I hate him."

"Your father? You don't hate him."

"Yes, I do. He hates me."

Allie smiled at the grass in front of her and pulled a blade loose. "Tracy, he definitely doesn't hate you."

Their eyes met for a moment. Tracy's were red and puffy.

"What do you know? He cares more about his stupid animals than he does me." She sniffled.

"That's not true."

"Then why did he yell at me when I hit the stupid horse? I . . . I didn't mean to hurt Prince."

"I know, Tracy. You want to know what I think?" When her question met with silence, she continued. "I think your dad is a kind man who speaks for the animals. He probably sees a lot of animals who have been hurt by cruel people."

Tracy frowned at the ground. Tears clung to her chin and wavered before they fell. She wiped her cheeks again. "But he cares about them more than he does me. He sent me and Mom away because of his stupid animals. He wouldn't have done that if he loved me."

"Oh, Tracy, I don't know what happened when your parents split up, but you can't take it personally. One thing I've learned is that you have to understand it has nothing to do with you. It's just the way things are."

"Oh *yeah?* Are your parents divorced?"

Allie shrugged. "I don't know."

"You don't know if your parents are divorced?" Tracy's voice swam in sarcasm.

"No, Tracy, I don't. I don't know who my parents are."

The girl stared at her. "You mean . . . you're adopted?"

"No. I was sent to live with my last foster parents when I was about your age, but they never adopted me."

Tracy frowned at her hands, and the tears slowed. "What was it like?"

Allie sighed, stretched her legs out, and leaned back on her hands. At least she had the girl talking. "It wasn't bad. I didn't know I was missing anything until I was older. I mean, if you have no idea what it's like to have a mother and father, you can't miss them. I had about fifty sisters and brothers over the years." She smiled at Tracy. "Then, when I was sent to live with the Taylors, I went to public school. That's when I found out that most kids had parents who loved them. For a long time, I thought it was me, I thought my mother had abandoned me when I was born because I was bad or ugly or something. It took me years to understand that it had nothing to do with me."

A hawk circled the pasture in front of them. Allie watched it move up and down with the wind currents. She felt Tracy's eyes on her.

"You're not ugly."

Allie smiled. "Thanks."

The hawk spotted its prey and climbed higher, then

tucked its wings and dove. Just before it hit the ground, its wings flared and it slowed, talons bared, and it disappeared in the grass.

"Dad thinks I'm still a kid."

She looked at the teenager. "That's a tough one, isn't it?"

Tracy nodded.

"I wish I could help you. I'm afraid I don't have any experience to fall back on. But, from what I've read, you have to give it time. It's really hard for fathers to let go of their children, especially their daughters."

The girl sighed. "I didn't really want to have sex with Tommy. I just wanted to make Dad understand that I could."

"I'm glad to hear that, Tracy. You're still a little young to be thinking about . . . having sex with someone. Believe me, there's plenty of time for that, no matter how it feels right now." Allie pulled her legs up and leaned forward. "Like I said, I'm no expert, but I think the only way your father is going to be able to let go is if he trusts you. And trust is something you have to earn."

Tracy nodded. "Yeah, I guess so."

Allie pushed herself up. "I've got cages to clean. You want to help?"

"Yeah." Tracy also rose, wiping her face one last time.

They walked side by side around the house. Tracy's gestures were so much like her father's, it made Allie smile.

"Dad's really mad at me right now."

"He was pretty mad, but I'm sure he'll get over it."

"Why do you call him Doc?"

Allie shrugged. "I don't know. I guess it helps keep things light."

★ ★ ★ ★ ★

Sam returned the sorrel to his stall, hung the lead rope on a nail, and dropped the door latch into place as he left the barn. At the faucet, he pushed his hat back and splashed water on his face. It helped a little, so he did it again before turning off the water. He draped his arms over the top rail of the corral and rested his dripping chin on the wood.

How could he be so patient with a wild horse and lose his temper so quickly with his own daughter? It physically hurt to yell at her. Afterwards, his chest tightened and his stomach ached. All he wanted was to hold her in his arms like he used to when she fell and scraped her knees. Life had been easy then. She'd been his pride and joy, his beautiful little girl. The world had been at peace when he rode behind the saddle, holding her in place and enjoying her giggles. Why couldn't it be that good again? Why did it have to change?

Sam sighed. There was nothing he could do about what had passed between them. He had to move on from here. As bad as it was, he was still confident that Tracy would come around. And they had only been together a little over twenty-four hours so far. God, it had been a long twenty-four hours.

Pushing off from the fence, he turned and headed for the house. It must be getting close to lunchtime because his stomach burned. Maybe he'd fix them all sandwiches and apologize over lunch.

As embarrassing as it was to have Allie see this side of him, he was thankful for her presence. She was good at catching him when he stumbled. Sam hoped he could make up for all she'd done, but he had no idea how he'd do that.

The back door popped open. "Sam, telephone. It sounds urgent." Allie held the door for him as he trotted in the house and to the phone.

"Yes?"

"Dr. Calvert, this is Mary Holden. Our dog is lying on the kitchen floor convulsing. His eyes are rolled back and his tongue is hanging out and I don't know what to do. What should I do?"

"Can you carry him?"

"I think so. David can help me."

"Pick him up and bring him over here. I'll be waiting in my office."

"Okay."

Sam hung up the phone, trotted to his room, grabbed a clean T-shirt, and headed for the bathroom. "Allie, I've got an emergency coming over. Will you help me?"

"Yes."

Sam left the door open a crack so he could talk to Allie while he washed his face and hands and changed his shirt. "As soon as they get here, I need to get the people out. Then I'll need you with me."

"Okay."

"Where's Tracy?"

"She's cleaning cages in your office."

Sam smiled. That was a good sign. "Will you get her out of there? She can help keep the family busy."

"Okay. I'll do that right now."

"Good."

Sam stuck his head under the running water and let it cool the back of his neck. Grabbing the towel from the rack, he rubbed his hair as he started toward the office.

It seemed only minutes until a car screeched to a stop in the driveway.

★ ★ ★ ★ ★

Sam walked slowly to the sink and washed his hands and face. Sweat marks stained the back of his T-shirt.

He turned and frowned. "Well, that's about all we can do."

Allie looked down at the big brown dog strapped to the table, an IV bag hanging above him. "Is he going to make it?"

Sam sighed. "I don't know. We'll have to wait and see." He motioned with his head as he dried his hands on a towel. "Come wash up and let's go talk to the family."

"What if he wakes up?"

"He won't, not for a while at least."

Allie lathered her hands and arms and rinsed off the soap. Dazed, she stared at the suds swirling into the drain.

Sam amazed her. In an emergency, he took calm and total control. When the teenage boy carried the convulsing dog in, Allie's first response had been to run away. The dog's entire body had twitched and jerked, his mouth had bled, and he'd yelped constantly. Sam had given her firm orders that were clear and direct, and she'd found herself following them without thinking about it. She still wasn't sure what all they'd done, but she knew Sam had pumped the dog's stomach and checked through the stomach contents. He'd sedated the animal, stitched up a cut in its lip where the dog had bitten itself, and hooked up an IV while explaining that the dog needed fluids.

Allie also didn't know how long they had been in the office. It felt like hours. Sam handed her a towel and she dried her hands. When she turned around, she found him watching her.

"You did good again."

"Thanks," she said, warming under his praise. "It must

be all the practice I'm getting."

"Yeah, it must be." He took the towel from her and tossed it into the hamper, then led the way down the hall.

In the den, a woman, her teenage son, and a much younger boy waited on the sofa. They all had cold drinks, and Tracy played cards with the youngest. Everyone stood up when Sam walked in.

"How is he?" the woman asked.

"I don't know, Mary. It looks like he's been poisoned, and I don't know if we got to him in time or not."

"Poisoned? Who would poison my dog?"

Sam ran his fingers through his hair and sat down on the edge of the overstuffed armchair. "What's the dog's name?"

"Butch," the youngest boy answered through tears.

"Was Butch out running loose recently?"

"I let him out this morning like I always do," Mary said, "and he came back an hour or two later. Then I went to the grocery store. When I got home, I found him on the floor. That's when I called."

"Did you feed him any raw meat this morning?"

"No."

"He had undigested bits of raw meat in his stomach. I took a sample to send to the county, but I'm sure they'll find poison. A few of the ranchers still put out poisoned bait for the coyotes. Unfortunately, they get more household pets than anything else."

Mary cringed. "That's terrible."

Tracy crossed the den and handed Sam a cold drink. He looked up at her. "Thanks, Trace."

She smiled at Allie as she gave her a can.

Sam took a long draw on the drink and then moved back a little in the chair. "I want to be honest with you. I've lost a lot of dogs to poison here. I don't know that Butch will pull through. We've done everything that can possibly be done, and I'll watch him tonight. If he makes it through the night, his chances will be better. I just don't want to get your hopes up. You understand?"

The whole family nodded.

Mary dabbed at tears with a tissue. "Thank you, Doctor. I know you've done all you can. What time should I call in the morning?"

"I'll call you as soon as I have any news," he said.

"Okay."

The woman ushered her boys to the door.

The youngest one turned back and looked up at Sam. "Tell Butch I love him."

Sam nodded. "He knows."

Tears welled in Allie's eyes.

As Mary was about to step through the doorway, Sam grabbed her shoulder. He waited until the boys were out of earshot. "Mary, if he doesn't make it, do you want me to take care of the body?"

The woman gulped and nodded. Tears spilled over to her cheeks and Allie wiped away her own as she walked into the kitchen, trying to find something else to concentrate on.

It was three-thirty and they hadn't eaten lunch yet. Tracy walked in as Allie was pulling ham and cheese from the refrigerator.

"Sandwiches okay with you?" Allie asked, working to keep her voice steady.

Tracy removed plates from the cabinet and nodded.

The car drove away, and Allie heard Sam's footsteps behind her as she sliced the ham. "We'll make sandwiches, if you need to watch him."

He touched the back of her arm tenderly. "Thanks." And then his footsteps faded in the hall.

Allie and Tracy fixed sandwiches in silence, both obviously fighting tears. As soon as they were done, Tracy started returning ingredients to the refrigerator and Allie picked up the plate with two sandwiches.

"I'll be right back," she said. She carried Sam's plate to the office. Trying not to look, she put the plate on his desk and turned around.

But she couldn't help it. She looked over at Butch, who was no longer just a big brown dog strapped to a metal table. Now he was a family pet, and there was a little boy who loved him. It was more than she could bear. Tears ran down both cheeks and Allie covered her mouth.

Sam got up from his chair and walked quickly to her, enveloping her in his arms. Allie pressed her face to his chest and cried. He held her tighter, moving slowly side-to-side and whispering into her hair. "It's okay, Allie. It's okay." He gently stroked the back of her head.

Allie wrapped her arms around Sam's waist and cried until she could finally stop the sobs. She lifted her head and wiped her nose and eyes on her sleeve. Then she looked up to find Sam looking down at her, his face kind and understanding.

"He's not going to live, is he?"

"I don't know, but it doesn't look good."

"It's so sad."

Sam reached up and wiped a tear from her cheek with his thumb. "You're just an old softy underneath, aren't you?"

Allie sniffed. "It kind of looks that way."

He released her. "Go eat your sandwich. I'll be out here."

She nodded and walked away from the office, gently pulling the doors closed behind her.

133

★ ★ ★ ★ ★

"You don't have to stay up with me. I'm used to these all-night vigils. Really, I'll wake you up if I need you."

Allie looked up from the book she was reading. Sam smiled when he realized it was *All Creatures Great and Small*, one of his favorites as a kid. That book was probably the reason he'd wanted to be a veterinarian in the first place.

"That's all right," she said. "I'll stay a little longer. I mean, if you don't mind—"

"I don't mind at all, I just don't want you to feel obligated."

"I don't."

"Good."

Sam leaned back in his chair and propped the magazine on his thigh. He was already two issues behind on *The British Veterinary Journal*, and another issue was due any day. There just never seemed to be enough time to do everything. He glanced over the top of the page at Allie.

With the lamp softly spotlighting her, she looked like she sat alone in the world. Everything around her vanished into shadows. He wanted to hold her again, to taste her precious lips. Recalling the promise of yesterday's kiss in this very room, his heart sped up.

Sam looked down at the journal, ashamed of his desires. At the moment, he sat in his office watching over a critically ill patient. How could he be so selfish?

And, yet, just knowing Allie was close was a comfort. Was it his imagination, or could he really feel her presence? She sat very still. Was she thinking about him?

Sam grinned when he realized they had both been working on the same page in their respective volumes for much too long.

Ten

Allie woke with a start, wincing at the pain in her neck. She pawed at the blanket that covered her as she worked to sit up. Where was she?

One dim light shone in the corner. Oh yeah, it was Sam's office. She'd sat with him until she fell asleep. He must have covered her with the blanket.

Allie stood and looked around, her gaze stopping on Sam's empty chair.

She turned and found the metal table also empty. The IV needle hung down with the tube looped over the top of the bag. Beyond the table, the exterior door wasn't quite closed.

Allie's heart pounded against her ribs. "Sam?"

Outside, the cold night air made her shiver as she stood on the step and searched the darkness. A faint light glinted from across the yard, and Allie followed a path that wound through shrubs and trees and into a small opening where a steady swishing sound came from near the light. As she got closer, she saw Sam, illuminated by a lantern, shoveling dirt. He placed one more shovel full and patted the top of the mound. Then he pushed the end of the shovel into the ground and leaned on the handle. Around him, she saw a circle of other mounds, some new

135

and some covered with patches of weeds.

"Sam?" Allie's voice was barely a whisper.

He turned around and squinted against the light. "Allie." Sam shook his head slowly.

Allie took the lantern from him and wrapped her arm around his waist. Sam dropped his arm across her shoulders. They walked back to the house in silence.

At the door, he turned off the lantern. They stepped apart and into the semi-darkness of the empty office.

"Damn, I hate losing them," he whispered.

There was nothing she could say, so she just nodded.

He sighed and started toward the door, guiding her with his hand on her back. "Thanks for your help, Allie."

"You're welcome, Sam."

"Good night."

"Good night." Allie tiptoed down the dark hallway to her room, wiping away fresh tears. It wouldn't be easy going back to sleep.

Allie put off getting out of bed the next morning as long as she could. She didn't want to be up when Sam called Mary Holden. By the time she crawled out from under the covers, the sun shone with midday intensity.

In the kitchen, she found Tracy washing dishes and coffee overheating in the glass carafe.

"Good morning."

"Morning." Tracy didn't quite turn around. "There's French toast in the bowl. You can heat it in the toaster."

"Okay, thanks." Allie removed the foil cover from the bowl and drew out two pieces. She'd never bothered with breakfast before meeting Sam, but she was getting used to it. As the toast heated, she filled her coffee cup and leaned against the counter. "How are you this morning?"

Tracy shrugged.

"That bad?"

The teenager rinsed a plate and placed it in the drain pan. She turned toward Allie with eyes red from tears. "I tried to talk to Dad this morning, but he's still mad."

"Are you sure?"

"Yeah. I tried to tell him I didn't mean to hurt Prince, and he just walked away."

"Hmm. Did he call Mary Holden about her dog?"

Tracy shrugged. "I just got up a little while ago."

Allie sipped coffee and frowned at the floor. "Tracy, I don't know for sure, but isn't it possible that your dad was upset about Butch when you tried to talk to him?"

"Why? He sees animals die all the time." Tracy started scrubbing a frying pan.

"True. But I think it still upsets him. Maybe he didn't want you to know that."

She stopped scrubbing and turned to Allie. "You think so?"

Allie shrugged. "I think it's possible." She placed her hand on the girl's shoulder and squeezed. "Give him a little time, Tracy. He may be your father, but he's only human."

The toast popped up, causing both of them to jump, and they laughed. Allie prepared her plate, carried it to the dining room, and sat at the table.

Sam walked in, buttoning his shirt.

"Good morning, Sam."

He smiled at her. "Good morning."

"How are you this morning?"

"Same as always."

Allie held a fork full of French toast poised in front of her mouth and dropped her voice. "You're lying." She looked up to find him frowning down at her.

As Sam shook his head, a half-smile appeared. He turned and walked to the kitchen. Allie could hear him, whether she wanted to or not. In this case, she was too curious not to listen.

"Tracy, I'm sorry I walked out on you this morning. I . . . I didn't—"

The phone rang. Sam's footsteps echoed through the wooden floor as he crossed the room.

"Hello . . . speaking . . . okay. Keep her calm and I'll be right there . . . no, just hold her where she is. If you get her excited, it'll get worse . . . okay."

Allie peeked around the doorway as Sam hung up the phone.

"I've got an emergency and I could use you both. Will you help?"

Allie nodded and glanced over to find Tracy doing the same.

"Put on jeans, long-sleeved shirts, and boots. I've got gloves for you. We've got a horse caught in barbed wire."

Allie dashed off to her room, the rest of her breakfast forgotten.

Sam pushed the truck as fast as he safely could. He let up on the accelerator when they hit a bad section of washboard, then sped on again when it ended. They still had three miles or so of gravel road before they reached the Cory ranch. Allie sat by the door with Tracy between them.

"You always have this many emergencies?" Allie yelled to be heard over the rattles.

"Summer's just getting underway," he yelled back. "Everyone's out and feeling their oats."

"Animals or people?"

"Both. Winter's a lot slower."

"Glad to hear it. This could age a person."

Sam smiled. The pace probably seemed a little hectic if you weren't used to it. Emergencies had been a part of his life for so long now that his heart rate barely increased. There wasn't another vet within a hundred miles, so he got all the calls.

He glanced over at Tracy. Pressing her lips together, she watched the road ahead of them with wide eyes.

"You okay, Trace?"

"Yeah." She smiled weakly.

Sam slowed and downshifted as he fishtailed into the driveway. He followed a narrow lane, lined with white fences, and stopped in front of the huge house. The Corys had the nicest place around.

"Don't slam the door," Sam said as he hopped out and pushed the truck door closed.

He grabbed his black bag out of the bed and looked across at Allie. "Get that small tool box, will you?"

She nodded and stretched to reach the handle.

Sam walked quickly around to the back of the house.

Samantha Cory waited at the gate with a teenage girl. They watched the pasture where her husband stood holding a horse in the bright sunshine.

"Dr. Calvert," Samantha Cory said, "I'm really glad you're here."

"Samantha." Sam shook the woman's hand, noting that it trembled.

She motioned toward the pasture. "Ed tried to get her out, but she just got more tangled." She glanced back at her teenage daughter. "She's Cynthia's filly."

"Her name is Jewel," Cynthia said from the fence.

Sam smiled at the girl with as much reassurance as he

could, then turned to Allie and Tracy. He motioned for Tracy to join him and knelt in front of his bag. Lifting out a bottle and syringe, he looked out at the filly once more. She couldn't be quite nine hundred pounds. As he filled the syringe, he gave Tracy instructions.

"When I tell you I need the sedative, you carefully take the cap off this needle and give it to me."

Tracy nodded.

Sam filled three more syringes. "These are anesthetics." He lined the syringes up in the side of the bag, then removed and opened the plastic kit. "We clean the cuts with this," he said, lifting one of the green bottles and replacing it. Then he wrapped the end of a suture through the curved needle. "When I ask for a suture, you do this and give it to me. Okay?"

She nodded again.

"Allie, get the wire cutters and both pairs of pliers out of the tool kit."

Allie followed his directions and he took the tools from her and shoved them in his back pocket.

Sam rose and pulled on his gloves. "Okay. We need to all remain very calm around the horse. She's scared, and it's going to hurt when we pull the wire loose. I can't give her the sedative right away, because I need to have her standing until we get her untangled. When you walk up to her, walk up to her head and talk softly. No sudden moves. Okay?"

Tracy and Allie nodded.

"Is there something we can do?" Samantha opened the gate for them.

"I'll let you know."

Sam picked up the black bag and started forward, taking a deep breath to lower his adrenalin level.

★ ★ ★ ★ ★

As they approached, Jewel's eyes got bigger. She began to move around when they were twenty feet from her, and barbed wire danced around her like a bed of angry, metal worms. Ed Cory stroked the horse's neck and glanced back at them.

Allie took deep breaths to calm the jitters making her hands shake.

Sam spoke in a soft, kind voice. "Whoa, girl, you're going to be okay." He placed the black bag on the ground and walked slowly to her, his hands low in front of him.

She was a beautiful horse. As they'd crossed the pasture, Sam had said she was an Arabian, about four years old. Whatever she was, she had a gray and white coat, and her nose, mane, and tail were dark. Her coloring made it easy to see blood on her legs and shoulder. Her nostrils flared at their approach.

"Ed," Sam said quietly, "good to see you."

"Thanks for coming out so quickly." Sweat dripped down both sides of Ed Cory's pale face. "I don't know how this wire ended up out here. We were fixing fence last week, but I didn't think we'd left any behind." He swallowed hard. "She's cut up pretty bad. I'd sure hate to have to put her down."

"I understand." Sam placed a hand on Ed's shoulder. "You've been out here awhile, haven't you?"

"Feels like hours."

"Why don't you wait back at the gate? We'll take it from here."

"That's okay. I don't mind holding her."

"I've got good helpers." Sam smiled. "Don't worry. I'll let you know if I need you. The fewer people we have out here, the better."

"You sure?"

"Yeah, we're fine, really."

Judging by the man's appearance, Allie guessed that Sam was trying to avoid telling him he was more worried about his health than the horse's. It probably wouldn't help to have Ed Cory pass out or have a heart attack while they were working on Jewel.

Ed nodded. As he traded places with Sam, he sighed deeply. "Okay." Without further discussion, he walked away.

"Tracy, stay by the bag. Allie, I want you to come up here and talk to her." Sam gave them instructions without changing his tone of voice as he let the filly smell his palm. Then, holding her halter in his left hand, he ran his right hand down her neck. Jewel visibly trembled.

"Allie, hold her by the halter like this. She's going to jerk her head around, so stand to this side. Don't let her turn around on me. Okay?"

Allie nodded and stepped forward. She spoke to Jewel in the same voice she used for Hattie, and the horse watched her with wide eyes. Once she had a firm grip on the halter and was rubbing the front of the horse's face, Sam started off to her side.

The horse jerked at the first snip of the wire, causing Allie to jump, too. She tried to relax, inhaling deeply as she continued to talk. The snipping went on for a long time.

"I've got most of the extra stuff out of the way," Sam said. "Just relax, but hold tight. The next one may hurt her a bit."

As promised, the next snip must have caused pain. Jewel jerked her head back and up, trying to back away. She whinnied and snorted as Allie fought to pull her head back down. The poor horse's eyes were wild.

Sam sat still as Allie worked at calming Jewel. After a

long minute or two, the filly quit struggling.

"Tracy, come here."

"Dad, I can't—"

"Okay. Don't worry. You hold the horse's head."

Allie glanced back at Sam out of the corner of her eye. "It's okay, I've got her."

"Allie, I need you to get this wire out of my back."

"Oh." Allie relinquished control of the horse to Tracy and walked around to Sam's back where wire protruded from a slice in his shirt, which was quickly turning red.

"Jesus, Sam, you're bleeding like crazy."

"Just pull the wire straight out."

"I don't—"

"Do it now, Allie. This is really uncomfortable."

Allie grabbed the wire on each side of the cut and lifted. Sam jumped a little, then rose slowly. His voice remained completely calm.

"How badly is it bleeding?"

Allie pulled his shirttail out and lifted the shirt. Blood ran freely down his back.

"It's bad."

She followed him to the black bag where he knelt on the ground and gave her a green bottle. "Pour this over it."

When she did, she heard him inhale sharply.

Then he handed her something that looked like a tiny bandage, shaped like a figure eight.

"It works like a Band-Aid, but it's really sticky on each end. Squeeze the cut closed and put this over it." Sam reached around his sides and lifted his shirt up to his shoulders. "Wipe the blood off with one of those rags just before you put the butterfly on." He moved his shoulders to loosen his back.

Allie's hands shook so badly, she almost couldn't peel

the backing off the bandage. When she finally had it, she pinched the separated skin together.

Sam's muscles tightened in response, but he didn't make a sound.

Allie dabbed away most of the blood and placed the butterfly bandage in the middle of the cut. It slowed the bleeding in the middle, but blood still flowed freely from each end. Sam handed her another one.

By the time she had the fifth butterfly in place, blood simply pooled like it would on a tiny cut.

Sam lowered his shirt slowly and stood up. "Okay, back to work."

Allie wiped her hands on her pants as she returned to her position at Jewel's head. They continued the snipping and calming routine until Sam informed her, with a sigh, that they were done. By then, Allie was trembling as badly as the horse. In the intense sun, the breeze felt almost cold as it evaporated sweat on her skin.

"Trace, I need the sedative."

Tracy brought over the syringe, uncapping the needle as she walked. Jewel only moved a little as Sam injected the sedative into the wide part of her neck. He handed the syringe back to Tracy and rubbed the filly, talking softly. "Okay, Allie, I've got her now. Step back out of the way for a minute."

Allie watched in amazement as Sam worked the horse to the ground in slow motion, with minimal protest from Jewel. She kicked up a bit of dust as she went down, but when the dust settled, the horse was on her side with Sam on top of her.

"Okay, Allie, come here and lay across her neck."

Allie knelt on the ground behind Jewel and stretched over the horse's neck just behind her head. Sam showed her where the windpipe was so that Jewel could breathe, and explained that the horse would have to lift her head to get up. They both rubbed and calmed the filly while they waited for the sedative to take effect.

Allie had her back to Sam. She shaded Jewel's eyes from the sun and rubbed her jaw. The horse quit snorting and her breathing finally slowed to what seemed like a normal pace.

Judging from the number of times Sam asked for sutures, he must have stitched a lot of cuts. It took forever. The sun heated Jewel's skin until it felt hot to Allie's touch. "She's burning up, Sam."

"Trace," Sam said, "go back to the gate and ask Ed for a bucket of cool water, a rag or sponge, and a blanket."

"Okay." Tracy trotted into Allie's field of vision as she approached the gate. Ed Cory took off at a run, nodding and pointing directions to his wife and daughter. They also hurried away.

"You all right?" Sam spoke from right behind Allie, and she looked back to find him sitting on the ground near Jewel's shoulder.

"I'm okay. The question is, how are you?"

Sam sighed. "I'm okay, too. All we have to do now is cool her down a bit, and wait for the sedative to wear off. You don't have to lean on her anymore."

Allie straightened and watched Tracy making her way back across the field. Water sloshed over the top of the bucket a couple of times before she slowed.

Tracy helped Sam wash Jewel down. They got off as much blood as they could, got her entire coat wet, and covered her with the blanket.

Sam grunted as he got up and walked back to his black bag, where he filled another syringe.

"One more shot, girl." He knelt by the horse's rump and gave her the injection. "Got to get some of this antibiotic into you." Then he rose again.

"Tracy, can you stay with her?"

"Yes."

"Stay by her head, away from her hooves. When she starts to move her head around, pull the blanket off and get out of the way."

"Okay, Dad."

Sam motioned to Allie. "Come on."

When she stood beside him, he draped his arm over her shoulders. "Time to take care of the vet," he said. "I feel like I just left the blood bank."

Allie was surprised to find Sam's step unsteady, and when she looked up, she was even more shocked by his frighteningly pale face. He leaned on her as they walked, and she held him tightly around the waist. Before they got to the gate, Ed ran out to them and took Sam's other arm. Together, they guided him to the shade of a giant cotton-wood where Samantha met them with a tray.

"I'm really sorry about this." Ed squatted beside them as Allie sat with Sam.

"Don't worry, Ed, it comes with the territory. We need to get the wire picked up before the horse comes around."

Ed nodded. "My son, Edward, just pulled up. I'll send him out there right now."

Samantha placed the tray on the ground beside them and Sam smiled up at her. "Chocolate chip cookies, my fa-vorite. Thanks."

"There's plenty more," she said, nodding at the heaping plate.

Sam munched on cookies and worked on a glass of milk as Allie and Samantha watched him.

"Would you two please quit staring at me? I'm okay, really. I feel better already." He grabbed another cookie.

Allie nearly laughed, giddy with joy at the color returning to Sam's face.

Sam smiled at her. "Keep an eye on Tracy, would you?"

"Sure." Allie got up and walked to the fence where she could see the horse and teenager. Ed's son picked up the wire, talking to Tracy as he worked. Tracy definitely smiled in response.

After a few minutes, Jewel raised her head and dropped it back to the ground. Tracy pulled the blanket off and stepped back. The horse raised her head twice more, then struggled to her feet. She stood in one place, looking woozy for a little while, then stuck her nose to the ground and walked away. Everyone smiled at each other, excited enough to clap, but they didn't dare for fear of scaring the horse.

Allie opened the gate for Tracy and Edward, who nodded with a quick, "Thanks." Edward carried Sam's black bag and Tracy picked up the toolbox as they walked on around the house. Allie turned to find Sam approaching, with Ed at his side.

"The sedative will completely wear off in a few hours. Keep an eye on the cuts and let me know if you see any getting infected. I'll be back in a few days. The sutures will dissolve in a week or so."

The two men shook hands again.

"Thank you, Dr. Calvert." Cynthia stood beside her father, and Ed put his arm around her shoulders.

"You're welcome, Cynthia. Take good care of her, she's a special horse."

The girl nodded, a smile beaming from her freckled face.

After saying their good-byes, Sam and Allie turned and walked slowly around the house.

"You're kind of a mess, Al."

Allie looked down at her pants, smeared with blood and dirt, and then at Sam who was covered with both. "I'm afraid you look even worse, Doc."

"Yeah? Then I've got first dibs on the hot water."

"Shouldn't we take you to the hospital or something?"

He shook his head as he pulled the car keys out of his pocket. "No, I'm sure you did a good job, and I'm caught up on my tetanus shot. But I think you better drive. I'm going to need all my strength for when you help me wash my back."

Allie looked up at him and found him grinning mischievously.

Sam fastened the last button on his shirt and winced as he tucked in the shirttail. His back had already started to stiffen up. Walking to the mirror, he pulled his comb out of his pocket and ran it through his hair. He needed a haircut. Just one more thing to find time for.

Assured that everything was buttoned, zipped, or straightened, Sam left his room and walked toward the kitchen.

"You two ready yet?" he asked.

Tracy stepped out of her room, pulling the door closed behind her. "I'm ready."

"Two minutes," Allie called out.

Tracy followed Sam into the kitchen, where he filled and drank a glass of water. She leaned on the counter, studying her fingers.

"Thanks for the help, Trace. You did really well out there."

She looked up at him and frowned. "I didn't."

"You did."

"But, when you asked me to help with . . . with the wire—"

"Tracy, it's okay. You did a good job."

Tracy dropped her gaze again and shrugged. "Thanks."

Allie walked into the kitchen behind him. "I'm ready."

The metamorphosis stunned Sam into momentary silence. When Allie had left for her room, she'd been grubby from head to toe, with her hair caked to her head and her face streaked with dirt. Now she stood before him as a vision in the light brown dress he'd bought because the color reminded him of her eyes. And her golden eyes glistened, taking away his strength. If his daughter hadn't been standing beside him, he might well have considered making a lewd comment.

"You look good," he said.

"Thanks." She did a little curtsey. "Let's go, I'm starving."

When they got to the truck, Sam held the door for Tracy and Allie, then slid in on the driver's side.

Allie leaned forward and looked at Sam with concern. "You sure you should drive?"

"Yeah, my back will heal, but the gear box won't."

She sat back. "I only ground it into gear once. I had to figure out the clutch, you know?"

"Whatever you say, Al."

"Oh, shut up, Doc."

He glanced over to find Tracy trying to hide a grin.

Eleven

When Sam stopped the truck in front of the Last Chance, they all climbed out. Sam scratched Blue's head and then followed Allie and Tracy, who walked together, talking.

Before they got to the front door, Bill pulled into the parking lot in his cruiser. "Sam! You got a minute?"

Allie turned back but continued to walk. "We'll meet you inside."

He nodded and stopped at the sheriff's car, leaned with both hands on the door, and spoke through the open window. "Hey, Bill. I don't have long, or I'll drop from hunger."

Bill smiled. "It won't take long. The woman who's staying with you, what's her name?"

"Allie Parker. Why?"

"Roger Disher hauled an abandoned blue Volvo in off the highway a few days ago. It's registered to Rick Tate."

Sam waited as Bill looked at him expectantly.

"You know, the guy who owns Tate's Kids?"

Sam shrugged.

"Well," the sheriff continued, "they found it just around the corner up on Route Eight."

"Hmm."

"Miss Parker hasn't said anything to you about a car?"

"No."

"Oh. I thought I knew where it came from, but I guess not. I'll have to keep looking."

"Yeah, I'll keep my ears open."

"Okay, Sam. Go eat."

"Will do."

Sam walked up the steps, frowning. A car abandoned on the road about the time Allie appeared did seem a little strange. But it must be a coincidence. If it were Allie's car, she'd have mentioned it, wouldn't she? Of course, it wasn't registered to her, anyway. And if she had been driving the car and hadn't mentioned it, she probably had a good reason. Sam pushed the door open and walked in, trying to ignore his own questions.

Tracy waved from a booth where she and Allie waited, and he crossed the dark room.

Tracy scooted over to give him room. "We ordered you a T-bone, medium-well."

Sam smiled. "Sounds perfect." He looked across the table at Allie, who frowned at her lap. "You all right?"

She nearly jumped at his words, then smiled up at him. "Yep, just tired."

Sam decided not to mention the car. Maybe the car had nothing to do with her. Either way, it was her business.

As soon as the soup arrived, Sam, even hungrier than he'd realized, dove in with enthusiasm. Moments later, with the bottom of the bowl staring up at him, he felt like his appetite had barely been whetted.

"That Edward Cory is kind of cute."

Sam frowned at Allie's words and looked over at his daughter to find her grinning. "Yeah."

"How old is he?"

"Just turned seventeen."

"Hmm, that's about right."

Tracy nodded. "And he'll be a senior. He skipped a grade."

"Oh, and smart, too."

"Yeah."

Sam shoved his empty bowl forward and frowned again. "Please. I don't think I'm ready for this conversation."

Allie pursed her lips together, trying to keep from grinning. When he looked over at Tracy, she rolled her eyes.

Sam sighed and ran his fingers through his hair. "Can't we talk about something easier for me to handle, like nuclear physics, or quantum mechanics?"

Tracy giggled.

Allie released her grin. "You're a piece of work, Doc."

"Thanks, Al. I think."

They all walked slowly into the house, too stuffed to move any faster. Sam stopped at the armchair and Tracy dropped onto the sofa.

Allie sat in the chair across from Sam's, leaned her head back, and closed her eyes. "Thank you for the wonderful meal."

"Yeah, thanks, Dad."

"You are very welcome. And thank you both for helping me today."

Allie smiled at the sound of Sam's voice filling the room with warmth and safety.

She was finally getting over the jitters caused by the sheriff's appearance. When things started jumping, it was like she had no past. She could easily pretend that Rick never existed when she stood beside Sam, helping him, listening only to his voice. Nothing else existed.

Allie took a deep breath and blew it out slowly. Walking into the bathroom earlier while Sam was in the tub had been difficult, to say the least. She knew he thought it was because she was shy, but it wasn't. It was because he was so amazingly desirable. As she cleaned carefully around the cut on his back, she tried, unsuccessfully, not to look at the rest of his body.

His wide, muscular back narrowed at his waist, and was as tanned as his face. He must work out in the sun without a shirt when no one was around. Allie had peeked over his shoulder while she worked. Soft, brown hair that matched the color of the thick waves on his head covered his long, powerful legs. She grinned at the memory.

"No rest for the wicked," Sam said. His chair squeaked as he rose. "I've got to check on the puppy, the cats, and the mare."

Allie opened her eyes to find Tracy also rising.

"I'll check on the puppy and cats for you, if you want," Tracy said.

Sam smiled and nodded. "That would be great. Make sure they have water and clean blankets for the night."

Tracy nodded and started toward the back of the house.

Sam stretched as he looked over at Allie. "Want to go with me to check on Hattie?"

She smiled. "Sure." Grunting in a most unladylike fashion, she pushed herself out of the chair and followed Sam through the door.

The sun had completely disappeared, but the sky wasn't yet dark. In the distance, the Rockies glowed a soft, eerie blue. Pine sweetened the cool night air, and crickets worked at making a racket. Allie inhaled deeply and smiled.

At the barn, Sam switched on the walkway light and picked up a flashlight from a shelf by the door. He walked to the stall at the end and shone the light on the floor.

"Talk to her, Allie."

Allie spoke softly to Hattie. The mare turned slowly in the stall. Sam kept the light on her as she did, then lowered it so as not to hit her in the eyes. Hattie walked to the gate and raised her head.

Allie scratched the middle of Hattie's face. "How much longer?"

"Not tonight, but soon. It's hard to tell with her; she's having a rough time. She's too old for this."

Sam turned off the flashlight and stood it on the floor by the wall. He leaned on the stall and turned to Allie. "You're good with horses."

She shrugged. "I've never been around them before."

"Then you must be a natural. You do well with Tracy, too."

"Tracy's easy. I was once a fifteen-year-old girl myself, you know. She wants you to think of her as an adult."

Sam cringed. "How am I supposed to do that?"

"I don't know. I think you just need to talk to her, tell her how you feel. Be honest with her, but make sure you listen to her, too."

He sighed and Allie turned to face Hattie. Even in the dim light, she could see the mare's eyes closing. Allie rested her head on her arm and listened to Hattie's even breathing.

"I've wanted to talk to *you* for a while now." Sam's low voice came from directly behind her.

Allie straightened.

"We started something a few days ago . . ." His hands rested on her waist, tentatively touching her, and he slowly urged her around.

Allie leaned back on the wall, looking up at Sam as her

heart began to race. He stepped closer, and spread his hands to grip her sides. Even with his eyes barely visible in the light, Allie could feel them on her, and desire wormed its way through her belly. She wanted him even more now than she had before.

He leaned forward, tilting his head, his breath stirring the air between them. His mouth covered hers gently at first, then quickly grew demanding.

Allie slipped her arms around his neck as he encircled her and lifted her completely off the ground. When he pushed her against the wall, she realized how aroused he was and her entire body trembled with excitement. She wrapped her legs around his hips, and Sam slid one hand down to hold her thigh. Allie pushed her fingers into his hair.

His tongue circled her mouth, again and again, and he groaned, his body vibrating like some giant cat purring. Allie's hand fisted in his hair and she held him tighter, wishing she could draw him closer still.

Somewhere back in the real world, the door to the barn creaked. "Dad? Allie?"

Sam groaned more quietly as he ended the kiss and slowly eased Allie down the wall. He held her until her feet touched the ground, then backed up, smiling at her.

She felt his breath on her face, hot and fast to match her own.

Tracy's voice came from inside the barn now. "Dad?"

Sam stepped to the side and leaned on the stall gate. "Over here."

Allie turned to face the horse, looking back at Tracy as she walked up.

"I didn't mean to interrupt anything," Tracy said.

"It's okay, Trace. How are the boarders?"

"Fine."

Allie straightened and squeezed Sam's arm. "I'm going to bed, and I think you two have stuff to talk about."

Sam nodded.

Allie touched Tracy's arm as she passed her, then closed the barn door and walked to the house, holding her chest and trying to catch her breath.

Sam lifted one foot to the top of an upside-down bucket and turned back to the mare. He took slow, deep breaths, trying to douse the flames that scorched him from head to toe. Did Allie have any idea what she was doing to him?

He needed to switch gears. The idea of talking to Tracy terrified him, but he knew Allie was right. Before, things had always managed to just fall into place. It wasn't going to happen this time without some help. And there was too much at stake. In three years, she wouldn't have to come back if she didn't want to. God, how could he live without seeing his daughter?

"Trace—" Where should he start? Allie said he needed to be honest, but it wasn't easy. Admitting to his little girl that he didn't know what to do was showing her a weakness he'd never revealed before. How would she react? He frowned as he looked over at her.

Tracy stood in the middle of the walkway, her hands tucked into her jeans pockets. She looked so tiny and vulnerable in the dim light. A shiver ran through him.

Sam turned and sat on the bucket. "Tracy, I don't know where to start. I want things to be good between us."

She walked closer and leaned against the wall with one shoulder.

He continued. "I'm sorry I didn't listen to you this morning. It wasn't you, I was tired and . . . well, I was tired."

"I know, Dad. It was bad timing."

"Yeah."

They were quiet. Sam frowned at his hands, then looked back up at her.

She watched him, also frowning.

"I'm so afraid of something bad happening to you," he said. "I want to protect you."

"I'm not a little girl anymore."

Sam flinched. "You're my little girl, Trace. I can't help it. You always will be."

Tracy turned to lean completely against the wall. She looked at her boots. "I'm *not* a child."

Sam ran his hands through his hair and leaned back. "I know." He couldn't help but smile when their eyes met. "What do you want me to do?"

Tracy shrugged. "I don't know, exactly. I want you to treat me like an adult. I want you to trust me."

"That would be a little easier if we hadn't gone through the episode in the parking lot."

Tracy looked away again. "I know, that was stupid. I was . . ."

"Acting childish?"

"Angry," she corrected.

Sam nodded.

"Sometimes I think you care more about the animals than you do me."

He stood. "God, Tracy, how can you—" The words caught in his throat. He leaned on the stall door again and took a deep breath.

"Why did you and Mom split up?"

This was the moment he'd dreaded for years. All the speeches he'd practiced disappeared in a puff of smoke.

Sam sighed. "Trace, your mom and I had problems we

couldn't solve. I'm sorry that things turned out the way they did."

Her voice was so quiet, he had to strain to listen. "Sometimes I feel like it was because of me. Do you care about me, Dad?"

"Oh, Tracy." He turned and stepped toward her, and she ran to him and wrapped her arms around his waist. His chest ached. "Tracy, I love you. I always have, and I always will. The worst day of my life was the day you left." Sam held her and felt her body shake with sobs. His own eyes filled with tears, but he fought them back as they stood together in silence.

When she stopped crying, Tracy backed a step away, wiped her eyes, and looked up at him. "Sometimes I guess I don't act like a grownup," she said.

Sam smiled as he brushed the blond hair from her face. "No one has to be a grownup all the time."

She smiled through her tears.

"Tracy, I can't promise that I won't treat you like a little girl sometimes, but I can promise to try harder. Is that good enough for now?"

She nodded. "I promise to try harder, too."

Sam hugged her one more time, kissed the top of her head, and released her. "Okay." He sighed as he turned her toward the barn door and walked with his arm around her shoulders. "I feel better. How about you?"

"Yeah."

"Good." In truth, Sam felt like he'd just been kicked in the stomach and he hoped it didn't show.

Allie switched off the lamp and pulled the comforter up to her chin. She shivered, but not from the cold night air. Sam had ignited a fire in her that continued to rage. Her skin felt icy by comparison.

She closed her eyes. She needed to go to sleep and quit thinking about him. There were several reasons why she shouldn't sleep with Sam. Unfortunately, she couldn't remember any of them at the moment.

Floorboards creaked as Sam and Tracy walked around the house, both getting ready for bed. Water ran somewhere, and then it stopped. Things quieted down, but Allie's heart raced on.

"Al?" Sam's voice accompanied a tiny tap at her door.

Allie threw the comforter aside and tiptoed quickly to the door. She opened it a crack and peeked out.

Sam stood dressed in sweat pants and a T-shirt, holding the doorframe, his head lowered, looking at her.

"Is something wrong, Sam?"

His answer was a whisper, deep with emotion. "Yes, Allie, something is very wrong. You and I are sleeping in different beds."

He watched her, waiting, standing perfectly still.

"Which bed would you suggest?" she asked.

"Mine."

Allie swallowed hard, resisting the urge to jump into his arms.

This was it. If she stepped through this doorway, there would be no turning back. She couldn't go to bed with Sam without opening her heart to him, and she guessed that it might be the same for him. It would hurt like hell when she had to leave. But, right now, the ache to be in his arms was greater than any pain she could imagine. Unable to deny the desire, she opened the door slowly and walked out.

Twelve

The floor creaked under their feet as Allie followed Sam down the hall. His room was farther away from the rest of the house than hers, which was probably why he'd suggested it. When they got to the door, Sam held it open for her, followed her in, then quietly closed it behind them.

Allie had never been in Sam's room. His bathroom opened to both his room and the hall, and she'd used the hall entrance when she went in to wash his back. One lamp shone by the bed and the rest of the room dropped into shadows.

The bed was brass. Not new brass look-alike stuff, but real, antique, brass. The mattress rose high off the floor, and was covered with a thick, blue comforter that Sam hadn't yet turned down.

As her heart hammered against her ribs, Allie realized she had no idea what to expect in Sam's bed. Her only experience with men had been with Rick, and sex with Rick had always seemed a bit like a battle. Although she'd enjoyed the closeness, the act itself hadn't really done much for her. But in the years they'd been together, Rick had never touched the emotions in her that Sam now stirred.

She could feel Sam close to her. Holding the metal bar

at the foot of the bedstead to anchor herself in place, Allie turned around.

He stood an arm's length away, looking down at her, studying her intently for a long moment before leaning forward. He kissed her lips tenderly, gently, his hands at his sides. Then he straightened.

"You look great in my T-shirt, Al," he whispered.

"So do you, Doc," she whispered back.

They both smiled.

Sam reached out and touched her left cheek, stroking her skin, tracing the line of her jaw. His fingers continued down the side of her neck and across her shoulder as if he were memorizing the feel of her, then slid slowly down her arm to her hand.

Allie's skin tingled under his heated touch.

Sam lifted her hand and laced his fingers into hers. He leaned over and kissed her gently again, then repeated the process with the other side.

Her knees began to shake, and she didn't think she could stand on her own much longer.

With both her hands in his, he pulled them up to his shoulders and released them as he leaned in for another kiss.

This one lasted longer, and Sam gripped the brass rail behind her, his arms against her ribs.

Allie held his massive shoulders, gently at first, then tighter as he urged her mouth open and circled her tongue with his, taking possession of her mouth. The passion of the kiss grew and deepened quickly, and Sam wrapped his arms around her, lifting her from the floor. With her legs around his waist and her hand a fist in his hair, they were back to where they'd left off in the barn.

He slid one hand under her to hold her up and the other behind her head to hold her close. The world melted away until there was Sam and nothing else.

They moved, but Allie didn't know where they were going and didn't care. She held him, his body vibrating again, and thought she might die from longing.

It took a moment to realize that Sam was sitting on the edge of the bed. He released her mouth and kissed her throat. Allie leaned her head back, her eyes still closed, floating in a haze of lust.

His hand moved slowly, sensuously up and down her back, his thumb tracing her backbone through the T-shirt. He was hard under her, and she pressed down on him. Sam drew in a sharp breath against her neck, flattening his hand on her lower back.

There was nothing between them but thin layers of clothing. Swimming in frustration, she gripped the shoulder of his shirt.

"Sam," she whispered, "make love with me."

He groaned again and drew her hips in tighter. "God, Allie, I've never wanted anyone so badly."

She kissed his lips, enjoying the hot, moist feel of them. Then she held her mouth near his ear. "Oh, Sam—"

The rest of the words died in her throat as his hand slid under her shirt. His touch on her bare skin opened a dark sea of longing beneath her, and she clung to him to keep from falling in. When his fingers touched her breast and gently crossed the nipple, she dropped her forehead to his.

Control drained away, but she didn't want it back. "Sam," she whispered.

And then his hand moved up to her shoulder and he pushed her back. Allie opened her eyes and frowned at him.

But she found him smiling, his eyes half closed. "Wait, Allie, wait."

"What is it?"

His eyes opened wider, so dark they looked almost black. He grabbed her hips and moved her back enough to relieve some of the pressure.

"It's been a long time since I've done this, and I sure as hell don't want to mess it up."

She smiled at him. "You're doing fine so far."

"Maybe, but I think it's supposed to last more than three minutes, isn't it?"

They grinned at each other and kissed tenderly.

"That would be nice," she said.

"Then you'd better get up."

Allie backed off of Sam's lap, grinning at his pained pout.

He stood and turned them both around. "I think it'll work better this way."

"Whatever you say." She sat on the edge of the bed, and Sam leaned over to kiss her again. His hot, ravenous kiss curled her toes, and she hated it when he stopped.

His hands ran up from her thighs, lifting the T-shirt with them and he pulled it over her head and tossed it on the floor behind him. He covered every inch of her with his eyes, smiling as he did. His chest rose and fell rapidly, and he sat on the bed beside her.

"Allie, you are beautiful."

With his words warming her heart, she turned to him and tugged on his T-shirt. Sam raised his arms and she peeled it off and dropped it. His chest was even more perfect than his back and she gulped. Muscles tightened and relaxed just below the surface of his skin as he moved, and the brown hair that lightly covered his chest was almost blond against his tan.

Allie touched him without really meaning to, spreading her palms on his chest. She saw his reaction at once as goose bumps rose on his skin.

He reached out and ran his fingers over her breasts, teasing the nipples as he crossed them.

She did the same to him, and he leaned into her touch.

Without warning, Sam grabbed her waist and pulled Allie up on top of him as he stretched out. She found his mouth and he wrapped his arms around her and rolled them both over. They stopped in the middle of the bed, his weight mostly on his elbows as he dove into another sizzling, consuming kiss. He eased her legs apart with his knee. She pushed up into him, he pushed back, and they groaned together.

The kiss went on and on, and ended much too soon. Sam moved to Allie's side, still holding her in his left arm, and trailed kisses down her neck. His right hand explored her body, sliding over her ribs and belly, and then pushing her panties to her knees. Allie kicked them the rest of the way off.

Sam's hand slid up her inner thigh, his touch hotter than ever. When he pressed his fingers to her, hinting at entering, she gasped, and he rose up and covered her mouth with his. He added pressure and released it, slowly, rhythmically, seductively, as he kissed her, backing her toward the abyss, until he'd pushed her too far.

Allie's body exploded as she dove off the edge of the world. She cried out into his mouth, thrusting desperately against his hand, pulling his shoulder into her chest. Sanity fell away and she floated, gloriously free, into an ocean of bliss. He continued to push, his shoulder tight as he held her down and rode the waves with her, falling into troughs, sliding over crests, slowing as her need slowed, and smiling against her lips as she finally stilled, gasping for air.

"Sam—" Allie opened her eyes as he lifted his face away

from hers. She wanted to tell him that she'd never experienced anything like this before, how amazed she was, how
incredible he made her feel—

"Are we still on the right track?" He eased his hand back
down her sensitive thigh, stroking her skin with his thumb.

Allie smiled and nodded. "Definitely."

"Good."

Sam rolled onto his back and opened the top drawer of
his night table. After a bit of fishing around, he rolled back
over holding a foil wrapper.

Allie propped her head on her hand and narrowed her
eyes. "Well, Sam, if you haven't done this in a long time,
how old is the condom?"

He frowned and squinted at the ceiling, counting silently. Finally, he smiled at her. "About forty-eight hours
old."

"Oh." Allie grinned, recalling the scene in his office. She
still couldn't believe she'd made the first move. "You want
some help with that?"

"No, sweetie, not this time," he said as he pushed his
sweat pants off.

She hadn't even caught her breath yet when Sam rolled
over, drew her to him, and started into another round of
sizzling kisses. Desire bubbled up again from the depths of
her soul, sparking a hunger that she thought had just been
sated. How could she still need him so desperately?

This time he parted her legs and settled between them,
fitting as if he'd always belonged there, kissing her mouth
and then her neck and then her mouth again.

His arms surrounded her loosely at first, and then tightened slowly as he continued to kiss her. Their tongues circled, and tasted, and stroked each other, and she drew him
in deeper. Their bodies rocked together, the synchronized

rhythm intensifying with each movement, her skin heating to the point of bursting into flames.

She couldn't believe what he was doing to her, making her feel as if her lust were new and unsatisfied. Suddenly, she needed him inside her, ached for him. She dug her fingers into his shoulders, pulling him closer, as soft sounds of longing rose from her throat. When at last he started in, she thrust against him, crying out, and he pushed her into ecstasy again.

This time his thrusts matched hers, and he pressed her to the bed with his weight, muffling his own cries into her neck. Allie held him with all her strength as their bodies melted into one.

They moved together through the firestorm of hunger and fulfillment, clutching each other, kissing and panting, rising and falling together, until the urgent need finally slowed and quieted. From some cloud below her, she heard him whisper her name.

When they lay still, Allie felt Sam's heart pounding against her ribs. She kissed his forehead, pulling the hair back from his face. With a huge sigh, Sam lifted his weight to his elbows and looked down into her eyes. He gently kissed her lips, twice.

"This must be illegal, Al. Or at least fattening."

She frowned playfully. "Is that a problem, Doc?"

"Hell, no," he answered.

Allie closed her eyes as Sam covered her mouth with his.

They lay silently entangled until necessity forced them apart. Sam returned from the bathroom with a glass of cold water. He offered it to Allie as they both crawled under the comforter.

She drank, returned the glass, and rolled onto her back,

dropping her arms out to her sides. "You know, I was tired before we started this."

Sam placed the glass on the bedside table and turned to face her, propping his head up on his hand. "I might have been, but I was too turned on to notice. I must admit, I'm starting to feel a little pooped now." He pushed a strand of Allie's hair off her cheek. "One thing I don't get, though."

"What's that?"

"The way you reacted at the lake the other day, when I was kidding around with you, I'd have sworn you were just a shy little thing. I'm beginning to think you're not so shy."

"You know, Doc, it's a good thing you're a hunk."

"Oh?"

"Yep. If you can't tell the difference between shy and choking on lust, you need to be able to fall back on your good looks."

She grinned at him, caressing him with her eyes until he couldn't help but kiss her. When he pulled his mouth away, he rolled back onto his elbow and smiled.

"So, how did your talk with Tracy go?" she asked.

Sam sighed. "I don't know. Okay, I guess. Neither of us yelled or cursed. It was definitely a step in the right direction."

Allie nodded. "Sounds like it."

He traced a circle around the top of her shoulder, enjoying the softness and luster of her skin. "I'm having a hard time with this, now that she's old enough to ask questions. She wants to know why her mother and I split up."

"Did you tell her?"

"I can't. How can I tell her that her mother was sleeping around? She doesn't need to know that."

"She was having an affair?"

Sam frowned into her eyes. He hadn't really meant to

say that. It was just that he felt so close to Allie, he forgot there were things she didn't know. He dropped his gaze back to her shoulder. "No, she wasn't having an affair, she was sleeping around. She said it was my fault, that I didn't pay enough attention to her. I don't know, maybe it was my fault." He sighed again and dropped his head to his arm.

Allie turned to look at him, and their eyes met. God, she had beautiful eyes. Sam rested his hand on her arm.

"What happened?" she asked. "Did you throw her out?"

He didn't really want to go into this. No, he hadn't thrown her out. He had been devastated when he found out about all the lies. The discovery had nearly killed him. Still, he'd asked her to stay, crawled on his knees to her, begged her and pleaded with her.

When she'd driven off, she'd taken not only his daughter, but also his dignity. How could he explain that to Allie?

"No, she left."

Silence grew between them thick enough to slice. He wanted to ask Allie about her past, but he couldn't. He'd promised to wait until she was ready to tell him, and he would keep his word. She said she didn't have any children. Had she been married before? Did she know the misery of a marriage ending? She seemed awfully young to be divorced.

"How old are you, Allie?"

"Old enough, Sam. Why?"

"I don't know, I'm afraid I might be robbing the cradle."

Allie laughed, then covered her mouth with her hand to muffle the noise. Grinning, she dropped her hand onto his shoulder. "Thanks, Doc. I'm twenty-nine. And you?"

"Forty-two, Al. That's quite a difference."

"Well, let's see, when I'm a hundred and twenty, you'll only be a hundred and thirty-three. That's really not a noticeable difference."

"Oh, thanks, I feel *much* better now."

"Good." Allie turned over and lifted herself to her elbow. She kissed him tenderly, and then sat up.

"Where are you going?"

"To my room," she said. "I don't think we're really going to do much sleeping together, and you have to work tomorrow."

Sam reached across the bed, snagged her with his arm around her waist, and pressed his lips to her lower back. "No, don't leave yet." He kissed her spine, and traced circles on her skin with his tongue, enjoying the sweet warm taste of her.

She shuddered, and then whispered hoarsely, "I thought you were tired."

Sam smiled into the back of her ribs. "I was, but I'm not anymore." He desperately wanted her again, and was surprised at the level of his desire.

Allie turned slowly, so that he kissed a ring halfway around her waist. When he got to her stomach, the muscles tightened.

"That tickles," she whispered. With her hands on each side of his face, she drew him up the front of her body and he left a line of kisses in his wake.

By the time he reached her face, Allie's eyes were half-closed, and her shallow breath warmed his skin.

Sam held his lips just inches from hers, thrilling at the anticipation.

She pulled him forward, and he covered her mouth, pressed her back to the bed, and wrapped his arms around her. As much as he wanted to just push her legs apart and dive into her, he held her and rolled them both over. "Your turn."

Allie immediately responded, spreading her knees and straddling him, teasing him with subtle movements. Maintaining control was delicious misery and his eyes closed for a moment.

"I hope you have another condom," she whispered.

"I bought a box."

"Oh? Pretty sure of yourself, aren't you?" She kissed his lips, and pushed down harder on him.

As soon as he caught his breath, Sam opened his eyes and grinned at her. "Wishful thinking is more like it." He pulled her in for another kiss. "To tell you the truth, I was too embarrassed to ask the kid at the counter for the singles."

They laughed quietly together and Allie sat up. Her hands ran up his arms, across his shoulders, and down his chest. Her touch amazed him, and he wrapped his fingers around her waist, ready to move her.

Allie grabbed his wrists and pushed them to the bed on each side of his head. She pressed her lips to his ear. "I thought it was my turn to be in charge."

"It is," he whispered back. "But you have to play fair."

"Ha!" She reached down and pinched his ribs.

He jumped, gritting his teeth against the desire to roll her over.

Allie grinned wickedly as she sat up and drew her fingernails down the front of his body. Sam closed his eyes and shuddered at the pleasure. Then he opened his eyes to find her waiting, one hand extended, palm up.

"What?"

She motioned toward the dresser with her head, and then moved with him as he rolled over to dig out another condom.

Straddling his thighs, she put the condom on him, not exactly with expert ease, but she managed to get it right. He tried not to notice how incredible her touch felt, afraid the result would render her work useless. Then she sat up and grinned triumphantly as she tossed the wrapper over her shoulder to the floor.

Her body absolutely blew him away. In the short time she'd been with him, she'd put on enough weight to make her look healthy, not overly thin as seemed to be the fad these days. Her breasts were real, and full, and filled his hands with a warmth that made him want to groan. And her rounded hips fit against him perfectly when she locked her long legs around him.

But it was her golden eyes that melted his heart. She studied him intently, her eyes glistening, strands of hair plastered to her temples from their lovemaking, and he was unable to speak.

Without warning, she rose up and took him into her more quickly than he expected, and Sam sucked a ragged breath through his teeth. She drew his hands up to her breasts, and he held her upright as she rolled her hips back and forth, her head back, her eyes closed.

He wanted to watch her for hours, to revel in her joy, but he knew better. Much too soon, he felt her body tighten in time with his own, and he drew her down to him, kissing her, holding her. Unable to take it, he rolled them both over and drew her into a powerful climax as he filled her with his seed and his soul, whispering her name as his breath.

She pressed her mouth to his shoulder to quiet her cries, and then panted against his skin as he held her.

Dear God, nothing could ever compare to the perfection of making love to her.

171

★ ★ ★ ★ ★

Allie lifted Sam's arm, heavy with sleep, and slid out from under it. He didn't stir. She sat on the edge of the bed and studied him.

The man was absolutely gorgeous. She couldn't believe how incredible he felt, or how much she wanted him.

When they'd made love the second time, she'd tried to play it cool, to maintain the upper hand, but as soon as she had taken him inside her, she'd lost it. He'd held her and kissed her, pushing just enough, holding back when he should. It was as if he were reading her mind. And when she took him over the edge, he'd hugged her, gasping into her shoulder, and then whispered her name until the waves of pleasure passed.

It occurred to Allie, as he kissed her, that they hadn't had sex—they had really made love. Feigning exhaustion, she'd turned over to hide her tears. Sam had wrapped her in his arms, pressed his cheek to the back of her head, and fallen asleep.

Allie stood slowly, tiptoed around the bed, and put on her nightshirt and panties. As tempting as it was to sleep in Sam's bed, she didn't want Tracy to discover what had happened. The teenager's words from the first night still made Allie's stomach knot. Now they seemed almost too close to the truth.

The door to Sam's room squeaked. Allie cringed at the noise, then tiptoed silently down the hall to her own room and her empty, lonely bed. She tried hugging the extra pillow to her chest and pretending it was Sam, but it was a pathetic substitute.

She'd almost told him about her past. There had been an opportunity, and she'd wanted to tell him, but she hadn't. The possibility that he'd think she was a fool, or an idiot, or worse, terrified her.

The reality of the situation was that now Allie cared more about Sam than she ever had about anyone, and she wished her past would just disappear.

"He deserves the truth," she whispered, her face pressed into the pillow. The next time they were alone, she would tell him about the night they met and about her past leading up to that night. Sam would understand. He would hold her and protect her and keep her safe.

Allie's sleepy brain knew that Sam would make everything all right.

Allie found Sam and Tracy having breakfast together at the table the next morning. It had to be the latest breakfast Sam had eaten since her arrival. His eyes lit up when he smiled at her and it was all Allie could do to remain calm as she sat. Without a word, he handed her the bowl of eggs.

Tracy covered her toast with jam. "Good morning."

"Good morning." Allie dropped a small spoonful of eggs onto her plate and took a piece of toast from the stack, too tired to digest any more than that.

Sam pushed his empty plate forward, held his coffee mug in both hands, and leaned back in his chair. "Will you two be okay without me for a couple of days?"

Allie frowned. "You're leaving?"

"Yep. Once a month I make the rounds at the shelters between here and Idaho Springs. Got to make sure everyone is fixed and healthy. It usually takes two days, more or less."

"Oh." Allie's heart sank at the thought of Sam leaving. She looked up from her plate to find him smiling at her.

"Why don't we all plan on a ride Sunday morning?" he asked.

Tracy perked up. "To the lake?"

"Sure. Does that sound okay?"

"Sounds good to me, Dad." She glanced at Allie. "Have you been to the lake yet?"

Allie nodded. "Once, but I was too busy being sore to really enjoy it."

"Then it's a date." Sam drank his coffee.

Allie felt his eyes on her while she ate breakfast, and it was all she could do to get one piece of toast down.

"I'll wash the dishes," Tracy said.

"I'll help you." Allie swallowed the last bite and stacked Sam's plate on hers.

He followed them to the kitchen, carrying the jam and butter. When Allie turned from the sink where Tracy was busy adding soap to the water, Sam winked at her and motioned toward the hall with a nod.

"I'm going to pack," he said. He walked from the kitchen, glancing back at her from the doorway.

Allie wiped her hands on the dishtowel. "I'll be right back."

Sam waited at the door to his room. When Allie walked by, he pulled her into his arms, lifting her off the ground, and carried her around the corner. His mouth on hers demanded her soul, and she gave it willingly. He held her against the wall, slid his knee between her legs, and pushed with his thigh. Allie groaned at the desire and dug her fingers into his shoulders. When he finally let her up for air, she clung to him, fighting to catch her breath.

"I'll miss you tonight," he whispered. His thick voice ran over her like heated syrup.

Allie nodded. She pressed her lips to his neck, and Sam tightened his arms around her. They stood together in the dark, touching and kissing.

"I wanted you this morning," he said, his voice low and husky. "I wanted to make love to you, Allie. Why didn't you stay?"

"Oh, Sam, I wanted to, but I couldn't."

His powerful tongue circled hers then teased her lips. He held his mouth to her ear. "I reached for you and you were gone."

"I couldn't stay. We aren't alone."

He groaned. "Think of me tonight."

"Yes."

If they had been alone in the house, Allie was sure they would have ended up in bed at that moment. Sam was hard against her, and it drove her wild to know how aroused he was. She felt cheated when they grudgingly parted.

He stood in front of her, one hand on her waist and the other on her cheek with his thumb stroking her skin.

She leaned back on the wall and looked up into his eyes. "I'm sorry you have to leave."

"Not half as sorry as I am."

Sam leaned down and kissed her one more time before releasing her. He backed away, moving toward the empty suitcase that lay open on his bed.

Allie took a deep breath and walked from his room without looking back. She made her way slowly down the hall, working on recovering before she entered the kitchen.

By the time she got back, Tracy was rinsing the last plate. Allie plucked a clean dishtowel from the cabinet and silently dried the dishes.

Thirteen

Sam stopped at the door, suitcase and black medical bag in hand. "I should be back tomorrow afternoon. I left a list of the shelters I'm going to by the phone. I don't know exactly how long I'll be at each, but if there's an emergency, someone will know where I am. I'll call tonight."

Allie nodded. "We'll listen for the phone."

"Yeah, if we can hear it over the party." Tracy stood behind Allie, grinning.

Sam raised his eyebrows. "You won't forget to feed Lucky and the other boarders, right?"

"Right," Allie and Tracy answered in unison.

They followed him out. With the bags tucked into the truck, Sam turned back to his daughter and kissed her cheek. She stood on her toes to meet his kiss and quickly hugged him with one arm. He didn't want to jeopardize the progress they'd made by hugging her back for too long.

"Look, Trace, you're not grounded anymore, but do me a favor and help Allie out before you go anywhere."

"I will."

"And use some of that common sense I know you have, will you?"

"Yes, Dad."

When he turned to Allie, she stepped back and extended

her hand. He held it, squeezing, enjoying the sunshine in her beautiful eyes. She obviously wasn't ready for a display of affection in front of Tracy, and Sam wasn't really sure he was either. He reluctantly released her hand and walked around the truck where Blue waited for him to drop the tailgate.

"Not this time, boy. You'll miss supper if you go with me."

The Lab skulked away.

Allie and Tracy waved as Sam pulled out of the driveway, and he waved back and watched them as long as he could.

This was the latest he'd ever started on shelter rounds, but he just hadn't been able to get up any earlier. As he recalled the details of the night, he grinned until he realized he was enjoying the memories more than he should. It wouldn't do to get caught incapacitated. Very purposely, he started through the list of shelters, trying to recall the patients he'd seen there last month. With all the excitement from the past week, the weekend had really snuck up on him.

Sam pulled into the parking lot of the Last Chance to grab a cold drink from the antique machine on the porch before heading out of town. Leaving the truck running, he trotted up the stairs, pulling coins from his pocket as he went, then he slipped in the quarters, opened the glass door, and extracted an orange soda. When he turned around, he nearly collided with the sheriff.

"Good morning, Bill."

"Good morning, Sam. Heading out of town?"

"Yeah, it's that time again." The two men walked down the stairs together. "How's Thor?"

"He still has a few sore spots, but now he's smart enough

to leave the porcupines alone."

"Glad to hear that."

"I'm still trying to decide what to do about that car. You remember me telling you about it?"

"Sure, I remember. What's the problem?"

Bill stopped in front of Sam's truck door. "I've asked everyone, and no one knows anything about it. The only stranger anyone has seen around is the woman staying at your place, and you say it's not her car. I ran the plates, and there's no report of the vehicle being stolen. I tried calling Tate's phone number, but no one answers. I even tried his office, but no one there wanted to talk to me. So, I've got a Volvo with a thrown rod sitting in front of the garage, and Roger has an engine for it. I guess I should call the Denver police and let them sort it out."

Sam opened his door and held it. "What did you say the owner's name was?"

"Rick Tate. I have his address right here." Bill extracted a small piece of paper from his pocket.

A knot formed in Sam's stomach. What if Allie had been driving this car and she was in some kind of trouble? She certainly seemed reluctant to talk about her life before last week. Maybe she was hiding from someone. Could it be this fellow, Tate? If the Denver police were notified, whomever she was hiding from might find her and take her away.

Sam felt like he needed to protect Allie, whether she wanted him to or not. The least he could do was keep Bill from notifying the police until he'd figured out how to ask her about it.

"Bill, give me a couple of days before you call, will you?"

The sheriff didn't seem the least bit surprised by the request, and Sam realized that Bill probably shared his suspicions.

Bill handed Sam the paper. "Here, you take this. But do me a favor and be careful, okay?"

Sam nodded. He tucked the address into his pocket and shook hands with the gray-haired sheriff. "Thanks." Then he climbed into the truck, took a long drink from the bottle, and eased the truck forward. Bill walked toward his car, glancing back only once.

Sam wasn't sure what he would do with this information. Maybe nothing. Allie had no reason not to trust him, so he was sure she'd tell him about her past sooner or later. He hadn't realized, however, that he would get so attached to her before she did. It didn't matter what she'd done or who she was—the possibility of her leaving terrified him.

He finished the cold drink and placed the bottle on the floor on the passenger's side. As the truck started up the hill out of town, Sam downshifted and sighed.

"Dammit," he muttered.

Searching for something to take her mind off of Sam's departure, Allie knocked on Tracy's bedroom door.

"Come in." Tracy had made her bed, and was placing a stuffed cat and dog on the pillow.

"You want to go for a walk?"

Tracy shrugged. "We need milk and paper towels. Why don't we go to town?"

Allied cringed. "I don't actually have any money."

"No big deal. Dad has an account."

"Oh. Okay."

"But we don't have to walk. My friend Sandy just got her license. She'd be happy to pick us up."

"You think so?"

Tracy nodded. "She's looking for any excuse to drive. I'll call her."

Allie followed Tracy down the hall and stopped in the bathroom. By the time she was ready, she found Tracy waiting on the side porch.

"Here she is," she said, pointing to the dust storm coming up the road.

Allie suddenly realized she was about to step into a car with a driver who had virtually no experience, and her mouth went dry.

But the ride wasn't bad, maybe because it ended so quickly. Before she had time to panic, they stood on the sidewalk, waving to the disappearing Ford Escort.

Allie smiled. "To the grocery store?"

"Sure."

"Allie! You better get in here and say hello, or I'll be offended."

Allie turned toward the beauty shop where Maggie stood, holding the door open with her foot. She had a pink comb stuck in the side of her hair and wore a neon-blue blouse over lime-green pants. The woman was nothing if not colorful.

Allie looked at Tracy. "Is a quick detour okay?"

"It's okay with me."

Maggie grinned at them.

Allie stopped at the door. "Maggie, do you know Tracy?"

"My word, child, you've grown again." The woman hugged the teenager. "Every time I see you, I'm shocked."

"Hi, Ms. Jenkins."

Maggie walked Tracy to one of the waiting chairs, her arm around the teenager's waist. She reached up and lifted a strand of Tracy's hair. "What's this? Trying to be radical by going natural?"

"I guess."

"Well, it looks great on you. Although, I must admit, I'd gotten used to the purple by the end of last summer."

Tracy blushed.

When Allie started to sit in the chair beside Tracy, Maggie grabbed her arm.

"Oh, please, sit here." She guided Allie to the hydraulic chair. "Will you let me cut your hair while we visit?"

"Maggie—"

"Oh, come on, I need to stay in practice, in case I ever get another customer." Maggie laughed and pulled Allie's hair back. She turned the chair to face the mirrored wall. "See how nice it would look? What do you think, Tracy?"

The girl nodded. "It would look good."

"On the house," Maggie said, eyebrows raised.

"Okay, okay." Allie smiled at Maggie's reflection. "Thank you."

Maggie tilted her head. "You look different today. Happier maybe?"

Allie shrugged at Maggie's much too perceptive comment as she tried to keep the color from her face.

Maggie worked with a flurry of spray bottles, scissors, and combs, and then more combs and a blow drier. Tracy drank a root beer while Maggie told stories about half the people in town. By the time the haircut was complete, Allie wasn't sure if Rob Barker was sleeping with Mr. Monroe's wife or Mrs. Phillip's husband.

Maggie spun the chair back to the mirror. "Voilà!"

Allie couldn't remember ever getting a better haircut anywhere. The dyed ends were gone, and the cut was long but perfectly shaped.

"Maggie, it's fantastic."

"Good. Maybe I haven't lost my touch after all." She lowered her voice. "I think Sam will like it."

Allie's eyes jumped to Maggie's in the mirror, and the older woman smiled and winked. Allie couldn't keep the blood from rushing to her cheeks this time. Fortunately, Tracy was absorbed in a magazine.

Allie rose. "We should go," she said. "Maggie, I can't thank you enough."

The woman waved off the thanks. "Oh, I have to keep these old fingers nimble. It's just dead around here."

Bells clanged as the door to the shop flew open.

"My word, what a surprise," Maggie said. "Here's a customer now. How wonderful to see you, Mrs. Price. Come on in. It looks like you need a trim."

Allie turned back to Maggie as she followed Tracy to the door.

Mrs. Price struggled to climb into the hydraulic chair. "I don't know what you're making such a fuss about," the elderly woman said. "I'm only ten minutes early."

Allie grinned and pulled the door closed behind her.

"It really does look great," Tracy said.

"Thanks. Should we go to the grocery store now?"

The teenager shrugged. "How about a video for tonight? We could get some popcorn."

"I think that sounds wonderful." Allie put her arm around Tracy's shoulders.

Together, they crossed the street. Allie felt stares from the townspeople, but tried to ignore them. No telling what the local gossip had her doing now.

"You must know everyone," she said.

Tracy nodded. "Most of them. Mom and Dad moved back here when I was four."

"Where did you live before that?"

The teenager smiled at her. "Hasn't Dad told you?"

"No."

"He used to be one of the main vets at the *world famous* San Diego Zoo."

"Wow."

"Yeah."

Sam took a key from Mrs. Richard's pudgy hand. "Thank you."

"Oh, Dr. Calvert, you know we're always happy to have you stay with us," the large, rosy woman said.

He nodded, too tired to get into an extended conversation, and scratched the miniature poodle that sat on the counter. The dog got so excited by his attention that she nearly fell off her perch. Mrs. Richards scooped Cuddles into her arms and grinned at Sam.

When he managed to get to Idaho Springs by the first night, he always stayed in the same motel and always got the room on the end because it was quiet. And, like always, his feet ached and he had to fight to keep his eyes open. The burger he'd had an hour earlier felt like a lead weight in his stomach.

Sam opened the motel room door, placed his suitcase and black bag against the wall, and fell backwards onto the bed. His back felt instantly better. If he hadn't wanted to call home, he would have closed his eyes and dropped off.

But he wanted very much to call home. He wanted to hear Allie's voice and pretend that he had her in his arms and in his bed. His hands shook as he dialed.

Tracy answered before the second ring. "Hello."

"Hey, Trace. How's it going there?"

"Good, Dad. How are you?"

"Tired, but okay. You got a pencil?"

"Hang on."

When Tracy returned, Sam read off the phone number.

"Okay, I've got it," she said. "Have you eaten dinner?"

"I had a burger. How about you?"

"Yeah, we ate after we fed all the animals. We're getting ready to make popcorn and watch a movie."

"Sounds like fun." Sam smiled at the phone.

"Yep. You want to talk to Allie?"

"Please. Thanks, Trace."

"See you tomorrow, Dad."

"Okay, Tracy. I love you."

"I love you, too."

The words filled his heart, as he listened to his daughter summon Allie to the phone. Allie's footsteps quickened his pulse.

"Doc? You're in one piece?"

"Yeah, Al, one tired piece. Of course, I wouldn't be nearly as tired if you were here."

Allie lowered her voice. *"Sam."*

"I mean it, Allie. Just thinking about all the things I want to do to you, and with you, is waking me up. Maybe I should drive back tonight."

"Don't you dare."

"Why not? Are you telling me you don't think we'd have fun?"

"Oh, it's not that. I just think a little anticipation is a good thing."

Sam groaned into the receiver. "I don't think so. It's too painful to be a good thing."

He could feel her smile across the phone line.

"I should be home by dinner tomorrow."

"Be careful on the road," she said. "We're anxious to have you back."

"I'm anxious to be there." He sighed.

"Good night, Sam."

"Good night, Allie."

Sam replaced the receiver and stared at it. Talking to Allie really had awakened him, and now he wanted very much to be with her. The whole situation was absurd. He was a grown man who could control his urges, and he'd see her in twenty-four hours. Actually, he had to admit that anticipation was kind of fun.

Sam rose slowly and started emptying his shirt pockets onto the motel table. The last thing he removed was the piece of paper Bill had given him, and he read it out loud. "Rick Tate, 1226 Cherrystone Lane, Littleton."

Was this someone who knew Allie? What if she really was in some kind of trouble? How could he protect her if he didn't know what he was protecting her from? How bad could it be?

It was less than twenty miles to Denver, but Littleton was south. Of course, it was too late for the traffic to be backed up, so it wouldn't take long to get down there. Would it really be spying? How could it be if he were doing it for her sake? Maybe he'd just take a quick look.

Sam picked up the keys and folded the address back into his pocket. He tried to ignore the feeling that he was sneaking around as he left the room and slid behind the wheel of the truck. The night sky threatened rain.

Tracy held an oversized bowl and Allie emptied popcorn into it. Together, they buttered and salted the treat and carried it to the den.

"You want a cold drink?" Allie tossed hand-towels onto the sofa and turned back to the kitchen.

"Sure."

She took her time getting drinks. Her pulse still raced from talking to Sam. Selfishly, she'd considered begging him to come home for the night. Nothing on earth could compare to the feel of Sam's arms or the taste of his lips. And his body—

This wasn't helping. Allie shook her head and walked back to the den. She handed Tracy a canned drink and popped the top on her own, then sat on the sofa. Tracy placed the bowl of popcorn between them and they dug in greedily.

"Good," Allie said with her mouth full.

Tracy nodded.

After several bites, Tracy wiped her hands on her towel and drank from the cold drink can.

Allie looked up to find the teenager studying her.

"How come you're not married?"

Allie wiped her hands and leaned back with a sigh. "I was." A white lie. The law may still see her as married, but she definitely didn't see herself that way.

"What happened?"

"I don't know, Tracy. I guess I married the wrong guy."

The girl frowned and took another sip from the can. "You like my dad."

"Yeah, I do."

"Are you in love with him?"

The question caused a lump in Allie's throat. Was she in love with Sam? It was true that when he walked into the room, everything else paled in comparison. He was a kind, wonderful, gorgeous man who treated her like someone special. And she ached to touch him, but it wasn't just the sexual attention that she wanted. She wanted to feel him close, to touch his skin, to smell him. When he got home, she'd lie in his arms and ask him for details about his trip just to hear his voice.

Maybe she was in love with Sam. Certainly she'd never

felt this way about anyone else.

"I don't know, Tracy, that's a tough question. I'm not sure I know exactly what love is."

"Weren't you in love with your husband?"

"Rick?" Allie sighed. "I thought I was . . ."

"Until?"

"Until recently."

"I think you're in love with my dad." Tracy smiled triumphantly.

Allie didn't know what to say to such a blunt statement.

"And I think maybe he's in love with you."

Her heart pounded. "Why do you say that?"

"I've seen the way he looks at you when he thinks I'm not looking. I mean, I'm only fifteen, but I'm not stupid."

Allie laughed. Tracy was definitely not stupid.

They munched on handfuls of popcorn.

How could Sam be in love with her? He was a prince, and Allie's life was no fairy tale. It couldn't possibly be true.

"Allie, I'm sorry."

"For what?"

"For what I said the first night I was here. I didn't mean it. I was really mad at Dad and I wanted to hurt him. I'm sorry if I hurt you, too."

Allie reached across the sofa with the hand that wasn't buttery and squeezed Tracy's arm. The teenager couldn't possibly understand how much the apology meant to her. The last thing she wanted was for Sam or his daughter to think badly of her. "Thank you, Tracy."

Tracy looked down, her face red from the honesty.

Allie was reminded again that this was Sam's daughter. She was so much like him—strong and yet tender.

"Which movie did you get?" Tracy spoke with her mouth full.

"*The Shining*—the original one," Allie said.

"Is it good?"

"You haven't seen it?"

Tracy shook her head.

"You said you like scary."

"I love scary."

"Then you'll love this. Let's turn out the lights."

"Okay." Tracy jumped up and skidded to the light switch.

Allie made her way to the VCR and pushed the tape in. She felt like she was having a slumber party and fought a powerful desire to giggle.

Fourteen

The drizzle stopped again as Sam turned off the truck. He rolled down the window and looked across the street at a pale blue, two-story house with neglected flowerbeds and several young trees in the yard. The only light on was a porch light.

Fear blossomed in his chest—fear of finding out something he didn't want to know. What if this was Allie's house? What if Rick Tate was more to Allie than just an acquaintance?

What the hell was he going to do now? He'd found the place, and it didn't look like anyone was home. Maybe that was for the best. Sam shook his head as he reached for the key.

He froze as a silver Audi drove up the driveway and stopped. The garage door opened and the car pulled in. Before the door closed, a man got out of the car and walked into the house.

Sam's entire body shook, and it wasn't from the cold, damp air. Lights came on inside, and a shadow moved across the curtains in the front windows.

Now he had to know.

Sam took a deep breath and got out of the truck. He walked slowly to the front door and stood for a while, listening to the beat of music from inside. Was he really going to do this?

He rang the doorbell.

The music volume dropped and the door opened. A clean-shaven man, about six feet tall and slender, stood in the doorway. He wore a tailored blue cotton shirt and designer pants, and his black hair was neatly clipped.

"May I help you?" he asked.

"Uh, yes, I hope so. I'm looking for Allison Parker. Is this the right address?"

"Do I know you?"

"Uh, no. My name's Sam Calvert." Sam shook hands with the man, noting his firm, confident grip.

"Why are you looking for Allie, Mr. Calvert?"

Sam's chest tightened at the use of Allie's nickname. He cleared his throat. "I work for the Reunited Families Institute. We reunite children and parents who have been separated."

"Oh? Someone's looking for her?"

"That's what I'm here to find out. Is Miss Parker available?"

"Well, no. She's, um, visiting friends for a few days. Maybe I can help you."

"And you are?"

"Her husband. I'm Rick Tate. Parker is Allie's maiden name."

Sam's breath escaped all at once. "I . . . I didn't know Allie, I mean Miss Parker, was married."

"Well, she is. Maybe I can help you, if you give me the details. You want to come in?" Rick stepped back, motioning for Sam to enter the house.

It was all Sam could do to keep from running. "No. I should wait for Miss . . . Mrs. Tate. When did you say she'd be back?"

Rick sighed and shoved his hands in his pockets. "To tell you the truth, we had a bit of a misunderstanding. She'll be back within a few days, though. She's staying with friends. Are you sure I can't help you?"

"I'm sure." Sam backed off the porch.

"Wait." Rick stepped through the doorway. "Do you have a card or something?"

"No, um, we have to maintain anonymity. I'll come back . . . thank you." Sam turned and walked quickly down the sidewalk. He couldn't catch his breath.

He jumped into the truck, started the engine, and pulled away from the curb with tires squealing. At the corner, he turned left and drove until he couldn't see where the hell he was going. There was nothing but darkness ahead.

Sam pulled over and got out, slamming his door behind him.

Rain fell in earnest now. He walked around to the front of the old pickup and leaned on the hood with both hands. His heart and lungs felt as though they'd burst as he panted for air. Cold rain did nothing to cool his over-heated skin.

Allie was married. And not to a monster, reeking of whiskey, greasy and snarling, but to a normal, average guy. That's all. Just normal.

Sam threw his head back and closed his eyes against the pelting rain. Icy drops stung, but they didn't wash away Rick's face. Sam saw himself, standing in the doorway of his own home as one of the men Lisa had slept with handed him the purse she'd left behind in the hotel room.

How could he possibly sleep with another man's wife? How could he care so much about her? How could he cause the same pain he'd suffered?

He couldn't.

Sam dropped his head to his arm and pounded his fist on the hood.

"Damn you, Allie." He tried to shout, but could barely hear his own voice. "Damn you."

"Jeez, Allie, that *was* scary. Turn on the lights."

Allie laughed as she hit the rewind button and then flipped on a lamp. "Here's . . . *Johnny!*" She jumped forward, imitating the character in the movie.

Tracy screamed and then laughed. "Okay, that's enough."

Still grinning, Allie returned to her seat on the sofa and stretched. She and Tracy had enjoyed the movie, overreacting and scaring each other like kids. She'd had almost enough fun to take her mind off of Sam.

But not quite.

"Did Dad say what time he'll be home tomorrow?"

"No, not really."

"I hope it's not too late."

"Me, too."

Tracy got up and grabbed the empty popcorn bowl. "I'll wash this tomorrow. I'm too tired tonight."

"Sounds good."

"Good night, Allie. And thanks again for the movie."

"Hey, it was your idea."

"Yeah, but you picked it out."

Allie nodded and smiled. "Good night, Tracy."

The red light on the VCR blinked on and off as the movie rewound. Allie dropped her head back on the sofa and closed her eyes.

As much as she missed Sam, she'd enjoyed the day with his daughter. When Tracy wasn't working at being a teenager, she was actually fun to be around.

Allie grinned as she ran her fingers through her hair. With the dyed ends gone, her hair was much softer. She hoped Maggie was right, that Sam would like it.

She really wished Sam were home.

From the shed where she filled dog bowls with food, Allie heard a vehicle in the driveway. Thinking it was Sam, she abandoned the bowls and walked quickly around the corner of the house.

A red convertible with the top down pulled up and stopped. It took a moment for her to recognize the driver as Edward Cory. He smiled as he got out of the car and walked to greet Allie with his hands in his back pockets.

"Hi. Is Tracy here?"

Allie pushed her hair off her forehead with the back of her hand. "Yes, Edward, she's at the corral exercising the horses. You want me to get her?"

"Oh, no ma'am, I'll go look for her, if that's okay."

"That's fine, go ahead."

The young man all but trotted to the barn.

Allie grinned. Edward was tall and thin, and would probably fill out nicely. He had a baby face and blond hair. *Cute* was the word that came to mind. When he disappeared into the barn, Allie returned to the food bowls.

She played with each dog as she placed bowls in the runs. When she fed Blue, he gave her a chance at a quick head rub before he backed away. The poor dog must really miss Sam because he didn't normally let anyone else within reach.

Allie closed the shed and walked into the house, leaving her rubber boots on the back porch. She felt sticky with sweat and dog slobber, and decided she wasn't ready to greet Sam. A shower wouldn't take long.

Two hours later, Allie watched Edward and Tracy stroll toward the red convertible, side by side.

"I'll see you tomorrow?" Edward stopped at the car and turned, his hands in his back pockets again.

"Maybe later tomorrow. I'm going riding with my dad and Allie in the morning."

"Cathy's having a pool party tomorrow at three. Will you come?"

Tracy shrugged. "Maybe."

Edward nodded, and got in his car. "See you tomorrow, Tracy."

"Okay." Tracy watched him back out of the driveway, returning his wave. Then she turned and ambled to the porch where Allie sat with her chin in her hand.

The sun had nearly set and there was no sign of Sam. Allie wasn't sure if she was worried or just missed him. Maybe both.

Tracy sat on the step below her.

"How is Edward this evening?"

"Okay, I guess."

"He's even cuter when he's all cleaned up."

"Yeah." Tracy glanced up at her and grinned. "You think Dad will let me go tomorrow?"

"I can't imagine why he wouldn't."

They sat together in silence. The casserole Allie had prepared for dinner was in the oven, drying out. There didn't seem to be much point in waiting for Sam. By this time, he should have eaten on the road.

Allie smiled at the teenager. "You ready for dinner?"

"Sure."

"Then, let's eat."

They both rose slowly from the porch, glancing at the empty dirt road that led in from town.

"You think Dad's okay?"

"I'm sure he is."

Tracy nodded. "I just wish he'd call or something."

"That would be nice."

"You want a refill?" Frank raised the glass coffee pot.

Sam shook his head and dropped his fork to his plate. He'd only eaten half the chicken-fried steak, but he just didn't have much of an appetite. What time was it, anyway?

He glanced at the Budweiser clock. Nine-thirty. Another hour and he could go home. Allie should be in bed by then. He couldn't face her tonight.

The bartender moved Sam's plate. "Can I get you something else?"

Sam sighed. "Yeah, Frank, give me a beer."

The man filled a glass and placed it in front of him without comment.

Sam drank slowly, turning the sweating glass in both hands between sips and staring at the dying foam.

Allie felt so close. Even knowing what he knew, he wanted desperately to hold her and kiss her and seduce her. But when he pictured her golden eyes, her face morphed into the face of the man standing on her porch, telling him that she'd be home soon.

He couldn't do it. It was killing him, but he couldn't do it.

Sam had run into Roger when he first arrived at the Last Chance and made arrangements for the mechanic to fix Allie's car and deliver it to the house. He played the scene out in his head, over and over again. He would hand Allie the keys and tell her that it was time for her to go home, that she had a husband waiting for her. He practiced so that he'd be able to say it. The words would be automatic; they wouldn't mean anything and they wouldn't break his heart.

But they were breaking it now.

By the time he drank the last sip of beer, the liquid was warm and it was ten-thirty. Sam rose from the barstool and walked slowly outside. The memory of Allie's face haunted him, along with the memories of her lips, her eyes, and her sweet, smooth skin. He slid into the truck and dropped his head to the steering wheel. He knew that memories of Allie would haunt him the rest of his life. How was he possibly going to survive?

Allie sat up in bed and listened to Sam's slow, heavy footsteps in the hall. He walked past her door, slowing a bit more but not stopping, and continued to his room. Allie's heartbeat thundered in her ears as she heard the door to Sam's room close.

She sat in the dark and waited.

The house was almost as quiet as death. Water ran for a minute, and then there was nothing. No footsteps. No knock on her door.

Nothing.

Maybe something was wrong. Maybe Sam had been hurt, or he needed something and was afraid to wake her.

Allie couldn't stand it. She threw the comforter back and tiptoed from her room. With her head against Sam's door, she tapped gently.

"Yeah?"

"Sam?" Allie pushed the door open a crack to peek in, but saw nothing in the darkness. "Are you okay?"

"Yeah, I'm just beat."

"Oh, okay. I'll see you in the morning."

"Yeah."

Allie pulled the door closed and stood in the hall,

wanting to throw up. Something was wrong. Whatever it was, Sam didn't want her help.

And he didn't want her. She walked quietly back to her room.

She wanted to run into Sam's room and tell him that she thought she might be in love with him. Instead, she could only lie in the dark with her tears.

He listened to her soft footsteps fade. The door to her room squeaked as she opened and closed it. And then there was silence.

Sam rolled onto his side and crushed the pillow to his chest, gritting his teeth against the pain. Allie's proximity salted the raw gash in his heart.

He needed to find a way to either heal by morning, or ignore the pain. He thought back to Tracy's little five-year-old face pressed against the car window. As soon as the car had disappeared, he'd fallen to his knees and sobbed, unable to bear it any longer.

But he'd found the strength to stand while Lisa and Tracy were there. Somehow, he had to find that same strength in Allie's presence tomorrow, or he'd never be able to let her leave. And he *must* let her leave, no matter how badly it hurt. He had no right to hold her.

By the time Sam rose the next morning, he still didn't know how he'd make it. The fact that he hadn't slept didn't help. He went about his chores, trying his best not to think about Allie.

Shortly after eight, he walked into the kitchen and refilled his coffee cup. Tracy stopped picking toast out of the toaster to kiss his cheek. The only thing saving him at the moment was his daughter's improved attitude.

"Good morning, Dad."

"Good morning, Tracy."

"You were late last night."

"Yeah, it was a long day." He sipped his coffee.

"Want some breakfast?"

"No, thanks, I already ate."

"Oh. You want some help cleaning the dog runs?"

"It's done."

"Saddling the horses?"

"What?"

"Do you want some help saddling the horses? The ride to the lake, remember?"

Sam frowned. He'd forgotten entirely about the ride to the lake. It was the last thing he wanted to do. "Look, Trace—"

"Aw, come on, Dad, you promised. You're not going to back out, are you?" Her eyes pleaded.

Just as things were starting to improve between them, he couldn't let his daughter down, no matter how painful it sounded.

Sam sighed. "No, Trace, I'm not going to back out."

"Good. Allie and I can pack the lunch."

Blood drained from his face at the mention of her name. He silently cursed himself for reacting. He had to do better. And a ride to the lake would not be easy to handle.

Water coursed through the old pipes for a moment, causing familiar creaks in the walls. Allie must be up. Sam gulped the rest of his coffee, ignoring the burn in his throat, left the empty mug on the counter, and headed outside.

"I'll get the horses ready," he said over his shoulder.

He felt like he was running by the time he made it to the door. No matter what his pace, he *was* running. He needed more time to compose himself before he faced her.

★ ★ ★ ★ ★

"I was just about to see if you were up." Tracy glanced up from a counter full of bread slices. "Eggs are in the pan, but they're probably cold."

Allie filled a coffee cup. It was all she could do to keep her puffy eyes open. "Thanks, Tracy, but I just want coffee."

Tracy returned to her job, slathering peanut butter on half the slices. Allie leaned against the counter, drinking coffee and listening to noises coming in through an open window. A dog barked from around the house, and birds twittered in the trees.

Tracy stopped her work and turned, frowning at the knife in her hand. "Allie, is something wrong with Dad?"

"Why do you ask?"

"I don't know, he seems kind of weird this morning."

"How?"

Tracy shrugged. "I don't know, he's just . . . serious. And he tried to get out of our ride to the lake. You think he's mad at me about something?"

"Oh, Tracy, I'm sure he's not mad at you. Maybe he's really tired from his trip."

The teenager turned back to the counter, scooping jam onto bread. "He's been up for a long time. He doesn't act tired."

Allie sighed. "I don't know what's wrong. Maybe he'll feel better after the ride."

Tracy nodded. "Yeah."

Allie finished off the coffee and refilled her cup. "Did you sleep okay?"

"Yeah, except for the dream I keep having about the guy trying to break into my room with an ax."

"I'm sorry, Tracy. I didn't mean to give you nightmares."

"Oh, it wasn't really a nightmare. All I can remember is laughing and eating popcorn while he's chopping at my door."

They grinned at each other.

"I should finish getting ready." Allie nodded toward the sandwiches. "You have this under control?"

"Yep. Go ahead."

Allie quickly squeezed the teenager's shoulder before she left the kitchen.

In her room, she placed her mug on top of the dresser, pulled open the top drawer, and stared at the socks. What was wrong with Sam? After their phone conversation night before last, she'd been sure she'd fly into his arms the moment he got home, and stay there for the night. Instead, she'd spent the night alone, crying herself to sleep.

When she got up this morning, she'd assured herself that he'd only been tired, and that things would be back to normal. It didn't sound like things were even close to normal.

Fighting monstrous butterflies in her stomach, Allie dressed for the ride. Something *was* wrong. A foreboding mushroomed in her soul.

Allie tucked sunglasses into her shirt pocket and carried her boots, gloves, and hat with her from the room. When she got to the den, she found Tracy with two large towels rolled into lunch bundles, putting on her boots. Allie did the same, and carried one of the towels as they walked together to the barn.

Three horses stood saddled and tied to the front corral fence.

"Which one am I riding?" Allie asked.

Tracy walked up to one of the horses and stuffed the towel in the saddlebag. "That must be your saddle on Prince."

"Oh, I guess it does look familiar. Brings back memories." Allie rubbed her backside as she walked to Prince. After patting the horse's neck, she placed her own towel in her saddlebag.

"How good are you at riding, Allie?"

"Not very. This is my second attempt."

Tracy chuckled and Allie shot her a playful glare. As Tracy checked out her saddle, Allie looked around. She didn't see any sign of Sam.

"I'm going to look for your dad."

"Okay. I'll check your girth for you."

"Thanks, Tracy. It sounds important."

"It is."

Allie walked to the barn door, pulled it open, and stepped through the doorway. In the darkness of the barn, it took a moment to see Sam's outline. He leaned on Hattie's stall, his chin on his forearms and one foot on an upside-down bucket.

"Sam?"

He visibly jumped and turned toward her, straightening as she approached. She couldn't see his face.

"Sam, are you okay?"

"Yeah. Just checking the mare."

"How is she?"

"She's okay."

As Allie approached him, Sam stepped to one side and started from the barn, obviously keeping her out of reach.

"Ready to go?" She heard the forced cheerfulness in his voice. He stopped at the door and held it open.

Allie sighed. Something was very wrong. She walked from the barn and to the horses, the flutter spreading from her stomach to her chest.

Tracy led Prince from the fence. "You want a hand getting on?"

"That would be nice. Thanks."

The girl went through the same motions Sam had a week earlier, lifting Allie's foot in her hands. The difference was that it was a slower process, and both Allie and Tracy grunted at the effort. But it worked. By the time Allie was set, Tracy and Sam were on their horses and the three of them headed for the trail to the lake. Sam rode in front, and Tracy and Allie rode side by side for the first part of the trip.

Tracy turned to Allie, pointed to Sam, and raised her palms, signaling a question. Allie shrugged, and Tracy frowned at her father's back.

As Sam pulled farther ahead of them, Tracy made the clucking noise and both Prince and her horse started trotting.

When they caught up and slowed to a walk, Allie turned to Tracy. "You have to teach me how to do that."

"What?"

"How to make that noise."

Tracy smiled. "Okay, but it probably wouldn't be a good thing to practice while we're riding, unless you want to trot all the way to the lake."

"No, that's okay, we can wait. I think the less trotting I do, the better off I'll be this evening." She focused on the trail ahead, trying not to worry about Sam.

Fifteen

Listening to Allie and Tracy talk as they rode was killing him. Sam tried tricks to keep his mind off his misery. He went through the entire skeleton of a horse, picturing and naming each bone, and then went on to each muscle. Without realizing it, he got lost somewhere and was recalling Tracy's fifth birthday party when they arrived at the lake. Who was that little redheaded boy who had been such a pest through the whole thing?

"Can we eat first? I'm starved." Tracy jumped off her horse and pulled the rolled towel out of her saddlebag. She held Prince's reins as Allie got down.

Sam dismounted slowly and loosened his saddle. "If you want to." He waited until Allie and Tracy were headed for the lakeshore before loosening their saddles and then walked slowly down the slope to join them.

Tracy had a towel spread on the ground in the shade and sandwiches and cans of root beer distributed around it. Sam sat on the ground and tried not to watch Allie kneel by the lake to rinse her hands. He looked down, pretending to study the sandwich he removed from a plastic bag.

Allie dropped her hat to the ground and sat across from him, folding her legs under her.

He glanced at his daughter. "Sandwiches look good, Trace."

"Thanks, Dad. It's your favorite, peanut butter and raspberry jam."

"All we need now is a little wine," Allie said quietly.

Sam looked up.

Allie watched him, waiting for a reaction.

He dropped his eyes to his sandwich. "Yeah." He could feel her staring at him, and was afraid to say any more for fear of losing control of his voice.

They ate in silence, except for the occasional song of a passing bird. Sam allowed his gaze to linger on the lake and the mountaintops, glistening in unobstructed sun. The only hint of the night's scattered thundershowers was an extra green tint to the grass.

When they finished eating, Tracy plucked up empty sandwich bags, tucked them under the corner of the towel, and brushed crumbs from her hands. "I'm going to wade in the lake."

"I'll go with you," Allie said.

Sam drank the last of his root beer as Tracy and Allie got up and walked to the water. When they sat to remove their boots, he took off in the opposite direction. He needed to get away from Allie. In spite of his preparation, he wasn't handling it well.

Sam sat on the edge of the cliff and closed his eyes. A steady wind blew up the valley, driven by mountain sunshine heating the ground. As it whistled in his ears, he imagined he was flying, floating on the wind. The trees and creek below were tiny, insignificant parts of the patchwork ground that he didn't have to touch.

A twig snapped behind him, and he straightened.

"Dad?"

Sam let out the breath he held, both relieved and disappointed that it wasn't Allie. "Yeah, Trace?"

"Can I talk to you?"

He turned and patted the ground at his side, and offered her his hand. "Of course."

Tracy held his hand as she sat. They both squinted into the wind and looked out over the valley.

"Are you mad at me?"

He winced. "No, Tracy. I'm sorry if I'm acting like I am. I don't mean to."

"Then you're mad at Allie, aren't you?"

Sam frowned at the toes of his boots. "It's not that simple, Trace."

"Can't you tell me what's wrong?"

"No, I can't."

"Why not?"

Sam sighed, and looked over at his daughter. When had she grown into the young woman sitting beside him?

He swallowed hard. "Sometimes things between a man and woman are no one else's business."

"Not even mine?"

Sam wrapped his arm around her shoulders and pulled her to him. "No, sweetheart, not even yours." He kissed the top of her head, and she rested it on his shoulder.

"Is that why you won't tell me what happened with you and Mom?"

"Yes."

"And it really wasn't my fault . . . that you split up?"

"No, Tracy. It wasn't your fault at all."

They sat in silence for a few minutes.

"I love you, Daddy."

Sam rested his chin on her head and held her tighter. "I love you too, Tracy."

"I really like Allie," she said, her voice soft and tentative.

Sam closed his eyes and let the call of the wind fill his head. He couldn't respond to his daughter's comment. One part of his heart was mending as another was being shredded. Damn, it hurt.

Allie watched a dozen tiny fish trying to bite her toes, long since numb in the icy water. She pushed the fish away, but they persisted. When she reached into the water, one actually swam into her hand.

A rock scooted across the ground somewhere behind her. She turned, shading her eyes against the sun, and found Sam and Tracy emerging from the trees, holding hands.

Allie smiled. She could only imagine what it was like to have a father who loved her as much as Sam loved Tracy, but she knew it had to be wonderful. At least things were working out between them.

Tracy waved to her. "It's time to go back."

Allie returned the wave and lifted her slightly blue feet from the water. Careful not to bend any toes backwards, she put on her socks and boots and rolled her pants legs down, giving her feet time to get feeling back into them before she stood.

At the picnic site, Tracy had the trash rolled into a towel. Sam led the horses over and handed Allie the reins to Prince's bridle. He didn't say anything when their eyes met.

She had no idea what she saw in his eyes, but it made her want to cry. Hiding her tears, she worked at lifting her foot into the stirrup.

Tracy spoke over the top of her saddle. "You need some help?"

"No, I think I can make it." Using muscle burn to take

her mind off of Sam, Allie struggled and pulled until she made it to the top of the saddle.

Tracy gave her a thumbs up and Allie nodded. Sam was halfway to the trees by the time she pointed Prince in the right direction.

The three of them rode down in silence.

When Allie climbed off of Prince in front of the barn, she knew she'd be sore, but not quite as sore as last week. Maybe it was possible to get used to this stuff.

"I'll take care of the horses," Sam said.

Allie shrugged. "Okay, I'll go hop in the shower."

"Dad," Tracy said, "can I go to a pool party that starts at three?"

"Where?"

"At Cathy Simpson's."

"I guess so, if that's what you want to do. I can give you a ride over there when you're ready."

"Thanks."

Allie and Tracy turned toward the house at the same time, but Tracy made it to the steps a lot faster than Allie did. Allie held her right hip as she walked. Riding made her feel eighty years old. A nice hot shower was exactly what she needed. Or, better yet, a soak in the miracle bath mix. Then, maybe she and Sam would get a chance to talk while Tracy was at the party.

Allie dropped sheets into the washer and turned the knob. As the washer filled, she poured in detergent. After this load, everything that had been in the clothes hamper would be washed. What would she do if Sam stayed hidden?

Allie made her way through the quiet house, searching the kitchen, dining room, and den. At the side door, she found Sam sitting on the steps, his elbows on his knees, studying something in his hands.

"Sam?" Allie walked out and sat on the steps above him.

His shoulders moved up and down slowly as he took a deep breath. "Are you married, Allie?"

"What?" A cold chill started up her spine.

"No, don't answer that. I already know the answer." Sam jumped up and paced back and forth in front of the steps, running his fingers through his hair.

"If you know," she said, "then why did you ask?"

"I guess I wanted to know how far you'd go . . . if you'd lie about it."

"I haven't lied to you." Allie clasped her hands together so that the trembling wouldn't show.

"You came to my bed when you had a husband waiting for you at home. How could you do that to him, Allie? How could you do it to me?" Sam spun around and stood with his back to her, his head down.

That was what he thought? That she would make love to him while she had a sweet, kind, loving husband somewhere waiting on her? How could he believe that?

He turned around, handed her a key, and stepped back, returning his hands to his hips. "You're free to go whenever you want to."

Allie studied the key, flipping it over in her hand. She looked back up at Sam, but he stared at the steps, frowning. Then she glanced down the driveway and saw her car parked beside Sam's truck. It hadn't been there twenty minutes earlier. Sam must have had her car repaired and delivered, and now he'd handed her the key.

He was throwing her out.

Moving in a fog, Allie rose from the steps and walked

into the house. In her room, she sat on the edge of the bed and looked around.

No, it wasn't her room, it was Sam's guest room. For a little while, she had made the mistake of thinking of it as hers. It wasn't, and it never would be. Tears started as she realized she would never have a real home.

The worst part was that she hadn't known what a real home was until she stayed in Sam's. Her whole life seemed to be one long series of discoveries of what she was missing and would never have.

What now? Did it matter? Allie wiped her eyes with the back of her hand. She stood up, took off the clothes she'd dressed in after her bath, folded them neatly on the bed, then put on her own jeans, shirt and sweater. She slipped the key into her sweater pocket.

Allie walked quietly from the house. Not wanting to run into Sam again, she looked around each corner as she made her way to the barn. Assured that it was empty, she tiptoed in and stopped at Hattie's stall. "Hey, girl."

The huge mare turned slowly, whinnied, dropped her head over the stall door, and closed her eyes. Allie rubbed the horse's jaw and face and hugged her.

"Good luck," she whispered into Hattie's mane.

Wiping away more tears, Allie walked quickly to her car and got in. It was all she could do to get the key in the ignition, but she couldn't stay another second. She pushed in the clutch and turned the key.

Sam raised his head at the sound of the engine cranking.

She was leaving. Allie was really leaving and he was letting her. No explanation, no discussion. She was about to drive out of his life and leave him empty.

He couldn't let her go. Not like this. No matter what, he

couldn't just sit here and let her leave.

Sam jumped to his feet and ran around the house. He didn't stop until he stood in front of her car, his hands on the hood, leaning forward as if to hold it in place. "No."

Allie sat behind the steering wheel, her eyes wide and her face glistening with tears. Her beautiful golden eyes stared at him through the windshield.

Sam took a deep breath and straightened. "Allie, turn off the car."

She did, and there was suddenly silence as Sam's heart tried to leap from his chest.

Allie rose slowly, standing between the open door and the car.

"I can't let you leave like this. We have to talk." He stepped around the car and stood in front of her. She held him in place with her eyes, and he had to look away from her to speak. "Allie, I did something I'm not proud of. I know I said it was your life and that I didn't need to know about your past. I guess I was wrong. I needed to know." He sighed and leaned against the car, studying the ground. "I went to your house, and I met your husband. I wish like hell I hadn't, but I did."

She just stood there, not moving, watching him. He looked up and into her eyes. Was it pain he saw in them, or anger, or sadness?

A car pulled into the driveway behind him, but he didn't care who it was. Before he could move, he needed to hear her voice.

"Allie, say something. Anything."

Her gaze moved past him, and her eyes grew wider.

"Allie—"

She stepped back and slammed the car door. "Tracy!"

"What?"

Allie dashed around him and ran down the driveway.
Sam spun around.

It took a moment to understand what he saw. A young
woman with red hair walked slowly beside Tracy, her arm
around his daughter's waist. There was blood on Tracy's
face.

Allie ran to Tracy's side and helped support her.

"Oh, God, Tracy!" Sam dashed to where they were and
they all stopped.

She looked up at him with one eye swollen and blood
running from her nose. "Daddy," she whimpered and fell
into his arms.

Sam scooped Tracy up and carried her into the house
where he gently placed her on the sofa. She cried, and tears
thinned the blood and ran down the front of her T-shirt,
staining it a sickening pink.

Sam knelt in front of her and pushed her hair back
enough to see her face. "Tracy, how badly are you hurt?"

She lifted her hand gently to her eye. "I'm okay," she
choked.

"Jesus, I need to get you to the hospital."

Tracy grabbed his arm. "No, Daddy, I'm okay." She
sniffed and wiped her nose, then frowned at the blood on
her hand. "Really, it's not as bad as it looks."

Sam looked around and found Allie standing behind
him, watching. "Allie, stay here with her while I get some
stuff."

Allie nodded and traded places with him.

Sam dashed down the hall and grabbed his first-aid kit
and a towel that he held under the faucet until it dripped
cold water. Then he ran back to the den.

Tracy sat on the end of the sofa under a lamp, and Allie
sat beside her, holding her arm. They both looked up at

him when he entered the room, and he knelt in front of his daughter again.

Holding her chin, he wiped the blood from Tracy's face. Her eye was badly bruised, but she could see out of it. Sam put gentle pressure on the bridge of her nose. "Does that hurt?"

"A little, but not too much."

"It's not broken." He sighed with relief. "Allie, will you put some ice in a towel?"

She nodded and trotted to the kitchen, and returned almost immediately with the towel.

Sam placed it on the side of Tracy's eye. "Hold this. It'll keep the swelling from getting much worse."

"Okay." She had nearly stopped crying.

"Any other injuries?"

The girl held out her right hand where scraped knuckles bled a little.

Sam cleaned her hand and bandaged it. He sat back on his heels and looked up at her. "Anything else?"

She shook her head.

"Tracy, what happened?"

She frowned. "I got in a fight."

"I can see that, but what happened?"

"I'm okay, Dad, does it matter?"

"Yes, it matters."

Allie touched the girl's shoulder. "Tracy, were you attacked?"

Tracy nodded.

"Was it a guy?"

She nodded again, and tears started down both cheeks.

"Was it Edward?"

Tracy shook her head. "No, he helped me." She wiped her nose with the back of her hand, and Sam handed her the towel. Tracy used it to wipe her eyes. "It was Tommy. He wanted me to leave the party with him and I said no." She glanced over at Sam and looked back at Allie.

"Tracy, did he rape you?" Allie asked.

Sam's daughter dropped her eyes to the sofa and his heart stopped.

"No," she answered quietly, "but he tried."

Sam jumped up. He would kill the bastard! Skin him alive or strangle him with his bare hands. Something slow and painful. "Where the hell is he?"

Tracy looked up at Sam, her eyes shimmering with tears. "I don't know, Dad."

"I'll find him," he said through clenched teeth.

Sam took off for his truck, but Allie caught him just outside the door.

She grabbed his arm and pulled. "Sam!"

He turned around.

"Sam, Tracy's okay. Don't do anything stupid. She needs you."

He took a deep breath. "Someone hurt my little girl. He'll pay."

"I understand, and you're right, he should pay. But she's okay. Are you listening to me?"

He nodded. "Yeah." Then he took another deep breath. "Will you stay with her?"

Allie nodded.

"Thank you."

She turned back to the house, and Sam continued to his truck. Fortunately, Allie had stopped him before he could kill Tommy Stanley. Sam knew that it wouldn't do any of them any good for him to end up in prison.

Allie held Tracy and let her cry it out. When she finally

did, Allie released her, but stroked her arm as they sat together.

"You think Dad will be okay?"

"I hope so."

"Me, too." Tracy wiped the tears away with the towel. "This was all my fault. If I hadn't been mad at Dad that first night, I never would have even spoken to Tommy, and none of this would have happened."

"Tracy, I know how you feel, but it's not your fault that Tommy's violent. Not at all. No matter what happens, you have to remember that."

The girl didn't answer.

"Please, promise you'll try. It's important to me."

"Why?"

Allie shook her head. "Because I really care about you."

The teenager sniffled, then looked up. "Allie, whose car was that you were in?"

She glanced out a window. "Mine."

"What were you doing?"

Allie didn't want to talk about this. Tracy had enough to worry about at the moment, and they were both worried about Sam. "It's not important right now."

"Were you leaving?"

Allie frowned at her lap.

"Promise you won't leave tonight," Tracy pleaded. "Please promise me."

She nodded. "I promise."

The girl sighed and rested her head on Allie's shoulder.

Allie closed her eyes. *Please, God, don't let Sam get hurt.*

Sixteen

The truck rattled as Sam drove home at a reasonable speed. He was anxious to check on Tracy, but the sight of her bruised face completely enraged him.

In the house, the den lights were still on but the room was empty. Sam started down the hall. "Tracy? Allie?"

Allie stepped out of Tracy's room, pressing her finger to her lips. "She's asleep," she whispered.

"Is she okay?"

She nodded. "Are you?"

Sam took a deep breath and blew it out. "You were right—I couldn't go after him. I went to the sheriff's office instead. Bill's on his way to pick up Tommy now."

"Good."

Sam tiptoed into his daughter's room. The lamp by her bed was the only light shining. He knelt on the floor and, leaning on the bed, pushed Tracy's blond hair back and studied her face. Her nose wasn't bleeding anymore. He checked her pulse. Nice and slow and even.

Sam leaned over and kissed his daughter's forehead. It terrified him when he realized she could have been seriously hurt, or killed. How would he have lived with something like that? How did parents make it through such a nightmare?

He kissed her again before slowly getting to his feet, then switched off the lamp and tiptoed from her room, quietly pulling the door closed. Sam dropped his head to the doorframe and closed his eyes.

Allie spoke quietly from beside him. "I promised Tracy I wouldn't leave tonight. I'll leave in the morning."

Her words initiated a new wave of pain. "Allie . . ." Sam turned his head in time to see her slip into her room.

Allie sat on the edge of her bed and let the tears fall, not bothering to wipe them away. They ran down the front of her neck.

She didn't even know exactly why she cried. Was it Sam's face as he stood in front of her car, or the pain in his eyes when he spoke to her? Or was it the pain in Tracy's eyes when she admitted feeling guilty, or her own misery at the thought of leaving?

Maybe she cried for all of it. There was just too much to be sad about.

Allie curled into a ball on the bed. Her soul was drowning, and she couldn't stem the flow. She pulled the pillow down and buried her face in it, and her body shook with sobs.

She heard Sam at the door, but she couldn't answer. All she could do was cry. The door to her room opened and Sam spoke to her. "Allie . . . no, Allie." His hand on her shoulder pulled her forward.

She wanted to tell him to go away, to leave her alone, but there were no words. Even worse, she needed his arms.

She'd hit the bottom of the universe, and she needed him. It didn't matter that he'd thrown her out.

Allie raised her head and let him pull her close. She slid off the bed and into his lap, and pressed her face to his chest. Sam turned so that he leaned back against her bed, sitting on the floor, and he held her, stroking the back of her head. Allie wrapped herself around him.

She cried until there was nothing left. Never in her life had she done that. It was as if twenty-nine years of tears were finally coming out, and Allie felt like she cried for hours.

She turned her head as she sighed away the last sob. Sam continued to hold her.

"Sam—"

"Shh, don't talk right now, Allie. I'm so sorry. Please forgive me."

She wasn't sure what she was supposed to forgive him for. Sam had been nothing but kind to her. At least, until this morning. And even when he was mad, he didn't yell at her. Allie had felt the sorrow in his words this evening in the driveway. He was right—she should have told him about her past. It just never seemed like the right time.

What she couldn't figure out, though, was how Sam had found out about Rick, and even met him, without Rick showing up. Maybe he was on the way. Maybe that's what Sam needed her forgiveness for—for turning her in.

The funny thing was that she didn't care. Nothing in the world could have convinced her to leave Sam's arms at the moment. She felt so safe. Listening to his heartbeat, she clung to his chest. All of her strength had left her body with the tears.

They sat on the floor for a long time. Finally, Sam loosened his hold on her. Allie straightened, sitting on his thighs, and wiped her cheeks with her sleeve.

"We need to get you out of those clothes, Al."

Allie looked down at her sweater, smeared with Tracy's blood. "Yeah, Doc, I always seem to look my best around you."

Sam reached up and pushed her hair back behind her ear. "I like your haircut."

"Thanks."

He eased the sweater off her shoulders and pulled the sleeves loose. "Come on. You go wash your face and I'll put this in the washer to soak."

Allie nodded and got up. She walked to the bathroom and splashed water on her face several times. When she dried her face and opened her eyes, she found Sam standing in the doorway behind her.

He backed into her room, pulling her with him. At the bed, he sat on the edge and positioned her in front of him. "Raise your arms."

Allie obeyed and Sam lifted her shirt off. Then he shook out the T-shirt he had given her the first night and put it over her head. Allie stuck her arms through the armholes. He picked up her feet, one at a time, and pushed off her tennis shoes. He unsnapped and unzipped her jeans and lowered them to the floor. She stepped out of them.

Sam stood. Before Allie realized what he was doing, he'd scooped her into his arms, and she wrapped her arms around his neck. She started to ask him where he was taking her, but realized it didn't matter. He walked out of her room, down the hall, and into his room. Gently, he placed her on his bed and raised the comforter for her to crawl under. Without a word, he went into the bathroom.

Allie watched and waited. When Sam finally came out, he had washed up and was wearing only his sweat pants. He crawled into the bed beside her, lay on his back, and pulled her onto his shoulder.

Allie draped her leg across his and rested her hand on his chest. His skin was smooth and warm and he held her tighter.

After a few minutes, Sam turned off the lamp. They lay together silently in the dark, and he kissed the top of her head and hugged her.

Allie listened to the air flow in and out of Sam's lungs until she fell asleep.

Sometime in the night, Sam awoke with a start. He thought he'd heard something—barking maybe—but when he listened, he heard only Allie's breathing.

Sam lay on his side with Allie wrapped in his arms. She felt so right there. Her body was warm and soft, and he pushed his nose into her hair and inhaled. She smelled better than any scent ever bottled. He kissed her shoulder.

Allie made a small noise and pushed back against him, and he kissed her shoulder again, letting his lips linger as he ran his hand down her side then back up under the T-shirt. He needed to touch her all over. He spread his fingers across her stomach and pulled her against him.

By the time she turned in his arms, he wanted her immediately. She did nothing to stop him when he covered her mouth with his. Before he knew what had happened, their clothes were off and they were tangled in each other's embrace.

They made love in the darkness, whispering, kissing, rolling together, and Sam couldn't imagine anything so perfect. He was desperate for her and lost the earth when he entered her. There was no beginning and no end to space or time, just Allie in his arms, over him and under him and wrapped around him, softly moaning. Intoxicated by the ecstasy, he didn't ever want to return.

Later, as they were drifting off to sleep again, Sam realized that, as much as he hated himself for it, he didn't care if Allie was married. He would probably go to hell for the pain he caused. He definitely deserved to, but he just didn't care. To have her in his arms, he'd gladly give his soul.

Maybe he already had.

Allie slid to Sam's side. She'd fallen asleep on top of him, and thought it must be difficult for him to breathe. He stirred a little, but didn't actually wake. She kissed his chest and nestled against him.

What had she done to deserve this? Making love to Sam was, as before, the most amazing experience she could imagine. He was kind and gentle and strong, and when he held her, he whispered to her that she was beautiful and wonderful and sexy. She didn't really believe him, but his words made her feel great.

And he knew exactly what he was doing. She'd never been to where he took her—never felt so satisfied, nor so hungry. No matter what else happened in her life, she'd always have the two nights she'd spent in Sam's bed to remember, to dream about.

Allie moved closer to Sam and closed her eyes. He smelled wonderful. His skin smelled like him, and nothing else. And a little like a crackling, romantic fire.

She must be dreaming the fire. Allie took a deep breath.

No, it was really there.

Lifting her head, she opened her eyes. She couldn't see anything, but definitely smelled smoke. When she sat up in bed, it was stronger, and she suddenly realized one of the dogs outside was barking.

"Sam."

"Hmm?" He tried to pull her to him.

"Sam, wake up." She grabbed his shoulder and shook it.

"What is it?" He propped himself up on his elbows.

"Smell the air, Sam. Am I dreaming?"

He bolted from the bed. Allie heard the light switch flipped, but nothing happened. Sam fumbled around near the bed and glass shattered.

"Damn. Wait, here it is." A small light flared when Sam switched on a flashlight.

Allie had already located her T-shirt and was searching for her panties when Sam threw the comforter back. They both put on the few clothes they had there, and Allie stood beside him.

"The electricity's out, Allie. You take this flashlight and head for the door. I'll get Tracy. Watch the glass." He pointed the light at the spot where the light bulb had broken when the lamp fell, then handed Allie the flashlight. "Go!"

They ran into the hall together, where smoke was actually visible and billowing from the direction of the kitchen. Allie stopped at Tracy's door when Sam pushed it open.

"Go on," he yelled as he stepped through the doorway. "Tracy! Get up!"

Tracy coughed, and Allie decided she couldn't leave them behind. She shone the light into the room.

Sam lifted Tracy off the bed, dragging her comforter with him. He trotted from the room and Allie led the way to his office. When they were outside, Sam placed Tracy on the ground and Allie knelt beside her. They all coughed.

The night glowed an eerie orange color and reeked of burning wood. Heat billowed from the sides of the house, and, as they watched, flames shot off the roof, reaching for the dark sky.

"Daddy, what's going on?"

"The house is on fire, Tracy. Are you okay?"

"Yeah."

"Allie?"

"I'm all right, Sam. We need to get the animals out while we can."

"Yes. Tracy, can you drive my truck?"

Growing flames illuminated the trio. Tracy nodded.

"The key's under the driver's seat. Pull it around the yard and back it up here, okay?"

Tracy got up and started around the house at a trot.

Allie followed Sam back into the office. He picked up the cordless phone, listened, then tossed it aside. "It's dead."

Without hesitating, Sam handed her a small cage, which she carried out, and he brought out a bigger one. They worked together until all the full cages and several empty ones had been retrieved. Tracy stopped the truck and Sam lifted cages into the back, stacking them on top of each other.

"Tracy, we need to get the dogs." Allie tugged the teenager's arm, and they ran around the house to the kennels.

The whole end of the house was engulfed, and flames rolled up the roof in balls, filling the night sky with glowing embers. Allie held her arm up to ward off the heat as she opened the runs. Tracy started back holding two dogs by their collars, and Allie followed her with the third.

As they passed the window to Sam's room, open several inches to let in the night air, Allie heard a long, sad meow, barely audible over the crackling fire. "Popsicle," she whispered. Smoke rose from the window, but flames hadn't reached that part of the house yet. When she handed the dog off to Sam, Allie turned back, picked up the flashlight from the grass, and dashed into the house.

"Allie!" Sam yelled. "Where are you going?"

"I'll be right back," she said over her shoulder as she hurried through the office.

The hall was much smokier than it had been just a few minutes earlier. Allie covered her mouth with her hand and stooped to walk under the worst of it. At the far end of the hall, flames crawled up the door to her room.

Sam's door was still open, and she hurried in. "Popsicle, here kitty-kitty. Where are you?"

A tiny meow from under the bed answered her. Allie dropped to her knees and shone the light around. Two huge devil's eyes reflected the light back at her.

"Come on, Popsicle. You're safe with me."

Terrified, the cat crouched into the smallest space possible against the far wall. Pushing the flashlight in front of her, Allie crawled on her stomach under the bed. There wasn't quite enough room to get on her hands and knees, but she slid easily on the wooden floor. She reached Popsicle quickly and pulled the trembling cat to her chest.

It was slower backing out, because she held the cat in one arm, but Allie finally made it. As she sat up and turned, she was startled to find flames licking the doorframe.

"Allie!" She barely heard Sam's voice over the roar.

"In here, Sam."

Popsicle dug her claws into Allie's shoulder and didn't try to escape.

Allie couldn't even see the top half of Sam's body as he ran through the doorway, and his legs glowed orange. He dropped to his knees beside her and took several deep breaths, then he pulled the comforter from the bed, wrapped it around her, and lifted Allie from the floor.

From under the cover, she felt Sam running. In a few seconds, he stopped and placed her on the ground. When he pulled the top of the comforter back, Allie saw a look of total terror on his face for a second. It faded quickly, and he hugged her.

"You scared the hell out of me," he said into her ear. "Don't do that again."

Allie shook her head against him. When he released her, she tried to hand Popsicle to him. They both had to work at getting the cat's claws out of Allie's shoulder.

With Popsicle in one of the cages, Sam called for Blue. The dog crawled out of the bushes at the edge of the yard. Sam grabbed him and tossed him into the cab of the truck, and Blue cowered against the passenger's door.

Sam threw his comforter over the truck bed. Tracy added her own to cover the last few cages.

Sam grabbed her arm. "Park the truck down by the road, but make sure it's out of the way." He handed her the flashlight. "Be careful, and meet us at the barn."

As soon as Tracy pulled away, Sam seized Allie's hand and started around the yard. Fire consumed his beautiful house like a hungry monster. The den collapsed as they passed it, sending a volcano of sparks upward. Sam jumped sideways at the crash, but continued without slowing.

It was hard to tell, with the waves of heat rolling off the house, but a steady breeze blew the fire toward the barn. Sparks landed on the garage, starting small flames visible from the ground. It wouldn't be long before the wooden garage was incinerated, and the barn would be next.

Sam released Allie's hand to pull the barn door open. He stepped in and back out again, and handed her a flashlight.

"Let the horses out into the pasture. Open the outer gate first, then get them out of the stalls."

Allie nodded, took the flashlight, and hurried out to the gate. As soon as she had it open, she ran back into the barn.

She shivered as she worked, partly because of fear, and partly because her arms, legs, and feet were bare.

Even inside the barn, the air smelled like smoke, and the horses snorted and stomped. Allie started with the closest stall and opened the doors.

Most of the horses bolted from their stalls immediately. She had to coax Prince out, staying far enough back that he didn't step on her toes.

When she got to the last stall, she opened the door. "Come on, Hattie. Here, girl."

Allie found the huge white mare lying on her side. The horse lifted her head to Allie's voice, whinnied, and dropped her head again. Allie tiptoed in, talking softly.

The horse breathed hard, her eyes wide. It must be time. Allie had no idea what to do. Leaving the stall door open, she walked back out.

The rest of the horses milled around in the corral, snorting and stomping. Allie pointed the light at the gate opening and shooed them all through. Once Prince discovered the escape route, the group followed quickly.

She returned to Hattie's stall where the mare still lay on the ground. Dust rose into the air with each breath she released.

"It's okay, girl. Sam will take care of you. Don't worry."

Allie ran from the barn, closing the big door behind her, and continued around the garage. She skidded to a stop, stunned by the sight that met her.

The house was little more than a flaming skeleton, with giant torches of burning aspen in the front yard. Sam and Tracy each had a hose that they used to douse flames on the garage roof, but they were losing the battle.

Seventeen

Allie ran to Sam and grabbed his arm. "Hattie won't get up!"

He stepped sideways, directing the water at a new flame. "She's on her own right now, Allie. Stay out here with us. If the barn catches, I don't want you in there."

"But, Sam—"

"Allie, this is the best I can do."

She nodded as she released him. Sam was right. The best way to help Hattie at the moment was to save the barn.

"What can I do?"

"Tracy's hose is short. There's another hose in the tack room. Add it to hers so she can reach the side of the garage."

"Okay." Allie ran back to the tack room, using the flashlight she forgot she still held, and dragged out a rolled-up garden hose. When she got to Tracy, she tugged on the teenager's shoulder. "We need to add this to your hose."

Tracy nodded. "I'll turn off the water. You put it on." She handed Allie the hose and ran off.

Allie started to unscrew the nozzle and stopped as water went everywhere. The cold water took her breath away when it hit her in the face. She squeezed the handle, pointing the water at the garage, until the pressure dwindled to nothing. Then she tried again to remove the nozzle. This time it worked, but she had problems finding the end of the new section.

Allie stopped and took a deep breath. She was so nervous, nothing worked. That certainly didn't help. As soon as the shaking in her hands lessened, she continued.

The hose section went on quickly, and Allie added the nozzle to the new piece. She yelled into the darkness behind her, "Okay, Tracy! Turn it on!"

Water pressure returned and she directed the stream at the closest fire on the garage roof. It flared up and fizzled out, and she turned to another. Tracy dropped to her knees on the ground beside Allie, panting.

A high-pitched whine rose against the background roar of fire. Allie strained to hear. The whine grew louder, and a wave of relief washed over her when she realized it was sirens. Help had finally arrived. Flashing red lights mixed with the orange glow as three fire engines lumbered up the driveway.

Allie leaned over and yelled to Tracy. "Tell them we're back here."

Tracy nodded, jumped up, and ran around the garage.

Allie moved aside when men in yellow suits appeared, dragging a huge white hose. One man yelled, but she couldn't understand a word. Suddenly, water gushed from the hose and the entire garage was quickly soaked. Water poured off the roof in all directions. Allie dropped the garden hose, put her hands on her knees, and worked at catching her breath.

"Allie, we have to move back." Tracy dragged her by the sleeve until they were well away from the garage.

Sam emerged from the back drenched from head to toe, but he didn't seem to notice. He walked directly to Allie and Tracy and threw his arms around both of them, hugging them to him as one. The three of them stood together in silence for a little while as firefighters swarmed the place, spraying everything. Allie felt Sam's chest rise and fall with a sigh, and he released them.

When the water hit the house fire, noise increased momentarily and the last of the frame collapsed. Billows of steam mixed with the smoke and the entire place hissed and popped.

The area grew darker and darker as flames slowly surrendered. After an hour, Allie could no longer see anything but outlines and small flares that jumped up the blackened spires where Sam's house had been only a few hours earlier.

The three of them stood together, Tracy and Allie on each side of Sam. He held their shoulders, and they locked arms behind him. Allie's spirit fell with the last crackles.

"It's horrible," she said. For the first time since the fire started, she didn't have to yell to be heard.

"It could have been worse," Sam answered.

"Sam! Where are you?"

Allie could just make out the sheriff's uniform in the light from the fire trucks before he joined them in the darkness. Her heart jumped, but she didn't have the strength to move.

"Bill, we're over here."

"Damn, Sam, that was quite a fire. We saw it from downtown. What happened?"

"I don't know. By the time we woke up, half the house was in flames and the phone was dead."

"Well, the Chief is checking it out. He says for everyone to stay away from the place until tomorrow when he can get a good look."

"Okay. But I've got a mare down in the barn, so I'll have to stick around."

Bill nodded. "I'll let him know. Meanwhile, you've got some of the townsfolk up front who want to make sure you're okay. Can you come out here?"

"Sure. Thanks, Bill."

Sam followed the sheriff, pulling Allie along by the hand, and walking with his arm around Tracy's shoulders. When they got to the driveway, Allie was stunned by the huge crowd gathered at the edge of the yard. They all cheered when Sam, Tracy, and Allie stepped into the headlights of cars and fire trucks.

Allie leaned against a tree and watched Sam accept handshakes and hugs, and talk to people. He wore only his sweat pants, and those were wet. How could he stand there and not look cold?

At the edge of the crowd, Tracy quickly hugged Edward Cory, and they spoke with their heads almost touching.

"You must be freezing," Maggie said, walking toward her holding a blanket. "Take this." The woman wrapped the blanket around Allie's shoulders and pinched it closed in front.

"Thank you," Allie said, enjoying the warmth.

When Maggie hugged her, Allie hugged back.

"Now, listen, I told Sam I've got room in the back of the store for the animals tonight, so he's driving over in a minute. I'll give him some clothes for you and Tracy. It won't be anything fancy, but it should beat walking around town naked."

Allie smiled at Maggie. The woman definitely had a heart of gold. "I can't thank you enough."

"Oh, don't worry about it. I just expect you to sit around

and talk to me once in a while so I don't lose my mind."

Allie nodded.

As Sam walked up, Maggie retreated after squeezing Allie's arm. "I'll see you later," she said.

Sam also donned a blanket when he stood in front of Allie and touched the side of her face. "You okay?"

"Yeah."

"I'm driving the truck over to Maggie's shop. You want to come with me?"

Allie shook her head. "I need to go back and stay with Hattie."

"Okay. If she starts to foal before I get back, just stay clear. She could hurt you without meaning to. You understand? I'll hurry."

"Okay."

He slid his hand behind her neck, reached down and kissed her tenderly on the lips, then smiled as he released her and turned away.

Allie stared at Sam's back. He had kissed her, not just in front of his daughter, but in front of most of the town. And he hadn't kissed her like a friend, he'd kissed her like a lover. Allie's heart pounded and her face burned. She gripped the blanket tighter as she worked at not chasing after him like a ninny.

Sam took three keys from Joe with a nod. Joe's Motel wasn't the Hilton, but it was the best place in Rocky Butte. "Thank you."

"Don't worry about it, Sam. The rooms are yours for as long as you need 'em. And if you need anything else, you just holler."

Sam shook the elderly man's hand and smiled. Joe meant what he said.

The cool night air held a hint of rain. Of course it would rain now. Mother Nature had a mean sense of humor sometimes. Sam shook his head as he climbed into the truck and drove it across the parking lot.

With the engine running, he opened the door to the last room and placed a bag of clothes on Allie's bed. Maggie said the bag was for both Allie and Tracy, but he'd let them sort it out. Pulling the door firmly closed, he jumped back into the truck and tossed the room keys on the seat. Blue's claws clicked against the metal truck bed.

Sam was driving by the sheriff's office when Bill trotted across the parking lot, flagging him down. He pulled in and slid to a stop.

"Glad I caught you. I've got some news."

"What's up, Bill?"

"First, the Chief told me he found signs of arson at your place. They found a gas can in the bushes, and your electricity and phone were cut at the pole."

Sam frowned. Who would want to burn down his house?

"Also, I had Tommy Stanley transported down to lock-up tonight. I just got a call a little while ago. He didn't show up."

"What?"

"Somebody ran my deputy off the road, shot up the radio and the tires, and left him out there. It took him two hours to walk in. I'm just glad they didn't shoot my deputy. Sam, the Stanley kid is loose and he's armed. He could be the one responsible for the fire. I've deputized a few men, and I've got them out there looking, and I've called the State Police. I'm doing everything I can to find him, but you better watch your back, because I'm sure he's pissed off at you."

Sam tried to shake off the disbelief. "Thanks, Bill. I've got to get back."

"Okay, I'll talk to you in the morning."

The old truck roared as Sam pulled out of the parking lot and headed to his house. Or, more accurately, to his barn.

Allie folded one of the horse blankets and pushed it underneath Hattie's head. At least she could keep the dust and hay out of the mare's face. Hattie's breathing was labored and rapid, and now and then she made a heart-wrenching grunting noise. Allie knelt beside her face and whispered encouragement.

Tracy walked up quietly. "I found rubber boots in the tack room. They probably won't fit, but it's better than being barefoot."

"Sounds good, Tracy."

"I also found more blankets. I don't know what else to look for."

Allie sighed. "I don't know, either. I just hope your father gets back soon."

As if because she'd willed it, Sam's truck thundered up the driveway, through the yard, and stopped near the door to the barn.

Allie walked to the stall entrance and leaned out. Sam strode in with Blue at his heels. He picked up a lantern Allie had forgotten she'd seen before.

"How is she?"

"I don't know, Sam. She's breathing hard, and she hasn't moved much since you left."

Sam pumped the small handle on the lantern, held a match to it, then adjusted the flame. When he stepped into the stall, Hattie snorted and raised her head.

"It's all right, girl," he said. "You hang in there."

Sam hung the lantern on a nail in the stall and inspected the horse, rubbing her and talking softly. The mare didn't calm down until Allie returned to her head and spoke to her.

Sam grinned. "Any time, now. Looks like we need to get comfortable. Tracy, there's a bucket in the tack room. Can you fill that with water?"

"Sure, Dad."

Sam leaned back against the wall near Hattie's tail and stretched his legs out. He smiled at Allie.

"Sam, I'm sorry about your home. How can you be so calm?"

"You know, Al, there's a big difference between a house and a home. I only lost my house tonight."

Allie frowned, trying to understand his comment. "But it was such a beautiful house."

"Yeah, but not as beautiful as you are."

Allie gulped and looked down at the horse. She couldn't believe she was tearing up again. She felt Sam's eyes caressing her face, and smiled against the tears.

"Oh, Sam, can't you give her something?" Allie sat against the mare's neck, stroking her face.

The horse made the most pathetic sounds, something between a groan and a grunt.

"No, I can't." Sam spoke softly. "My bag was in the office. Besides, she has to push the foal out, at least at first. If I gave her a sedative, she might not do that. And the birth has started now."

"Sam—"

"Allie, you remember what I told you about horses? They can sense fear. You need to stay very calm, because you're the only one who can help Hattie stay calm. She's old, but she's done this before, and it's a natural process. We're just going to help her along a little."

Sam's voice at least calmed Allie, and she tried to pass it along. Hattie closed her eyes and pushed her head against Allie's leg.

"Tracy, come in here and stand behind me, and bring the bucket of water," Sam said.

Moving slowly, Sam draped blankets over Hattie's legs and tucked them around her hooves. He explained that it was to keep her from kicking one of them accidentally. Hattie didn't even react. Just as Sam settled back down, the mare opened her eyes, raised her head, and grunted.

"This is it. I think I see a hoof."

Hattie dropped her head. Allie rubbed her jaw and neck. "You're doing good, Hattie." The horse grunted again.

"Yep, I see the hooves." Sam sighed. "At least it's coming out the right way. Keep it up, girl."

There was silence, broken only by Hattie's heavy breathing.

"Damn," Sam muttered. "She's not pushing. Tracy, get down here. Kneel right here. That's it. Now, hold both of these hooves and pull. Not hard, and don't jerk on them, just apply slow, gentle pressure like this. That's it."

Allie couldn't see exactly what was happening, but what she could see didn't look at all pleasant. Sam seemed to be reaching inside the horse, and Hattie's eyes opened wide. Allie continued to talk to her and rub her.

"Damn," Sam muttered again.

Allie wished he wouldn't do that. Her heart was pounding hard enough already.

"The cord's wrapped around its head. Wait."

Allie held her breath as Sam grunted and moved.

"Okay, now. Pull, Tracy. Good, that's it. One more pull, but not too fast."

Hattie's huge belly moved like something from a horror movie, and Allie wanted to throw up. Yet, as much as she didn't want to know, she couldn't help but stretch to see what Sam and Tracy were doing.

The two of them pulled a wet red and black mass from Hattie, and, as Allie watched, it seemed to pop free. Sam placed the little body quickly on a blanket beside him and wiped its head and face with a towel.

"Daddy, he's not breathing."

"I know, Trace." Sam leaned over and covered the tiny horse's nose and mouth with his hands and mouth and blew. Allie stretched farther. After five breaths and long pauses, she saw a tiny hoof twitch.

"He moved. He's alive! He's breathing." Tracy's voice was choked with tears. "Oh, Daddy, he's alive."

The two of them hugged quickly over the top of the now-squirming foal.

Allie dropped back down, watching Hattie and fighting tears. The mare closed her eyes again, and Sam explained to Tracy how to wash the foal.

Allie leaned down to whisper into the mare's ear. "You did great, Hattie. You have a beautiful baby. Now you have to hang in there so you can take care of him, you hear? Don't give up."

The horse opened her eyes and looked up at Allie, then closed them again. Her breathing slowed a little, but remained steady. Allie rested her head just behind Hattie's ears.

She heard Sam and Tracy moving around. Then Sam walked up to Hattie's head, carrying the baby horse. He placed the small thing on the ground and stepped back.

"Allie, give her some room to move now."

Allie backed to the wall and watched. Hattie's nostrils flared as she snorted and opened her eyes. She lifted her head once, then threw her head forward and rolled onto her stomach, folding her legs under her. She pressed her nose to the tiny form and snorted again, then she licked it.

Allie looked up to find Sam and Tracy leaning over the wall, grinning. Sam motioned to her with his head, and Allie slid up the wall. She walked quietly around the edge of the stall and out to the walkway. When she looked back in, Hattie was working hard at cleaning her foal.

"Good job, both of you," Sam said.

Allie leaned back on the wall and covered her mouth with her hand. She shook as she thought about what she had just witnessed. Not only had she been a part of the miracle of birth, but she'd watched Sam breathe life into a little baby horse, and now he stood there calmly grinning as if he'd just made coffee.

"Dad, I—"

Sam put his hand on his daughter's shoulder and leaned down to look into her eyes. "What is it, Tracy?"

"I don't know." The teenager wiped her eyes.

Sam hugged her to his chest.

"Dad, Mom says terrible things about you sometimes. I used to believe her. I'm sorry."

Sam kissed the top of his daughter's head. "I know, Trace. It's okay."

Allie felt like she was listening to someone else's confession, but she didn't want to disturb them by moving.

Tracy pushed back to look up at her father. "I never really thought about what you do before tonight. It's pretty cool."

Sam smiled at her. "Sometimes it is."

"Dad, if I became a vet, could we work together?"

Sam hugged her again and closed his eyes as he spoke. "You have lots of time to decide what you want to do, Tracy. No matter what you choose, I'll always be proud of you. And if you decide you want to be a vet and work with your old man, I can't think of anything that would make me happier."

The two stood together for a long time before Sam released his daughter and looked down at her. "Right now, though, you need some sleep."

Tracy nodded.

Allie was sure Sam had forgotten she was there until he looked over at her and smiled. "Why don't I take you two to the motel? I'll come back here and watch Hattie for a little while to make sure she's okay."

"Sorry, Doc, but there's no way I'm going to sleep anytime soon. Why don't you take Tracy to the motel and I'll stay here? I have my car. I can come get you if there's a problem."

Sam took two steps down the walkway, his hands on his hips. He must want to say something.

"Actually, I don't want to leave you here alone." He looked at both of them and then back at the floor. "I ran into Bill earlier. The fire was arson."

Allie gasped. "Arson? Someone did this on purpose?"

Sam nodded.

"But, who? Who would do this?"

"I don't know for sure, but Tommy Stanley escaped from custody before the fire started."

"Oh, Sam."

"So, I don't want either one of you here alone. I'm not too worried about the motel. It's in the middle of town."

Allie pressed on the sides of her head with her palms.

Everything seemed to be happening at once. The man who had attacked Tracy had probably burned down Sam's house and might be lurking in the bushes, waiting to attack them? It was all becoming too much to deal with.

"Al? Are you okay?"

Allie dropped her hands and sighed. "Yeah, Doc, I think I'm getting a headache."

Sam laughed. "If that's the worst injury we end up with from this night, I'll be thrilled."

Allie nodded. "Let's take my car to the motel so Tracy can have it if she needs it. We can both watch Hattie for a while."

"Good idea."

Tracy stepped forward. "Allie, I don't have a driver's license."

Allie wrapped her arm around Tracy's shoulders and led her from the barn. "Promise not to hit anyone?"

Tracy nodded.

"Okay, then, you drive it to the motel so you can get the feel of it."

Sam stopped at the barn door. "Come on, Blue."

Eighteen

Sam followed the taillights of the Volvo into town. Tracy got better at driving the car as they approached the motel, and was an old pro by the time she parked it. Sam parked beside her, grabbed the room keys, and slid out of the truck.

"You're in room three, Trace." He handed her a key. "I'm in two and Allie's in one. Oh, and there's a bag of clothes for you two in Allie's room. They're from Maggie."

Sam stopped at the sidewalk where five bags leaned against the wall by his door. He peeked into several. "Well, it looks like we've all got clothes." It touched him the way the people in this tiny town always came through in a pinch.

Taking a deep breath, Sam unlocked his door. "I need a quick shower. You two want to check through the clothes and see what goes where?"

Allie scooped up two bags. "Sure. We'll dump them on my bed. You go ahead and I'll bring something over for you to wear." She motioned to Tracy to follow, and Sam handed Allie the keys as she passed him.

The shower felt heavenly. He was filthy, first from the fire and then from the foaling. Joe had delivered shampoo and a bag of other goodies already. Nice guy.

Sam stood under the water until he started feeling over-heated, then turned off the water, dried off, and wrapped the towel around his waist. He was halfway through shaving when he heard Allie open his door.

"Sam?"

"In here."

She stopped in the doorway to the bathroom.

Sam raised one eyebrow at her in the mirror. "No comments, please. I feel just a little underdressed here."

Allie grinned.

He smiled at her reflection. "Let me finish shaving, will you? You distract me and I'll probably slice open my throat."

Allie turned back into his room. "Your clothes are on the bed. I'll be in Tracy's room when you're ready."

"Okay." Sam was disappointed when he heard the door to his room close. He liked having Allie with him, and the thought of being in a motel room with her was devilishly exciting.

Clean, dressed, and shaven, Sam tapped on the motel door.

"Who is it?"

"It's me. Sam."

Allie opened the door. Tracy had just climbed into bed, dressed in a flannel gown that made her look like a little girl.

Sam pulled the covers up to her chin and kissed her forehead. "Tracy, I am so thankful you're safe."

She smiled up at him.

"You get some sleep and we'll be back soon. Don't open the door for anyone else, okay?"

Tracy nodded. "Don't worry, I know what to do. I live in a big city, remember?"

Sam looked down into the mirror image of his own eyes.

He loved the way hers sparkled. "I can't help it, I was hired to worry about you. It's my job." He kissed her forehead again, then rose and turned off the lamp by the bed. The bathroom light made a decent nightlight.

At the door, he turned back. "Good night, Trace."

"Good night, Dad."

Sam followed Allie to the truck and climbed in. A drizzle fell on the windshield as they drove.

Allie walked in front of Sam to the barn. She waited while he lit the lantern then followed him to Hattie's stall.

"Now, that's a sight I wasn't sure I'd see," Sam said. "You did good, Hattie."

The mare stood in the middle of the stall and the tiny foal balanced on shaky legs, nursing. Hattie nuzzled his back. He was now a shiny black.

Allie leaned on the top board. "Oh, Sam, he's so cute."

Sam slid his arm around her waist. "Actually, he's a she."

"Oh."

"What do you think her name should be?"

Allie looked up at him. "Me?"

"What, you don't think you can name a horse?"

Allie smirked and then looked back down at the baby horse. The foal's little black tail twitched and she almost fell over. Hattie steadied her, and the foal continued to nurse.

"I think you should name her Last Chance. And you should call her Lady Chance so she'll grow up thinking she's special."

"Good name. Last Chance it is, a.k.a. Lady Chance. And she is special."

Allie looked up and found Sam studying her. His eyes

twinkled in the lantern light as they ran across her face and shoulders and back to her eyes. This was the same man who had thrown her out less than a day ago, and then made love to her. In all the excitement, she'd nearly forgotten—at least the leaving part. Had he simply changed his mind? Did he expect her to go along with his decision without question? Allie twisted free of his arm and started toward the barn door.

"Allie, where are you going?" Sam followed her, holding the lantern up.

She stopped and turned around. "Sam, I'm confused."

"About what?"

"About you. About us."

Sam lowered the lantern and frowned down at it. "I bet you are. We need to talk, don't we?"

Allie nodded.

He walked around her, grabbing her wrist as he did. "Come on, I know where."

Outside the barn, Sam turned off the lantern. The pale blue sky provided just enough light to see. He grabbed her arm again and led Allie to the tack room, then inside and toward a ladder that went up the wall.

Allie climbed into the darkness. "Sam, I can't see anything."

"Just move over and hang on a minute." Sam also climbed the ladder and she watched his shadow cross in front of her. When he pushed open the upper doors, soft light flooded the hayloft. Sam returned, stood in front of her, and offered Allie his hand. She took it.

They crossed the half-full loft and Sam sat on a bale of hay, holding Allie's hand as she sat on a bale near his.

Sam studied her fingers for several moments before he spoke. "Allie, when I found out that my ex was sleeping with other men, it nearly killed me. If it hadn't been for my daughter, I don't know what I would have done. And it wasn't just that Lisa was having sex with them, it was more that she was lying to me. I always try to be truthful, and I guess I just don't expect people to lie to me. That's probably why it shocks me when they do, you know?" Sam looked up. There was enough light in the loft to see the honesty in his eyes.

He dropped his gaze back to her hand. "Anyway, when I went to your house the other night, I went up to your door and met your husband." Sam shook his head. "I just kept seeing myself with the roles reversed, and I hated it. God, I hated what I'd done." Sam frowned at her hand. "But when you started to leave, I realized that I didn't care how much pain I was causing. It doesn't matter how much I hate what I'm doing." Sam slid off the bale, pushed Allie's knees apart, and knelt in front of her, wrapping his arms around her waist and pressing his face to her shoulder. "I plan to do whatever I can to convince you to stay with me, Allie."

The desperation in his voice frightened her a little. Allie held the back of his head and his shoulders and rocked back and forth. They stayed that way, in silence, as the sun started to color the sky. Finally, Allie pushed him gently away, and Sam sat back on the floor, looking up at her.

"Sam, there are some things I don't understand. And there are a lot of things you don't understand." She slid off the bale and sat on the floor in front of him. "You told Rick you knew where I was?"

Sam shook his head and cringed. "No. I lied to him. I said I was looking for you."

"Who did you say you were?"

"I think I said I represented members of families separated at birth who were trying to find each other."

Allie got up, walked to the loft doors, and studied the horizon, now pink with a hint of orange. "And where did he say I was?"

"He said you two had an argument and you were staying with friends. He was sure you'd be back in a few days."

"So, that's what you thought? You thought I'd had a little spat with my husband, run away from home, and what, slept with you as a diversion? To take my mind off my little problems?"

Sam frowned at his hands. "No, I didn't think that. I . . . I don't know what I thought. All I know is you're married, and you didn't tell me."

"Actually, if it were possible, I would have already filed for divorce."

Sam's eyes jumped to hers.

Allie turned and walked around the loft as she spoke. "I didn't tell you about Rick at first because I couldn't. For several reasons. Now . . . well, things are different. I might as well tell you the whole story." Allie tucked her hair behind her ears. "The last time I saw Rick, he was having sex with his secretary in his office."

"Allie—"

She held up her hand. "No, Sam, let me tell you the rest of it. I want you to know the truth. One of the funny parts of the whole thing was that I hadn't slept with Rick in over a year. He simply needed me to maintain his image. Nothing more." She turned to Sam. "You see, I don't handle being lied to very well, either. I left his office and drove away for good."

Allie sat on a bale, facing the open doors. "I've spent some time reflecting on my marriage since I've been here, and how I could have let it all get so out of hand. By the time I left, I had no access to money and no friends to turn to. Rick made sure I depended on him for everything.

"I worked hard to put myself through college. I have a degree in education, and I worked with the special ed program. As you probably know, Rick owns Tate's Kids. They sell educational supplies, among other things. It's a very wholesome business. Five years ago, I went to him to ask for a donation to the school, and we ended up having dinner." She watched a thin cloud of dust settle to the floor at her feet.

"Rick told me I was pretty. No one had ever told me that. I liked hearing it. When he asked me to marry him after only three weeks of dating, I agreed. I know it sounds absurd, but he pegged my weak spots early and made good use of them. He knew how much having my own home and family meant to me. That's exactly what he promised. He even talked me into investing all of my savings in our house. He said he had to put it in his name for tax purposes.

"There was one condition on our marriage: Rick had to have total control. He didn't put it that way, but he did tell me he expected me to quit work so I could raise the kids. He said he was a little old-fashioned. At first, I thought old-fashioned was charming.

"It took a while to realize that control was more important to him than anything. He created a perfect public image to go with his company. The world saw him as a caring, wonderful family man who took his wife with him everywhere. I was expected to stand quietly, only speak when spoken to, and serve refreshments when we had guests. It must have worked, because by our first anniversary he'd opened three branch outlets and business was booming.

"I'm not saying that I didn't do it all willingly. I've studied the psychology books, I know the names of the syndromes. But when you're in the middle of something like that, it doesn't matter what your head knows. And I didn't have anything to fall back on—any person in my life who loved me like you do Tracy and made me believe I was special. I think he knew instinctively that he could control me with my own doubts. He stopped telling me I was pretty. He told me when to cut my hair, what dress to wear, how to apply my makeup. When I tried to ask him about the business, he said I would never understand it, so I shouldn't try. Every day, I lost a little more confidence. And there was no one to tell me he was wrong, that I was a worthwhile person.

"By the time our second anniversary rolled around, he started spending more and more time at the office. I planted gardens and painted and found furniture for him to buy. It didn't even dawn on me at first that I had no money. Rick set up a small household account that he replenished weekly. If I wanted anything else, I had to ask.

"But he knew me. Whenever I started to question things, he talked about our home. He promised me that things would soon be right for kids. And he stayed away more and more. After three years, I barely saw him."

Allie closed her eyes for a moment as she thought back on the fears and doubts. "I wanted to go back to work, so I asked him if I could. That was the first time he ever really yelled at me. I don't mean the kind of yelling most people do, but a murderous, irrational yelling like he hated my guts and could barely keep from hitting me. I was terrified of upsetting him after that.

"Finally, after five years of marriage, I was desperate. The morning of the day I walked into the bar, I approached him again about work, with the same result. That evening, I decided I'd try to make up by surprising him at the office with dinner. He had to work late again. That's when I found him with his secretary. He acted like *I* was in the wrong for being there. He ordered me home.

"I'm sure that when I didn't show up, he reported his car stolen. He's not going to just let me leave. It would ruin his image. I'm really not sure how far he'll go, which is why I was afraid to tell you about it at first. I was afraid you wouldn't believe me and would turn me in. Then, when I started caring about you . . ."

Allie plucked a piece of hay from the bale and rolled the stalk between her finger and thumb.

"It's the lies that hurt. He told me he was too busy with work to be interested in sex, but I was sure I just wasn't attractive anymore. I now realize that he was probably busy with other women. And I was left as a prisoner, his perfect little housewife to show off to the world. I wonder if he had any intention of ever letting me have children. I don't know if he told me the truth about anything.

"I guess I was stupid to believe it all for so long, but it's easy to fool yourself when you want to, you know? The one thing that I wanted, more than anything else, was a home— a place to call my own, a place where I belonged. And I wanted my husband to love me. Unfortunately, the home wasn't any more real than the marriage. It was only an image."

It all sounded even worse in summary. Allie sighed. "I had a housemother at St. Mary's who said we should always try to look on the bright side of things." Allie looked down. "If Rick hadn't betrayed me, I wouldn't have met you and Tracy. A lot of good things have happened to me here, and it was all because I was running from the lies. You saved my life, you know. That night at the Last Chance, I didn't know what I was doing. I would have died outside in the cold. You were my guardian angel. I'll always be thankful that you were there." Allie sighed again and stood. There was no way she could make him understand how much he'd done for her. He'd also made her believe she had something to offer the world.

"So, you see, Doc, I'm stuck. I don't have the money to file for divorce, and I might even have the law out looking for me as a missing person or a car thief. I have nightmares that he'll catch me and lock me in my room for the rest of my life, and no one will ever know I'm there."

She turned around and found Sam leaning back against a hay bale, his knees up to support his elbows, frowning at his fingers. He started to say something, then closed his mouth and shook his head. When he looked up at her, the sunrise reflected off his green eyes and the tears on his face. He looked down again.

Allie walked over and knelt in front of him. "Sam, I didn't tell you all that so you'd feel sorry for me. I just want you to know the truth." She placed her hand on his cheek.

He turned his head and pressed his lips into her palm and closed his eyes. When Allie took her hand away, Sam wiped his face with the back of his hand and took a deep breath. "I don't feel sorry for you, Allie. It hurts me to know the pain you've endured. And it really hurts to know that I've caused some of it. I shouldn't have assumed any-thing. I should have talked to you. I hope like hell you'll forgive me some day." Sam extended his hand as he stretched out his legs.

Allie took his hand and he pulled her onto his lap. As she wrapped her legs around his hips and her arms around his shoulders, Sam buried his face in her neck. Allie put her head on his shoulder and held him, never wanting to let go.

"Why do you care about me?" she whispered. "I don't understand it."

"God, Allie, how can I not? You're the most incredible woman I've ever met. You're kind, and caring, and strong, and sexy as hell." He tightened his arms around her and pressed his lips to her skin.

After a few minutes, Sam released her and turned her around. He positioned Allie in his lap, and she rested her head back on him. With his arms around her, they watched the sun rise. He kissed her head every few minutes.

"You know, Sam, if you don't quit saying nice things to me, I might start to believe them."

"You better believe them. I told you, I never lie. At least not to you."

Allie smiled. Even with all the bad things that had happened in the past twenty-four hours, the entire world seemed perfect at that moment.

Sam mixed vitamins into the feed, then emptied the bucket into Hattie's trough. The mare just watched him without backing away. Maybe she was finally losing some of her fear. She'd made it through in better shape than he'd expected her to, and she'd even passed the afterbirth fairly quickly. Now all she needed was time with her foal.

He latched the stall and left the empty bucket beside the door. Allie rubbed the mare's head one more time and then joined him.

With his arm around her shoulders, Sam and Allie walked out of the barn. Her arm felt great around his waist, and she drew circles on his side with her fingers. He kissed the top of her head. At the truck, Allie started to open the door. Sam pushed it closed, trapping her in his arms. When she turned around and looked up at him with her golden eyes, he captured her mouth. Her arms were instantly around his neck and her lips parted for him.

He already knew Allie's taste and craved it when he wasn't kissing her. His eyes closed as his tongue circled hers, and he slid his arms around her waist and pulled her to him. He was hard before her body touched his, and feeling her only made it worse. Sam pushed his knee between Allie's and groaned into her lips. When he pulled his mouth away, her sweet breath caressed his face.

"Allie, I want you constantly." He pushed her against the truck, careful to avoid the door handle.

"I'm having the same problem, Sam."

He grinned when she opened her eyes. Her lids were heavy with desire.

"I didn't say it was a problem."

"No, I guess you didn't."

He leaned into her for a kiss that burned his soul. He needed to be closer.

"You know," he said, "I have a motel room."

"What a coincidence. So do I."

"Your place or mine?"

"Mine. It's more private."

"Hmm."

He kissed her one more time before tearing himself away. When he got in the truck, Allie rested her hand on his leg.

They drove slowly past the pile of ashes that used to be his house. Here and there, pieces of blackened pipe rose from the heap like bony fingers from a grave. The horror of it in daylight made him want to throw up.

What he had told Allie was true—it was just a house that had burned in the night. Still, it wasn't easy to take. The pencil marks on the back of his closet door were gone, the one that he had drawn for Tracy's height at four, and the mark she'd made at the top of his head as he held her. And all the pictures, and the stuffed animals he had given her over the years. Some things could never be replaced. For the first time since the fire started, anger and sadness welled up in him.

When he pulled out of the driveway, Sam glanced over at Allie. How could he be unhappy with her by his side? Remembering her words about wanting a home more than anything, he covered her hand with his and pulled it up to the top of his thigh. She looked up and he winked at her.

Allie's smile felt almost as good as her hand did.

When they got to the motel, Sam stopped in front of Tracy's room and listened for a moment. "She must be asleep," he whispered.

Allie nodded. She couldn't image Tracy not being asleep after such a long night. If not for the desire Sam had sparked in her, she was sure that she, too, would be unconscious. But the thought of lying in Sam's arms sent a rush through her that pushed her eyes open and turned up the corners of her mouth.

Sam opened the door and followed her in. When she turned around, she found him walking slowly, deliberately toward her with a wicked grin on his face. He didn't stop until he'd backed her onto the bed and was on his hands and knees above her.

"Right where I want you," he said, raising one eyebrow. She loved the way his eyes glistened and his lips parted when he lowered his head to kiss her.

Sam had to be at least as tired as she was, but he took his time undressing her. He followed the hem of her T-shirt with his mouth as he slowly stripped it off of her. Allie couldn't believe the desire that crackled through her body.

The first time they'd shared a bed, it had embarrassed her when Sam pushed her into ecstasy and she lost control. But he'd looked so pleased with himself that she'd decided to relax and enjoy it. How could she complain? She closed her eyes and sucked in a sharp breath when he nibbled a spot on her shoulder that she didn't know was sensitive.

By the time his mouth returned to hers, she was desperate for him. She raised her knees on each side of his hips. "Sam," she whispered, "take off your clothes. Please."

"Not yet," he whispered back, his breath hot on her ear, "I've got plans."

They both jumped and then froze at the knock on the door. Sam frowned down at Allie, then backed off the bed, and Allie dashed into the bathroom, leaving the door open where she could hear.

Sam opened the door. "Bill, come on in."

"No, thanks, it's a little late. Or early, I guess. Anyway, I just wanted to let you know we got Tommy."

"You're kidding. How?"

"Well," the sheriff said, "you could have knocked me over with a feather. Ron brought him in."

"Ron Stanley, his father?"

"Yep. I swear, I think he really feels bad about the fire. Says he's taking up a collection of household goods and food. Hell, he already had a sign to put in my window."

"Wow."

"Yep, I guess some folks are never too old to change."

"Well, thanks for stopping by, Bill."

"No problem. See you tomorrow."

Allie heard the door squeak as if closing, but then it sounded like it opened again.

"Daddy?"

"Tracy? What are you doing up?"

"I heard Sheriff Walker," she said. "I just wanted to tell you good night."

"Good night, Trace." He kissed her.

"And tell Allie good night for me."

"Allie?"

Tracy giggled. "Dad, I'm not stupid, you know. And this is her room."

"Tracy—"

"Don't worry, your secret's safe with me."

There was a funny silence before the door squeaked again. Then Sam appeared in the bathroom doorway. "Looks like we've been found out."

"Oh, Sam, I'm sorry." Allie wondered how she'd get back to her room now without being seen by the rest of the town.

"Well, I'm not."

Before she realized what was happening, Sam scooped her into his arms and carried her back to the bed where he dropped her unceremoniously. "Now," he said, crawling back on top of her and kissing her mouth quickly, "where was I?" He frowned teasingly, and then grinned. "Oh, yeah."

She groaned with frustration as he slid out of her grip and off the bed, but when his mouth followed her pants as he pulled them over her hips and knees, the frustration turned into quivering expectation. With her pants and panties gone, his mouth moved to the inside of her thigh, touching off a fuse coiled through her body that she'd never known existed. Every muscle tensed, aching for more as his mouth moved slowly higher, fanning the spark. Allie clutched the bedspread in her fists.

And then his hot, demanding mouth covered her and she

cried out as the spark touched off an explosion that ripped through her, burning up all the oxygen, pulling her breath out in gasps as electrical charges ran up the backs of her thighs. Her body arched into him and back, uncontrolled, in blissful agony as he continued to draw out the wondrous torture, until at last the flame died down and she lay in an exhausted heap.

When Sam started back up her body, his clothes were gone, and the feel of his warm, smooth skin revived her as he wrapped himself around her.

"My God, you're so beautiful," he whispered. He kissed her and pulled her closer to him.

For the first time in her life, she truly felt beautiful.

The sun was well up as they completed the round of lovemaking. Sam lay on top of her, kissing her face, pushing himself into her with long, slow strokes. He whispered against her lips, his voice deep and hoarse, "I love you, Allie."

As he filled her, she held him close and whispered back, "I love you, Sam. I love you."

She finally understood exactly what it meant.

Nineteen

"Allie, you don't have to do this. We can get someone else to do it for you."

"I know." Allie took a deep breath and blew it out. "I think I need to." She pushed the truck door open and hopped out carrying the envelope, then closed the door and walked around to the driver's side.

Sam rolled up his sleeves to his elbows, and then flexed the muscles in his arms as he clenched and opened his fists.

"What are you doing?" she asked.

Sam stood tall and looked down at her. "I'm working on looking intimidating."

"Why?"

"That's what I'm here for."

"Oh." She ran her gaze up and down him twice, and smiled. "Okay."

He grinned and stuck out his left elbow, and Allie looped her arm through his. They walked slowly up the walkway to the front door of the house that she had once called home. How could she have ever thought of it that way? Music from inside assured her that Rick was there, and her heart rate doubled.

On the porch, Sam winked at her and stepped back a little. He leaned down and spoke softly in her ear. "I'm right behind you, sweetie."

Allie smiled. His statement was more reassuring than Sam could possibly imagine. She rang the doorbell.

Rick opened the door and staggered back a half a step.

"Allie! Where in the hell have you—" He looked up at Sam. "Hey, I know you. You're the guy from that agency, what was it?"

Allie held the envelope out to Rick. "I suggest you sign this."

"What's going on here?"

"Rick, these are divorce papers. If you don't sign them, I'll file them anyway."

Rick glared through narrowed eyes that darted back and forth between Allie and Sam for a few seconds.

"If you think I'm going to agree to this, you're dead wrong. You are not going to ruin me, not after all the shit I've been through. If you don't—"

As soon as Rick grabbed Allie's arm, Sam was on him, squeezing and twisting Rick's wrist and leaning close to the smaller man's face. "Keep your hands to yourself and watch your mouth," Sam said, in a low, threatening voice.

Rick stepped back and Allie walked past him.

"Are my clothes still in my room?"

He didn't answer.

"Rick, I suggest you sign those papers while I pack. You get everything except my clothes and the car, but that's a one-time offer. In spite of what you did, I have no desire to ruin your business. At this point, I just want you out of my life. But if you push it, I'll take you to court. I'm sure the press would love the juicy gossip about scandals in the office of Tate's Kids." Allie turned and left Rick standing in the living room with Sam right beside him, looking absolutely murderous. If it had been anyone but Sam looking at him that way, she might have been concerned for Rick's safety.

Allie smiled to herself as she walked down the hall.

"The sandwiches are perfect," Tracy said. She pushed the corners of the bread back together and grinned at Allie.

"Good."

Sam put three plastic cups on the towel and held up a bottle, still wrapped.

Allie raised her cup and smiled. "Wine?"

"Nope." Sam unwrapped a large green bottle, and covered the top with the towel to muffle the pop. "Champagne."

Tracy picked up a cup. "And I get some, too?"

"Just enough for a toast." Sam poured a little champagne in Tracy's cup, then half-filled Allie's and his own. He balanced the bottle on the ground and raised his drink.

"Here's to my wonderful daughter, who I will miss tremendously when she leaves me tomorrow." He smiled at Tracy, then moved his gaze to Allie. "And here's to the beautiful woman who is just crazy enough to agree to marry me."

"What?" Tracy's face lit up as she turned to Allie.

"Drink first, questions after." Sam tapped his cup to both Tracy's and Allie's.

They all drank.

Tracy wiped her mouth with the back of her hand. "When?"

"When what?" Sam frowned.

"*Dad*. When are you getting married?"

"Does that mean you approve?"

"Only if I'm here. When are you going to do it?"

Sam smiled at Allie and then at his daughter. "We were

257

thinking about Thanksgiving, during your vacation from school."

"Great!" The teenager turned to Allie. "Do I get to help plan or something?"

Sam had assured Allie that his daughter would be happy when they told her, but there had been a seed of doubt in Allie's mind. Tracy's reaction swept it away.

"I was hoping you'd agree to be my maid of honor."

"Oh, Allie!" Tracy jumped to her knees and she and Allie hugged over the top of the picnic.

As Tracy sat back, Allie squeezed her hand before releasing it. Over the past two and a half months, she and Tracy had become close friends. It was still a little strange thinking of the teenager as her stepdaughter. *Friend* was easier to handle.

"We can work out details on the phone when you talk to your dad."

"Sounds perfect." Tracy looked down at her cup and back up, her eyes moving back and forth between Sam and Allie. "I'm really happy about this. You guys are cute together."

"Cute?" Sam looked wounded.

"Yes, Dad, *cute.*"

"Oh."

Allie reached over and touched his arm. "It's okay, cute is good."

Sam grinned at her.

The three of them had just started eating sandwiches when the approach of horses drew their attention. Edward and his sister, Cynthia, rode into the clearing. They dismounted and led their horses as they approached the picnic.

"Hi, Dr. Calvert. Miss Parker. Tracy." Edward nodded

to each of them. "We didn't mean to interrupt lunch."

"That's okay, Edward. Would you two like to join us?" Sam motioned to the pile of full plastic bags. "We have plenty of sandwiches."

"No, thank you. We're riding to the top of the ridge trail today."

Sam nodded. "Hi, Cynthia. Jewel looks good. You must be taking care of her."

The girl beamed as she stroked her horse's neck. "Yes, sir."

They all smiled at each other, and Allie guessed, by the glances Tracy and Edward exchanged, that this meeting was not an accident.

Edward looked down at the ground and blushed. "Um, Tracy, can you come with us? I mean, is it okay with you, Dr. Calvert, if Tracy rides with me and my sister?"

Tracy nodded at her father, her eyebrows raised expectantly.

"If you want to, Trace. We'll meet you at the house in a few hours?"

"Thank you, Dad." The girl jumped to her feet.

"But only under one condition."

"What?"

"You take some of these sandwiches."

Tracy grabbed three of the sandwiches. Edward said polite good-byes to Sam and Allie, and he and his sister followed Tracy to her horse. Allie and Sam watched the three of them gallop from the meadow.

Sam sighed as he took a bite of his sandwich.

"You did good, Doc. I didn't even see you flinch."

"I'm trying, Al."

Over the course of the summer, Allie had watched Sam adjust to the idea of his daughter dating. Edward was so much like Sam that Allie wasn't the least bit worried. Maybe her confidence had helped Sam handle it.

They ate in silence for a while.

"One more week," she said.

"Yep."

Allie smiled at the thought of the grand opening of the new office. Sam had insisted on making the event into a party, and Maggie had helped plan it. The new place would be quite a bit different from the old back room. The office even had a parking area and was separate from the house, which also approached completion. Though she loved working on it, Allie enjoyed the break from painting walls.

Sam filled their cups and they sipped champagne.

Allie watched brown waves of hair dance around Sam's head in the gentle breeze. "Aren't you at all excited about next week?"

He smiled, drained his cup, and crawled over to her. Taking her cup away, Sam kissed her as he eased Allie back to the ground. He lay beside her, his head propped on his hand, his leg over hers. "I'm more excited about tomorrow night."

"Why?"

"Because we get to try out our new bed. It's being delivered tomorrow."

Allie laughed. "Sam, we don't even have a dining room table yet."

He traced a line down her neck and chest with one finger. "We can eat on the floor, Allie, but I'm anxious to get you back in a real bed."

"Sam." Allie squirmed free and sat up. "We may not be alone out here."

He also sat up, crossed his legs, and looked at her. "Allie, there's something I've wanted to tell you for a long time."

Her heart raced at the serious note in his voice as she sat facing him. "What is it?"

Sam looked down at a piece of grass that he twisted in his fingers. "After I got divorced, I devoted myself to my work. I knew there was no way I would ever open my heart to anyone again. I couldn't imagine that it would be worth the pain. And I thought I was happy." He shrugged. "I was happy enough."

He looked up at Allie with eyes as green as emeralds. "Then you came along. I don't know why, but I was given one last chance to find out what happiness really is. I'm sure I don't deserve it, but I'm grateful. Allie, I love you so much, and I want to make you happy. I want us to have a perfect home together. I know how much it means to you." He touched her knees.

His words tore her into delirious shreds. Unable to answer, all Allie could do was smile as she crawled onto his lap and locked her legs and arms around him. She hoped he felt her emotion in the burning kiss they shared.

Sam wrapped his arms around her and groaned.

When he released her mouth, Allie pressed her lips to his ear. "I love you," she whispered. "*You* are my home, Sam, and I'm way past happy."

They kissed again, and she felt him getting aroused as he held her tighter and the kiss deepened.

After a minute, Allie pushed on his shoulders and leaned back. Sam opened his eyes, pouting and smiling at the same time.

"You know, Doc, you've got a one-track mind."

"Only when you're around, Al. Is that a problem?"

Allie smiled. "Oh, hell no." She slid her arms back around his shoulders and dove in for another scorcher. Sam slipped his hands under the back of her shirt.

About the Author

Sarah Storme grew up in New Orleans, the motherland of jazz and romance. After a year at Emory in Atlanta, she dropped out and moved to Alaska, where she enjoyed a taste of the Wild West pipeline days. Three years later, Sarah returned to the Lower 48 and earned a Master's degree in engineering from the University of Texas at Austin. As a civil engineer for the government, she has lived all over the United States, but considers both Alaska and Louisiana home. She's married to her own personal hero, has a fantastic job in Santa Fe, New Mexico, working for the Forest Service, and has finally stumbled onto the joy of her life—writing. Her first romance, *Emily Again*, from Warner, was released in December 2001, followed by *Wild Montana Hearts* from Echelon Press in 2003, and *Just Kiss Me* from Echelon Press in 2004. She also writes mysteries under the name S. H. Baker, and the first of her Dassas Cormier Mystery Series, *Murder in Marshall's Bayou*, from Zumaya Publications, has been recommended for an Edgar Award.